Kinship

TRUDY KRISHER

DELACORTE PRESS

Published by
Delacorte Press
Bantam Doubleday Dell Publishing Group, Inc.
1540 Broadway
New York, New York 10036

Copyright © 1997 by Trudy Krisher

Library of Congress Cataloging-in-Publication Data
Krisher, Trudy.
    Kinship / Trudy Krisher.
        p.   cm.
    Sequel to: Spite fences.
    Summary: In 1961 fifteen-year-old Pert, who lives with her mother in Kinship, Georgia, meets her long-absent father and discovers the true meaning of home.
    ISBN 0-385-32272-0 (alk. paper)
    [1. Mothers and daughters—Fiction. 2. Fathers and daughters—Fiction. 3. City and town life—Georgia—Fiction. 4. Georgia—Fiction.]   I. Title.
PZ7.K8967Ki   1997   96-35480
[Fic]—dc21   CIP
                                                                AC

The text of this book is set in 12.5-point Adobe Garamond.
Manufactured in the United States of America
September 1997
BVG   10   9   8   7   6   5   4   3   2   1

To Bev,
friend and family,
and to Lella,
family and friend

Part One

Alice Potter,

The bottles on my bottle tree is just like family. They gots names and stories.

My bottles is beautiful. They different every day. They change, don'tcha know. It depends on the light and the weather and the breeze and the *m-m-mood* of the person what's doin' the lookin'.

Some folks says the breeze rustlin' through the bottles sounds like chimes or handbells. Some folks says people's tears finds they way into the bottles, and when the wind skips across they lips in a certain way, it sounds like cryin'. I 'spect that's right in Pert Wilson's case. She were restless, that'un. Couldn't never seem to sleep at *n-n-night*. When she were just a bitty thing, I could hear her *c-c-calling* out in the middle of the night, calling for her daddy. Funny thing about that. Most children calls out for they mama, don'tcha know.

The bottles on my bottle tree is just like family. They gots names and stories. I 'spect my bottles got spirits, too. Don'tcha know that one of 'em's named for Pert Wilson?

1

I always stopped at the crest of the hill on my way home from school to say hey to Lucinda Adkins. The high school was way over in the east end of town, and Lucinda was inside the white cemetery in the west. I liked to rest on top of her cool marble slab under the leafy oak. I'd tell her how much my feet ached and how I envied her that long nap. I'd had trouble sleeping since I was a kid. Tossed and turned near every night. Lucinda'd been sleeping since 1868.

When we was kids, my brother Jimmy and me had stood together at the crest of this hill in the only winter in recent memory when it had snowed in Georgia. Jimmy and me didn't have a ride back then, neither. Other kids managed to bring sleds with rope pulls and red runners; Jimmy and me only had a strip of cardboard. I didn't need to reach fifteen to know I couldn't head out of Kinship if I didn't have a ride.

Lucinda Adkins wouldn't know about cars, of course. She wouldn't know about the way a boy like Jimmy flipped through car magazines, eyes spinning like hubcaps. She couldn't really have known anything about the ways of Kinship, Georgia, in 1961, a time when both the high and the humble had cars. Peter Matlack owned the Ford dealership and bought both him and his wife, Margaret, a new car every year. Henry Pugh, my friend Maggie's daddy, lost jobs now and again but kept his pride shiny by polishing his chrome. Zeke Freeman had abandoned the trading cart he used to push down Fenwick Street, which separated north from south and white from colored; now Zeke traded from a teardrop trailer hooked to the back of an old Dodge with a rusty muffler that scraped the street. Even crooked Jim Bob Boggs had wheels before he went to jail: If you was going to rob the First National Bank of Kinship, you couldn't do it without a getaway vehicle.

"Lucinda," I mumbled, looping my fingers into the curves of her graceful *L*, "if both the high and the humble in town have cars, where does that leave us Wilsons?"

Lucinda Adkins wasn't much for talking, but I was grateful for the way her marble cooled the back of my legs all the same. It was like our Frigidaire when I stuck my forehead in the tiny freezer, fetching ice cubes for Rae Jean, my mama. I gave the marble a pat and looked back over my shoulder to Fenwick Street, the main street in town, with the bank and the grocery store and the Civil War statue of General John B. Gordon at the other end.

Then I looked down the hill. I could see the turpentine plant and the textile factory and the housing project on the far west end. When Mayor Cherry was getting reelected last fall, tooting his horn from his Lincoln, he bragged on the new houses down there that folks called Kinship Acres and Gram called cracker boxes. Riding around Kinship with his top down, Mayor Cherry bragged on the dripping red meats that lined Sam Shriner's meat case, hauled in from places like Gainesville and Raleigh on frost-lined refrigerator vans.

Shaking hands like a pump handle, he bragged on Clarence Adkins's sawmill, hauling logs off to places like Birmingham and Memphis on long flatbed trucks. Handing a shiny plaque to Lucy Tibbs, the switchboard operator, Mayor Cherry bragged on the way Lucy dispatched cars: police cruisers to patrol the Trailways station and the pool hall, delivery trucks to deposit new furniture in the suburb called Fenwick Acres to the east, and Frank Alhambra's taxis to provide colored maids from the south side of town to iron and polish for the white ladies who sat proud as their houses in mansions to the north. Kinship, Georgia, Mayor Cherry claimed, was a town on the move.

From the crest I could also see the familiar pines and the flat patch of red dirt that most folks called Happy Trails and that I called home. The trailers in Happy Trails was set all whomper-jawed and every which way, like fallen pick-up sticks. I could see their shapes like toasters or cough drops. I knew they had names like Vagabond, Wanderlust, and Travelodge, and every one of those ten tin cans had a story. Myra and Emil Highwater, Trailer 7, had a picture on their what-not shelf of the Seminole tribe they left behind in Florida. Said no self-respecting Seminole could hold their head up under the laws of the reservation now. Said they'd rather live away from the tribe with dignity than within the tribe without it. Charlie Hale, Trailer 10, had never been married, but he was the only one in the park with a kid besides Rae Jean, who had Jimmy and me. Charlie's younger brother and sister-in-law and three kids was killed in a head-on on the Macon Highway ten years ago. Pee Wee Hale, the nephew named after Charlie, was the only one in the family to survive. Sophie Mulch, Trailer 4, had never been married, neither. Her fiancé up and left her standing at the altar. Rae Jean said folks had marveled at Miss Mulch. Said Miss Mulch was a real lady. She had finally lifted her veil, folded her hands, turned to the congregation, and said, "Well, you folks are welcome to join me at a nice supper in the church hall, and I guess that Hugh Mulligan is just going to miss one fine meal." Later on, Miss Mulch found out that Mr. Mulligan had run off to Talladega and married her twin sister.

Wilsons, Trailer 5, we had a story, too. A mama with no husband; two kids with no daddy. Only Daddy hadn't really died, he had done what was worse: He had kept on living, but he was gone just the same.

I wanted wheels as bad as my brother. But Jimmy wanted wheels to ride *around* Kinship. I wanted them to ride *out*. Fact was, although near all the folks who lived in Happy Trails felt like kin somehow, the trailerites I envied most was the ones who'd up and left. Some of them was magicians and dog trainers and construction workers who followed the jobs from site to site. Veronica Hussle had been a finalist for the 1947 National Trailer Coach Queen; she left Happy Trails after her husband, Stanley, said it was tough being married to royalty and he wanted a divorce. Señor Morales, who had a black mustache that curled up on the ends, was an elephant trainer who followed the Ringling Brothers' tents to Sarasota each winter. Mingus Swift had a trailer that looked like a diner; he had moved to Ollie Trout's trailer park in Florida. I envied the freedom that was their lives; like the letters of the alphabet, anything in the world could be made out of them.

Sometimes you didn't much like the folks who lived

around you. They was like annoying relatives who stayed to visit too long. Like your own kin, you learned the things you had to ignore if the family was ever to have a day of peace. You learned that Alice Potter could be more'n a mite bossy and that Gene Nugent wouldn't ask you inside his trailer to catch some cool from his brand-new air conditioner if you was sweating in hell (which was the same thing as Kinship in August). You learned that if the wind was rising out of the west, you would choke on nosefuls of smoke sharp with ketchup and vinegar from the Coateses' barbecue pit. And if you got within arm's reach of Miss Mulch you'd be plunked back in math class: She'd set you figuring whether the Bon Ami cleanser with her coupon was cheaper than the special sale at Shriner's Grocery without.

But you also learned to love the music of Alice Potter's bottles across a spring breeze. You learned that Gene Nugent would let you sit and pout in his '49 Fleetwood Cadillac if you needed to, and that once you helped Sophie Mulch with a shopping problem, she'd turn on the only TV in the trailer park and let you watch soap operas for as long as you wanted. And you could trust that just as soon as you was down to your last pack of graham crackers, Odette Coates would show up on your doorstoop with a plate of barbecue.

Maybe folks in Happy Trails wasn't very happy—and we sure wasn't blazing any trails—but there was things you liked about the place just the same. You liked the clever gadgets in the trailers, like the stepstool that folded down out of the wall or the dining-room bench that folded into a bed. You liked playing in the abandoned school bus that Esther and Alvin Beezle once raised five kids in, before they moved to Troy. You liked the sound of rain on the tin roof and the sight of moonlight on a silver dome, and the way Rae Jean gathered the neighbors around on lawn chairs of an evening to set and talk, the night lit up by our old Christmas-tree bulbs strung from poles and winking like colored fireflies in the darkness.

But there was more'n a few things to dislike about trailer living. Sometimes a rough wind would shake the sides of the trailer in the middle of the night and you'd wonder whether you'd wake up the next morning in Munchkinland like Dorothy. Sometimes you hated the lack of privacy and had to go off to the woods to be alone. Sometimes you was reminded just how close you was connected: If your hairbrush fell down your toilet, you could back up your neighbor's tub. Sometimes you got plain fed up with dollhouse living. Your big brother couldn't stand full up in his own home; he had to crook his head. Living in tiny places with names like Kozy Koach or Spartanette reminded you that you wasn't yet living a real life, only a miniature version of it.

When I stood up, I was always careful with my feet. Whether it was icy or muddy or wet or dusty, I made sure to keep my feet off Lucinda's stone. That marble was her eternal home. I knew homes was supposed to be special, but it would take this fall to show me the reason why. Right now, I was caught in the feeling that the Wilson trailer was just like us: something supposed to be mobile that stood stock-still.

Sophie Mulch,

TRAILER 4

Oh, *laws,* a trailer court's the dullest place in the world, and I'd have died of boredom long ago if it hadn't been for Pert Wilson. I had the only TV in the court, and when we could, we'd watch the soaps together. We played a game about them. Pert made it up, bless her heart. We'd count the number of lies the people told each other in every episode. When Pert first thought of the game, we used to count a half-truth as a whole lie, but there got to be so many of them, we couldn't keep up.

A trailer court's no place for a child. I swannee, there wasn't a swing or a slide in sight. You'd cut your feet if you went barefoot, which Pert did spring and summer. I bought her a new pair of school shoes every fall. Took the bus to the Thom McAn in Troy together. Rae Jean put up a fuss about it the first year I did it, but I said it was my pleasure. I'd retired from schoolteaching some years ago, and buying Pert Wilson new school shoes helps an old lady keep her corners up.

I swannee, I thought of Pert Wilson as my grandchild and Rae Jean Wilson as my daughter. Rae Jean, bless her sweet heart, had more than her share of heartache. Her husband ran off right after Pert was born. He sent her money now and again, and most folks thought Rae Jean lived on the hope that he'd come back. But I'd bet my last nickel that Rae Jean only wanted him back because of Pert: Pert Wilson missed her daddy like the devil.

Laws, but Wilsons made me feel like kin. Had me over when they played Monopoly. I swannee, it was the closest thing they ever had to money in their hands. Pert gambled like a sailor, buying up everything in sight till she'd gone broke. They always let me be banker, and I never bought cheap properties like Oriental Avenue or Baltic. Bought only greens and blues. Park Place, Pennsylvania Avenue. I liked to see my dollars spent on improvements to my properties, so I was pleased as punch when I could buy a house or a hotel.

I swannee, Happy Trails could use a few improvements, too. I wish the police would catch those vandals that slashed the side of my trailer last spring. I had the only leather-sided trailer in the park. Bought it with part of my teacher's retirement. Now it looks like a vinyl sofa with the foam rubber popping out. While they're at it, I wish the police would get rid of those Weevils over in Lot 3. Those chickens peck and squawk day and night. Whoever heard of letting chickens run around in the front yard? Something bad's going on over there, but I can't figure out what. Makes it hard on the rest of us in Happy Trails trying to live a decent life.

2

Rae Jean and me got the same routine near every day. First Rae Jean sinks into the sofa in the front room and lays the little heart-shaped pillow behind her head. I'll have the ice cubes jingling in the glass before she can say "Gee, Pert, a cold glass of iced tea would just about hit the spot right now."

Then Rae Jean slips off her shoes and rubs her feet together. The nylons crinkle like a soda-straw wrapper. Rae Jean wears stockings to work every day, even in summer when it's hot enough in Kinship to melt the poles. After I bring her tea, Rae Jean sighs and says, "Whew, but I'm *dog* tired today, Pert."

Then we both laugh. When Rae Jean laughs, she shows teeth that still look like baby teeth. Bright white and tiny. Everything about Rae Jean reminds me of a doll.

That little joke about being dog tired is another one of our routines. Rae Jean works for Doc Jackson. He's both a people doctor and an animal doctor—an M.D. and a D.V.M. His office in town has two doors: front door for the people and back door for the animals. Rae Jean goes in the back door. She's the vet assistant.

After our joke, Rae Jean reaches for the little book called

Good Tidings from the end table next to the couch. My gram picks up a new *Good Tidings* for Rae Jean every Sunday after mass. As soon as Rae Jean opens her book, the cat jumps onto the back of the couch and plays with Rae Jean's ears. Then Rae Jean reaches her hand behind her to bat at Mittens's paws while she reads. After she's read a few paragraphs, Rae Jean looks up over the top of her *Good Tidings* and says, "How was your day, Pert?"

Mostly I rush right out with my report. That the Highwaters was behind in their rent but they'd be paid up by Wednesday. Or that the Bijou, the movie theater where I work, was showing a matinee on Saturday. Or that I'd got a letter from Maggie, my friend who'd gone off to Atlanta.

But one day near Easter last year I couldn't think what to say when Rae Jean asked how my day was. I didn't know how I was going to tell her that Nympha Claggett, my home ec teacher, was coming over.

Miss Claggett had come up to me in the hall and announced how she'd be paying us a visit Saturday morning. What bothered me most was her reasons: My grades . . . and my home. "Poor grades are often a sign of a bad home environment, Pert Wilson," she had said, shaking a finger fat as a drumstick. I knew what she meant by a bad home. Living in a trailer court. Having no daddy. Being a Wilson.

Like most folks in Kinship, Nympha Claggett had the wrong ideas about trailer parks. Most folks thought trailerites was gypsies or outlaws, either dancing through the world or shooting it up. But the trailerites in Happy Trails was folks who had unpacked their suitcases and decided to set a spell. Charlie Hale could afford to stay put, for the construction business in Hayes County was steady, and he didn't need to follow the jobs from place to place. Gene Nugent never left his trailer except to bowl on Friday nights or to walk his dog, Sarge. The Highwaters dragged their canoe to Pearl Lake day after day and didn't seem interested in fishing other waters. The Coateses had a steady business in barbecue, and Farley Ewing was fixing to build a business in homemade puzzles. Wilsons, of course, couldn't just up and leave: we was too down-and-out. But it wasn't on account of where we lived.

"Shoot, Miss Nympha," I'd muttered, watching her turn and traipse off. "Ain't you never heard how folks think it's rude to just invite yourself on over?"

Rae Jean rattled the pages of her *Good Tidings* to get my attention. "So how was your day, Pert?" she said again.

"Oh, it weren't too bad, Rae Jean," I said, stalling for time. "Had a substitute in history."

"That all?" Rae Jean asked.

I wondered if I could just get out of this whole thing. I'd been good at getting out of things my whole life. "That's about it, Rae Jean," I said. I was stuck. Rae Jean Wilson never lied, and Pert Wilson tried not to, but Pert Wilson didn't always succeed. "That's all" would have been a lie, but "That's about it" was still pretty much true.

"Got a phone call today at work," Rae Jean said, setting the *Good Tidings* beside the iced tea. "It was Nympha Claggett. She's comin' over for a visit tomorrow mornin'. What's that about?"

I saw the sweat dripping down the sides of the iced-tea glass and felt a damp spot forming down my own back. "What'd she *tell* you it was about?"

"Just that she's comin'." Rae Jean had wide blue eyes. Not

14

a dark blue. A pale blue. The color of blue that peeks through the sky after it rains.

"Didn't you ask her why?" I was dodging now. It felt like keep-away. Getting rid of the ball as fast as you could.

"I reckon I did ask." Rae Jean took the pillow from behind her neck and sat up. Mittens jumped from the couch and then gave a long stretch like someone that had just woke up. Rae Jean folded her legs under her skirt sidesaddle and reached for her tea.

"Said I should ask you." Rae Jean took a couple of swallows. "That's why I'm asking."

What was so hard about this was that Rae Jean hardly ever got mad at me. She never scolded, never yelled, never laughed at me, never made me feel shame. Said the only trouble I ever caused was the trouble I caused for myself.

I figured as how I was going to have to talk. I reminded myself that I was good at talking. Gram always said so. Said I could talk the antlers right off a deer. I knew it was true. I could talk my way *into* some things (like free admission) and *out of* others (like detention).

I took in a deep breath. "Miss Claggett has this idea, Rae Jean. It's a dumb idea but she believes it anyway." Rae Jean and I both knew that folks in Kinship believed all kinds of dumb stuff. "She says that bad grades is usually on account of bad home conditions. And she promised to visit the home of every freshman girl who was getting a bad grade in home ec."

Rae Jean's pale blue eyes narrowed a wink. "So how bad *is* your grade, Pert?"

"Miss Claggett thinks it's bad. Bad enough to pay a visit. It's my lowest one this marking period."

Rae Jean plumped up the heart-shaped pillow. "Weren't you doing just fine in Miss Claggett's class?" I had made that pillow for Rae Jean when we'd done the sewing unit. I'd designed the shape my own self and trimmed it with white eyelet and even stitched the initials right in the center by hand: They said RJW and JWW.

"Did fine with sewing, Rae Jean. But we're doing cooking now."

"Cooking? Pert Wilson's having trouble with *cooking*?" Rae Jean sat straight up and the shoulders of her blouse slipped backward. Her eyes lost that dreamy, sleepy look they sometimes had.

I hung my head. It sure did sound like a fish story. I'd had a job at Elmer Byer's drugstore up in town before all the commotion about serving coloreds at his lunch counter. Elmer Byer fired me for taking orders from them and giving them a seat. After that, I took the job at the Bijou Theater. But at Byer's Drugs, I'd been a waitress and short-order cook. I could do most any kind of grill work. Hamburgers, BLTs, grilled cheese, fried-egg sandwiches. Course, I didn't cook much at home. Jimmy and me ate a lot of TV dinners.

Rae Jean straightened the collar of her blouse. Then she said, "What grade are you getting, Pert?"

"A low one."

"How low?"

"Way down there."

"How far down?"

"An F, Rae Jean," I said, staring at the floor and watching the yellow marks in the linoleum leap like tiny flames. "I'm getting an F."

Gene Nugent,

TRAILER 9

Rae Jean doesn't know her daughter smokes. But I've seen Pert Wilson slipping off into the woods for a cigarette lots of times. I usually go out at night to walk Sarge. That's my black Lab. A dog's better company than most people, if you ask me. Sometimes I see the red tip on the end of Pert's cigarette like a signal flare.

Got a metal plate in my head after I got back from Korea. On permanent disability now. Used the plate to screw the two parts of my brain back together. Works fine, thank you. The hell of it was it was one of my own buddies did it. Thought I was the enemy and fired away.

Best thing about living in a trailer court is that nobody bothers you. I watch people, but I don't say much. Watched the Weevils for years. They're running a bookmaking operation, if you ask me. All those people coming in the back late at night, dropping by the trailer court, nosing around. This court'd be perfect if it wasn't for that criminal element.

Only time I go out is Friday nights. That's my bowling night. It's all the people contact I can take, thank you. Almost made it to the state championships last year. Would have, too, if I had made that split on the last frame.

I can see Pert Wilson smoking out there now. I figure she's entitled to whatever pleasure she can snatch. She's had a full plate of trouble. Always liked the way Pert walked. Tall and proud. Tucking the newspaper up under her arm and

17

sashaying across the court. Always admired the gal. Knew what it was to hold your head up and not give in to the shame. Since she was a tiny thing, Pert's brought me my newspaper every day. Always give her a Goo Goo cluster for the effort. Like the idea of putting something sweet in her life, even if it is just chocolate and peanuts.

3

That Saturday morning last spring we got up with the chickens, and Rae Jean and I cleaned for a long time. We didn't talk.

As Rae Jean emptied Mittens's litter box and shredded up fresh newspapers, I thought of my daddy. Gram had noticed the name Samuel James Wilson on a *Tribune* list of people with unclaimed bank funds. Samuel James Wilson was my granddaddy, my daddy's daddy. I didn't understand how people could forget that they had money in the bank, but Gram said most of those people on the list was dead, with either no relatives or relatives that didn't give a lick about them. Gram said that Rae Jean, as my daddy's wife, ought to march up to the bank and claim that money herself.

I didn't know much about my granddaddy. Only that he was a carpenter who had raised nine kids, lost his right thumb in an accident with a circular saw, drank too much, and died right before Jimmy was born. But hearing my granddaddy's name made me wish two wishes: that my daddy would come back home to claim that money, and that my daddy would decide he wanted to stay.

Alice Potter was friends with a granny woman who had

taught Alice about ESP, and Alice had taught me. ESP stood for extrasensory perception; it was a belief that people could communicate without words, by just wishing or trusting. You couldn't prove ESP; you just took it on faith.

ESP was about people who got shivers up their spine and decided not to take an airplane that afterwards happened to crash. ESP was about people knowing their great-uncle was sick even though he lived three thousand miles away and they hadn't talked in twenty years. ESP was about a fifteen-year-old girl who'd been sending her daddy messages ever since she was small. She'd close her eyes tight and see the stars on the back of her eyelids and say, *"If my daddy can hear or my daddy can see, help him receive this message from me."* Then she'd tell him things she wanted him to know: that Rae Jean needed a better job or that Jimmy was fixing to drop out of school or that she was tossing and turning in bed at night.

Mittens leaped off the back of the sofa and brushed Rae Jean's ankle as Rae Jean moved to clear off the coffee table. I had brought Mittens to Rae Jean years ago. I had found her when she was just a kitten. She was lost and wailing like a banshee. When I picked her up she was light as a sack of gray dustballs, and she was shivering. I made a sling from my T-shirt and carried her home like a baby. Rae Jean loved her right off. She named her Mittens on account of her four white paws.

I'd always liked watching Rae Jean with animals, and I was grateful she'd found work with Doc Jackson. She got the job because she was anxious about Jimmy and me. She'd been having to leave us at night while she worked the desk at the Sleepy Time Motel, and it worried her sick. She knew she needed a steady day job.

Doc Jackson let her start by cleaning cages and sweeping and giving the animals their medicine. But after a while, he decided to teach Rae Jean a few vet things. Now Rae Jean knows a slew about animals.

Rae Jean kept on straightening up while I followed behind with the feather duster. After she turned over the middle cushion of the couch so you couldn't see the tea stains, she rassled with the afghan Gram had made for the family, finally laying it flat out across the back of the sofa. I liked it that way: it showed off Gram's neat stitches and it hid the rips both.

"You never seen such a dumb way of cooking as Miss Claggett has, Rae Jean," I said. The feather duster swirled and flared like a cancan skirt. "Patty shells. Would you believe the last thing we had to fix, Rae Jean, was patty shells? Miss Claggett says people from the best homes always eats patty shells." I think Miss Claggett wished she was from one of the best homes herself, but everybody in town knew her type: too poor to paint and too proud to whitewash.

I glanced at Rae Jean out of the corner of my eye. "Now who in their right mind this side of the White House is ever going to have cause to eat a patty shell?"

"You are, Pert," Rae Jean said.

I stopped dusting. "Why, Rae Jean?"

"Because you're going to pass home ec." I saw a black newspaper streak on Rae Jean's right cheek at the place where the dimple appeared when she smiled. You couldn't see the dimple now; Rae Jean was not smiling. She never once looked at me. She just turned away and started picking the dead leaves off the spider plant.

Something that was hard to swallow stuck in my throat.

It felt like a ball of flour and water and lard. But I knew it wasn't really dough that was caught there. Part of it was guilt at disappointing Rae Jean. The other part was shame about the pile of things that Nympha Claggett tried to teach me that was different from the life I led in Happy Trails. Like putting different colors on the plate. Miss Claggett said to think of a dinner plate like an artist's palette: red tomato over here, green asparagus over there. Hadn't she ever enjoyed an all-white meal of mashed potatoes, noodles, and white rolls with gravy like the one Jimmy and me fixed last Thanksgiving when Rae Jean was called out on emergency at the vet's? What was so important about those different colors anyway? Didn't they all just mash up together in the same stomach?

I moved to the end table next to the couch to dust up under Jimmy's insect collection and my handprint ashtray. Rae Jean had kept both of them there for years as if they was pieces for a museum. Jimmy had made the insect collection in sixth grade. He and Rae Jean had roamed the fields around Kinship, turning up rocks and catching the bugs that tried to wiggle away. Jimmy had mounted the insects on cardboard, covered the whole thing with Saran Wrap, and labeled each of his specimens in dark black lettering. It was the last time Jimmy Wilson ever showed any interest in school.

I picked up the handprint ashtray and dusted under it. Then I looked at it hard. I had made it for Rae Jean when I was in kindergarten. The ceramic was rough and ragged, but there was my five-year-old handprint left in the clay like a fossil. The best thing about that handprint fossil was that my fist was unclenched.

I couldn't remember much about the years before kinder-garten. All I knew is what people told me. What they talked about most was the fruit crate. Rae Jean had wanted a crib for her babies, a white crib carved with scrolls and curlicues like you saw on thrones. She'd had to settle for a fruit crate padded with a quilt crocheted by Gram.

I wondered how my daddy had felt about that fruit crate. Or about the red-faced squawling baby with the balled-up fists. Mostly about the baby, I reckon. Mostly I wondered how my daddy had felt about that baby.

I'd never known my daddy. Never even seen him except in that one wallet photo Rae Jean had framed for me. It showed his face in profile. He had dark blue eyes and a strong square chin. He'd looked like a handsome young boy with wavy black hair and a sweet but crooked smile.

I straightened one of Rae Jean's paint-by-numbers pic-tures hanging on the wall. The picture was of a white poo-dle. Most folks don't know how many shades there is in white, but Rae Jean knew every fancy name for them—like alabaster, pearl, and eggshell. There was something about Rae Jean's paint-by-numbers pictures that made me sad. I thought of her setting at the kitchen table on a Saturday night. I thought about the way she dabbed colors onto the white cardboard, laying dots in the places where the number guides said. When I thought of Rae Jean like that, my heart got soft; she reminded me of a schoolgirl trying to do just what the teacher said. Month after month. Year after year.

Fact was, I knew all kinds of things about my mama, but I only knew one thing about my daddy. The only thing I knew for sure about him was that he'd disappeared.

The only other baby story I'd ever heard about me was the

one where my daddy looked me over when the nurse brought me, squawking and screaming, to him before he signed the birth papers. Rae Jean said he'd wrote *Perty* on the birth certificate because I was the prettiest baby in Georgia.

I straightened the corners of Rae Jean's picture of *The Last Supper*. She kept it over her shrine. It was the only paint-by-numbers that wasn't an animal.

I heard Jimmy rustling around in the kitchen. He had to be at the Texaco station by seven, and he was always late. "I'm runnin' a little late, Rae Jean," he'd say every morning, same as today. "Could you touch up my work shirt real quick?" It was another one of our routines.

"Touch up your own shirt, Jimmy Wilson," I shouted this morning. "Can't you see your mama's busy?"

"It's all right, Pert," Rae Jean called. "It just won't be pressed as nice today."

I could hear her rushing around in the bedroom, pulling up the spread. The trailer was too small for an ironing board. If you wanted something pressed, you set a piece of cardboard on the foot of the bed, and got down on your knees to iron. Whenever I saw Rae Jean kneeling over my brother Jimmy's shirt, I could feel a tiny pile of kindling starting to smolder inside me.

Jimmy was running water for his coffee. He left the trailer every morning with a cup of instant coffee in his thick hands. He made it from hot water straight out of the tap.

I followed him to the kitchen sink, scolding like a nag. "Don't forget to take that girlie calendar of yours off the wall," I said. Jimmy Wilson had only two things on his mind: cars and girls. He *had* the girl, Sue Ellen Jenkins, but

24

he didn't have the car. If I could have picked one or the other for Jimmy, I knew I'd prefer the one with wheels, the one that didn't make all those whining sounds.

"Yes, Miss Bossy," he said over his shoulder. "Wouldn't want Miss Claggett to think that family life was about anything more than cooking and sewing." Then he looked me in the eye and winked. I punched his arm.

When Jimmy left, I went back to the front room while Rae Jean ran around the kitchen, cleaning up Jimmy's mess. I could hear Rae Jean's slippers slapping back and forth at her heels as she moved the few steps between the stove, the sink, and the refrigerator.

"And peas, Rae Jean," I called to her, getting on my knees in front of the couch. "You should hear the way Miss Claggett carries on about peas. Took a whole period last week to teach us how to shell 'em." I was peering under the sofa, and I wiggled my duster under it to sweep out the dust bunnies.

Rae Jean padded into the front room, slung the dish towel over her shoulder, and grinned. "Well, Pert, honey, no teacher's going to see any home that's better than ours is. I'm right proud of the job we did."

Then she put on her pink skirt, pink high heels, and pink angora sweater that she wore only for special occasions. I combed my hair in a side part to cover the fact that my roots needed peroxiding again, and I rubbed the scuff marks on my white flats with a piece of chalk.

When we returned to the front room, Rae Jean gave it a quick once-over and then frowned. She put her index finger to her mouth. "That ashtray, Pert," she said, bouncing her finger off her lips while she thought, "the handprint ashtray on the table. You'd better put it away."

"Why, Rae Jean?" I said. "What's wrong with it?"

"Wouldn't want Miss Claggett to think we smoked."

I put the ashtray in the cupboard, and Rae Jean moved to the corner of the room to straighten her little shrine, then mumble a prayer. The shrine was a high kitchen stool covered with a white sheet. On it was a statue of Jesus, a rosary, a glass candlestick with a white beeswax candle, a hanky Rae Jean used for a head covering, and a Holy Bible. Sometimes Mittens ran under the cloth and bumped the statue over; it was the only time Rae Jean ever got annoyed with her.

Rae Jean and Jimmy and I was the only RC family in Kinship, and when we was small, Rae Jean used to make us kneel down at that shrine for Sunday prayers. Now that Frank Alhambra had started the taxi service, we drove all the way to Troy every Sunday for mass at St. Jude's. Whenever Rae Jean couldn't figure things out, she fiddled with the silver cross on the chain around her neck and then mumbled a prayer to Mary.

After she prayed, Rae Jean ran to the bedroom and returned with her perfume bottle, squeezing the spongy bell so that squirts of perfume drifted all over the front room.

Then we sat like statues on each end of the couch, listening to the drip, drip of the bathroom tap that always needed fixing, staring at the dead bugs of Jimmy's insect collection, breathing in the sharp, sweet smell of Rae Jean's perfume, and waiting for the arrival of Miss Nympha Claggett.

Iris Breeding,

TRAILER 1

My Carter was the one to live here first. Carter Breeding was
sent to Kinship on a scholarship from a university up
Nawth. University of Chicago, it was.

When I first met him, I was working at my uncle Sam's
grocery store in town. I was visiting for the summer and
earning money for junior college. I'd never heard tell of an-
thropology *in my life*. My Carter's a cultural anthropologist.
He studies things like kinship patterns and customs that are
just common *say-ince* to people that aren't professors.

But it's lonely in Happy Trails. I've been trying to help my
Carter with his work, but it's the most piddling work *in this
world*. I'd much rather be sewing curtains or aprons or learning to crochet with Wilma, Rae Jean Wilson's mama. Wilma
sits and talks now and again. I told her about my hope for a
baby and what all, and she taught me to crochet a baby
afghan.

This morning, I looked out my window and saw a lady
tripping through the mud to call on Wilsons. A big black
pocketbook banged at her side, looking like Gene Nugent's
bowling-ball bag. The lady heaved herself up the concrete
stay-ups, and I've never seen anybody so fat *in this world.*
"Yoo-hoo," she called out, "it's Nympha Claggett."

I saw Rae Jean open the door, and I think she said something like "Good morning, Miss Claggett. How nice to see
you."

4

"Nice to see you, too, Mrs. Wilson," Miss Claggett said, her tiny eyes scurrying like mice into every corner of the front room. She wiped her muddy shoes on the oval mat that lay by the door.

"Here, now, can I take your purse?" Rae Jean said. "And won't you come on in and sit down?"

On the way to the couch, Miss Claggett tripped on the edge of the throw rug and walloped her shin on the coffee table something good. Clutching her shin with one hand and the arm of the couch with the other, she lowered herself onto a cushion, and I thought I heard the sound of seams giving ever so slightly.

"Whew," she said, dropping her purse beside her with a thud and peeling off her white gloves. She took them off dainty-like, one finger at a time, the way she showed us in that class on etiquette. Then she spit on her palm and began rubbing her shin with the spit.

Rae Jean took the seat to the right of Miss Claggett on the couch, and I sat on the footstool to her left.

I leaned forward on the stool. "Can I get you some salve, Miss Claggett?" Miss Claggett's gloveless hands waved me away. "Are you sure you're all right? We got Ben-Gay and Bactine in the bathroom." Fact was, I was sorry she wouldn't let me help. I figured showing her some Red Cross nursing skills might do something for my grade.

"I've never been in a trailer before," Miss Claggett said. "It's something like riding in one of those Pullman cars on a train, isn't it?" She folded her gloves together and set them on her lap. "Everything all squinched together. Bed pulling down from the wall. Card table pulling out from the windowsill." She was still reaching to touch the spot on her shin, but at least she had stopped spitting. "I never thought about how it could be right dangerous in here. What with everything so close and all," she said.

Rae Jean offered, "A trailer's not so bad when you get used to it."

I wanted to put in a good word for trailers, but fact was, lots of times I felt cramped as a chick in an egg in here. But I didn't want Miss Claggett to think of trailers as a bad environment. "Trailer, houseboat, apartment," I said. "Home's just anyplace where you've got kin. It don't feel crowded when you all get along."

Miss Claggett reached into her big bag and took out her grade book, a steno pad, and a pen. She started writing something down. I hoped it had to do with what I said about home and kin, but I was afraid it had something to do with her shin and the coffee table.

"Before we get down to business, Mrs. Wilson," she said, fanning the air with the grade book and sniffing, her nose a-going like a basset on a trail, "I've got to compliment you on how nice it smells in here. It's not Pine-Sol, is it?"

"Thank you, no, Miss Claggett," Rae Jean said. "Evening in Paris."

I could feel a tiny kettle of hope beginning to simmer in my chest. "Rae Jean keeps a house real good," I said. "You ain't seen nothin' like it in a place without a maid."

Nympha Claggett looked up from her writing. "Who?" she said.

"Rae Jean."

"Who's that?" Miss Claggett looked startled.

"What do you mean 'Who's that?' You're sitting right next to her. Rae Jean's my mama there."

"You call your mother by her *first name*?" Nympha Claggett started fanning herself with the stenographer's pad.

I looked at her straight on and said, "It's her name, ain't it?" Nympha Claggett was dumb as a mule and made twice the salary.

Rae Jean made a motion with her hands like smoothing wrinkles out of sheets. "What you need to see, Miss Claggett," she said, soft as a kitten, "is that Pert and I have a special kind of relationship. It's so special that we call each other by our first names."

My mama was trying to shush me with her hands, but I wasn't going to leave her stranded like this. I said, "It ain't like most mothers and daughters. We're real close. Sort of like sisters. It seems silly to call a sister anything besides a first name, don't it, Rae Jean?"

"Oh, I see," said Miss Claggett. She was writing something down fast as lightning. "And while we're on the subject of names, Mrs. Wilson." Then she looked up from her writing. "You are *Mrs.* Wilson, aren't you?"

Rae Jean slowly blushed the color of newborn hamsters.

I went straight to red: A familiar fire was sweating up my insides. "Of course she's *Mrs.* Wilson," I said. "How'd you think she'd come to have us kids if she wasn't married?"

Then I passed Miss Claggett the heart-shaped pillow with the initials RJW and JWW on it. "Made this pillow in honor of them," I said. "That's Rae Jean over there," I said, pointing to the RJW. "That's my daddy," I said, pointing out the JWW. "Made that in your own sewing class, Miss Claggett."

Rae Jean saw that Nympha Claggett was getting my goat, so she stepped in, quiet and calm. "We don't really know if we can expect James Wilson back, Miss Claggett. He's been gone right long. Ever since Pert here was born, in fact." Rae Jean fingered the silver cross she wore around her neck. Then she leaned forward. "But we hear from him now and again. And we *are* married, Miss Claggett."

Rae Jean wasn't lying: We did hear from Daddy now and again. Five times he sent Rae Jean fifty dollars, once from West Virginia and four times from Tennessee. Another time he sent me and Jimmy a winking crystal from a cave he'd crawled through in Kentucky. One time he even sent me my own letter. It was written on a piece of white business paper that said SPEEDY AUTO PARTS, CHATTANOOGA, TENN. at the top. Next to the words was a wheel with wings that looked like it was streaking across the page. The letter said:

HEY PERTY HON—

*HOW YOU BEEN—TRIED TO GET A TRAILER PARK
MANAGER TO BUY ONE OF MY ELECTRIC
HOOKUPS—SAID HE ALL READY HAD A GOOD
HOOKUP BUT SAID HE MIGHT TAKE A GANDER AT*

31

*MY SHOWER SYSTEM—HE'S LOADED WITH MONEY
AND IT LOOKS LIKE HE'LL BE GIVING ME SOME OF
IT—I'LL TALK TO HIM AGAIN NEXT WEEK*

*BET YR PERTY AS A PITCHER BY NOW—JUST LIKE YR
MAMA—*

I'LL SEE YOU ALL QUICK AS A JIF—

YOUR DADDY—J. W. WILSON

I had read the letter so often that I knew it by heart. My favorite part was where my daddy said he would see us "quick as a jif." It was like a favorite line in a poem. But so far, a jif meant at least five or six years.

Miss Claggett said, "I didn't mean to imply, Mrs. Wilson . . ." And then she broke off and fished around for words. "It's just that family situations seem to be changing nowdays. People getting married and then divorced and then remarried and all. Things are more difficult in families today, don't you think?"

I figured I could stick in my two cents as well as Rae Jean. "I don't think so, Miss Claggett," I said. "Things is simple as pie around here with Rae Jean in charge."

Miss Claggett pulled a hanky from her pocketbook, pressing it down the side of her nose, wiping up sweat. "Well, that may be, Pert," she said, the sweat making damp spots on the hanky, "but I can't help seeing the changes in Kinship, what with all the broken families and all."

I didn't like those words: *broken families.* Maybe the folks in Happy Trails had been stomped on like cigarette butts, but they wasn't broken.

I looked Miss Claggett square in the eyes and my words came steady. "Our family ain't *broken*," I said.

Miss Claggett quickly looked away, patting the back of her neck with her hanky. When she was done, she slipped the hanky down the front of her dress. I never saw anyone in the world wet as Nympha Claggett.

Rae Jean put her hand on Miss Claggett's arm and gave her a sweet smile. I could see the dimple deep in her right cheek. "Well, now, Miss Claggett," Rae Jean said. "I'm sure you're not half as interested in Pert's family as you are in how she's doing in your home ec class, isn't that right?"

"Yes, Mrs. Wilson. I've been right worried about your daughter here." Nympha Claggett picked up her grade book and waved it around while she talked. "Pert's grades were fine when we were on sewing, but now that it's cooking, she has slipped. Frankly," she said, slapping the grade book down on the table, "Pert's getting an F."

"I know," Rae Jean said, and Miss Claggett's eyes widened in a look of disbelief. I saw that she had hoped to surprise Rae Jean with this bad news. "Tell me, Miss Claggett, what the problem seems to be."

Miss Claggett fidgeted. The polka dots on her dress wiggled first to the left and then to the right. "Well," she said, refusing to look at me, "she has no interest in cooking. Stares out the window half the time. After we spent days on presentation, she refused to arrange things artfully on the plate with any attention to color." As she talked, the end of her hanky flashed out the front of her dress like a rabbit tail.

"And she dumped cayenne pepper in the white sauce as a joke. Ellen Russell said so." Finally Miss Claggett looked at me and glared. "And now she's flunked the major test on the four food groups."

I glared back while Rae Jean rose from the couch, moved behind my stool, and placed her hands firmly on my shoulders. Inside, I was steaming. I'd had about enough of Nympha Claggett. First she had to get all over my family. Now she was all over me.

I held my tongue while Rae Jean rubbed my shoulders. Her hands was like a blanket on my fire.

"Miss Claggett," Rae Jean said, "I appreciate everything you've told me, and I thank you for that information. Now, it seems to me that the most important thing might be the fact that Pert failed that test on the four food groups. Is that right?"

Nympha Claggett shifted her weight, and the rabbit tail flashed out again. "Well, yes," she said. "Yes, perhaps it is."

"Was that test what brought Pert's grade down to an F?"

"Well, yes," she said again. "It was. It was the last straw."

"So the most important thing Pert needs to do to get a passing grade in your class is to pass that test on the four food groups. Is that so?"

Nympha Claggett picked up the grade book lying on the table. She licked her thumb to flip through the pages and then ran her fingers down a column in the book and then across at a line of grades. She frowned over what she saw, as if it was a trick question on a quiz. "Well," she said, "I suppose if she can pass that test, then she can pass the class this marking period."

Rae Jean took her hands off my shoulders and moved to

sit next to Miss Claggett on the couch again. She perched on the edge of the cushion and leaned over at Miss Claggett. "Tell me," Rae Jean said, "does she actually have to take another *test* on the four food groups?"

Miss Claggett picked up her grade book and hugged it to her chest. She looked scared that Rae Jean might try to steal it from her. "I don't know what you're getting at exactly, Mrs. Wilson."

I didn't know exactly what Rae Jean was getting at, neither.

Then Rae Jean jumped from the couch and started pacing. "I was just thinking," she said. "Pert and Jimmy do most of the cooking here at home. I'm often tired out after a day with Doc Jackson. And Pert's really a wonder with the meals around here, let me tell you. It's amazing what she can do with the things in my Frigidaire."

Rae Jean's high heels made her legs look long and graceful, and as she twisted and turned in her pink sweater and skirt, she reminded me of a dancing ballerina on a music box. "It's nearly magic what Pert can do," Rae Jean went on. "I've watched her time and time again. It doesn't matter what all's in the fridge. Doughnuts. Pickles. Grape jelly. Pert can wind up with the best meals. She manages to get every food group represented somehow."

What was Rae Jean talking about? Half the time we ran out of milk and I had to make it from the powdered stuff in a box Rae Jean kept on a shelf. Sometimes we put it on graham crackers if we ran out of cereal, too. Lots of times *that* was supper.

Rae Jean gave a little twirl, and then she clapped her hands. "Oh, don't you see, Miss Claggett?" she said. "Let

Pert *cook* for you! Let Pert fix you something to eat. Of course, she'll have to make sure she has all the food groups there and all. Would that be okay with you, Miss Claggett? Would that help Pert pass cooking?"

I got up from the stool and crossed to Rae Jean. "But, Rae Jean," I said, "we're out of near 'bout everything. I can't cook for Miss Claggett on the spot like this right now!"

Rae Jean grabbed me by the shoulders and stood still. She looked at me straight on. "Pert Wilson," she said, "you've got to pass that test if you want to have a life outside of this trailer court for any part of the rest of this year."

I couldn't believe what I was hearing. Was Rae Jean fixing on grounding me if I didn't pass that test? I'd never been grounded in my whole life.

Then Rae Jean said something truer than a threat. "I've seen you make something out of nothing a million times. Your daddy's the same way. I know you can do this, Pert."

"Frankly, Pert," Miss Claggett said, "I think your mother here's got a great idea. You'll save me the time of making up a whole new test, and I'll save *you* the time of having to come in after school to take it. Besides, I'm already here. There's just no time like the present."

"But, Miss Claggett," I protested.

"You heard Miss Claggett, honey," Rae Jean said, and she pointed to the kitchen. *Git!* her eyes said, and I saw the way the blue turned to gray; strong and tough as steel.

Charlie Hale,

TRAILER 10

I'd got back from the construction site in Latonia early. It was raining so hard we'd had to quit working on account of the mud. I can't see why so many of those day workers are dishonest. Right now some of them are stealing new plumbing fixtures from the site over in Kinship Acres; then they sell them for twice what they cost. I could have sworn one of the workers in Latonia was James Wilson, even though I hadn't seen him since high school. Same black head of hair. Same strut. Same way of reaching into somebody else's pockets to make a buck without having to work for a living. Everything the same except for the beard. I was likely wrong. I could barely see through the sheet of rain.

I sat by the kitchen window picking dried mud from my boot treads with a pocketknife and looking out for Rae Jean. You'd be amazed what a quiet man can see. I confess when Rae Jean smiled and that dimple dug into her right cheek, I wanted to reach out to pet her.

I *b'lieve* I saw Nympha Claggett out by the sign that says Happy Trails Trailer Court. I could see Rae Jean and Pert through their trailer window. Rae Jean smoothed her skirt and Pert fluffed her hair. Then Miss Claggett heaved herself up their concrete steps.

When Rae Jean opened the metal door, she was wearing a pink sweater that looked like cotton candy. I'd seen people come to her door before. Social workers. School officials.

Rae Jean hated the way they looked down on her, but she always treated them real nice. When Jimmy dropped out of school, the superintendent had paid a personal call. I could have told him he didn't need to worry with Rae Jean in charge. She worked steady. She went to church. She never went to bars. She was strong. I confess you'd find it hard to *b'lieve* to look at her; she was just a bit of a thing.

Sometimes I'd sit at the kitchen table with her while she studied Doc Jackson's animal books. She had trouble with lots of the words, so I told her if she'd call them out, I'd look them up in the dictionary for her. I confess it worked like a charm. Rae Jean had started with Doc Jackson's book on cats. I never would have *b'lieved* cats had so many different kinds of worms. First word I'd looked up was *integumentary.* That's skin.

I was never much for words. I was more for doing. Words are something I always trip over. Like my own big feet.

When folks think of Charlie Hale they think of masonry, plumbing, drywall.

They don't guess at the things I see.

Or that I know what it is to dream.

5

I opened the refrigerator and stuck my head inside. It was practically empty, and it smelled like a mix of sour milk and the coolant Jimmy used in cars. I lifted a covered dish of tuna fish, sniffed, and put it back; blue fuzz was growing on the surface. It looked like we had a pitcher of tea, a dish of leftover grits, a jar of grape jelly, half an opened can of chicken-gumbo soup, a few slices of drying bologna, and a jar of French's mustard with barely enough for a single swipe across a hot dog. A couple of butter pats was left in the butter dish, and Jimmy had drank only half a quart of the milk. A tomato sat on the counter next to a loaf of bread that had only four slices left, one of them an end.

I was hopping mad.

I wiped the cat hair from the top of the dinette and went for napkins. Shoot. We was out of paper napkins and paper towels both. I went to the bathroom, picked up three washcloths, and stuffed them through some old curtain rings that might pass for napkin holders. I set them on the dinette next to the plastic dishes Rae Jean had ordered special from the coupon on the detergent box.

I slapped the skillet across the stove. I watched the butter bubble and brown, and I slid the knife through the tomato. As I worked, mad as a hornet, I thought about how I'd like to use that hot grease and that sharp knife on Nympha Claggett. Would I cut her up and then fry her? Or would I fry her first and then cut?

I heard Rae Jean's heels click across the floor. Her head peeked around the door frame. "'Bout ready, Pert?" she said.

"Almost," I grunted. I was *almost* ready. Except for the part that was most important to me, the only part that would give me satisfaction. Nobody oughta dare to cross Pert Wilson because Pert Wilson was always one to cross 'em back. I huddled next to the sink, working on a special blend from the cold white milk in the milk bottle, the deep-blue milk of magnesia bottle fetched from the bathroom, and the tiny amber glass of vanilla flavoring. Then I rubbed my hands together, moved to the doorway, and announced, "Lunch is ready, ladies."

I pulled back Miss Claggett's chair and seated her across from Rae Jean. The dinette was shoved next to the window, and you could only set three at the table at once. We usually ate in the front room off our laps.

"My, what a view you've got here," Miss Claggett said, looking out the window. "This is like lunching on a dining car, passing all the tire heaps and rusty junkyards along the way." I couldn't tell whether Miss Claggett was admiring our scenery or insulting it.

"And what nice napkins you've got here, Pert," she said, removing the washcloth from the curtain ring and laying it on her lap. "They look kind of familiar. Where'd you get them?"

I couldn't tell her I got them straight from the bathroom,

so I just agreed with her. "Ain't they special? They're thick and thirsty. Great for wipin' up barbecue."

Rae Jean cleared her throat. "May we have a moment for a blessing, ladies?" she said. Rae Jean crossed herself and then stretched out her hand to take mine. I could feel a current pumping through our fingers the way it always did when Rae Jean, Jimmy, and me held hands over grace. It made me feel safe, as if the circle of hands was keeping the dark things away from my family.

Miss Claggett looked puzzled, so I reached over and took her hand; it was damp as dough.

I stood up. "Now, if you'll pass me your plates, ladies, we can have somethin' to eat." Then I filled their plates by the stove and set them down on the table with a little curtsy. Rae Jean smiled. Miss Claggett tried to.

The sandwiches was hot and steaming. Miss Claggett lifted the lid of the bread. I'd given her the two good pieces. Rae Jean and I had open-faced sandwiches. Rae Jean had the one other good piece of bread, and I had the end. Miss Claggett asked, "What's on the menu today, Miss Wilson?"

I sat down and said, "Grits sandwiches."

Nympha Claggett looked like she had chomped on gristle.

I tried to help. "Ain't you never had a grits sandwich before, Miss Claggett?"

"No, Pert," she said. It was clear she was telling the truth. "Never."

Rae Jean piped up. "Well, then, Miss Claggett," she said, "you're in for a treat."

Rae Jean and I dug in, and Nympha Claggett looked confused. "Don't I need some silverware, Pert?"

"Heck, no, Miss Claggett," I said. "Grits sandwiches is best with two hands. You can really wrap yourself around 'em that way."

Miss Claggett stared at her sandwich and then moved her damp white hands in the direction of her plate.

"Would you like some ketchup, Miss Claggett?" I asked. "Or some pepper?" I slid the ketchup bottle over to her and the salt and pepper shakers. The salt shaker was a mama pig. The pepper was a daddy.

"No, thank you, Pert," Miss Claggett said.

I jumped up from the table as I saw Miss Claggett take her first bite. "Oh, bless me," I said. "I near forgot our drinks."

While I was pouring the mixture at the sink into a cold glass, I saw Nympha Claggett swallow a nibble of food and then lay her sandwich across her plate. She looked tuckered out. I set the milk down in front of her.

Suddenly Mittens jumped on the table. I hadn't seen her coming. She landed right on her favorite spot. Right on the windowsill at the edge of the table.

Nympha Claggett jumped from her seat, sending the plastic plates sliding.

"Get off of there, Mittens," Rae Jean said, lifting the gray ball of fur from the table. "I do apologize. But you know cats and windows, Miss Claggett," she said, carrying Mittens to the bedroom.

Miss Claggett looked like she didn't know the first thing about cats and windows.

When Rae Jean returned, she used her washcloth napkin to dust the spot where Mittens had landed. A few strands of fur floated across the table. "Now, then," Rae Jean said, propping her elbows on the table and smiling across at Miss Claggett, "let's get off the subject of pets and talk about this nice meal Pert's fixed us here."

Nympha Claggett settled herself in her seat again. The polka dots across her chest was thumping in and out. "Yes, Mrs. Wilson," she said. "That's a good idea. You promised to tell us about the four food groups, Pert. I'd like to hear how you'll do on this test your mother proposed."

I took a deep breath and studied my plate. "Well, now, let's see," I said, wiping the melted butter off my chin.

I pointed to the half sandwich left on my plate. "There's the bread-and-cereal group, Miss Claggett. The bread part's there," I said, pointing to the toast. "Any dummy knows that's the bread group." I gave a quick glance to Miss Claggett. "But the grits is the cereal part of the bread-and-cereal group. Grits, Miss Claggett," I said, "is about the finest food in Georgia. Grits is real good for you, too, Miss Claggett. Grits got more vitamin C than orange juice. That's a fact."

Miss Claggett wrinkled her brow. She thought she knew everything there was to know about vitamins.

"And the bologna in there," I said, lifting the lid of Miss Claggett's sandwich, "that's your protein group. Your meat. Your chicken. Stuff like that." I didn't tell her how I had cut the dried part of the bologna away.

Miss Claggett stared at the bologna. Then she took a fat finger and peeled away some of the casing still stuck to the edges of her slice. She dropped the wiggling casing on the plate like a worm she hadn't wanted to touch.

"And your tomato in there," I said, "now that tomato's a little more challenging. I'm sure it's part of the fruit-and-vegetable group, Miss Claggett. But I'm not sure as to whether it's a fruit or a vegetable. What do you think, Miss Claggett? Do you think tomato's a fruit or a vegetable?"

Miss Claggett had pulled her hanky from her chest and started swabbing her neck again.

"Dear me, Miss Claggett," I said, "you're looking a little peaked. Why don't you drink some of this nice cold milk here. Made a nice milk drink special for you. It's your milk-and-dairy-product group, Miss Claggett. Cold milk sure can stop a sweat."

I watched her gulp half the glass, and she seemed to cool down a bit. "Go on, Miss Claggett," I urged her. "There ain't nothin' better for you than vitamin D milk. They call it bottled sunshine."

I watched her finish the milk; the red fire that ate at my insides cooled as I watched.

"That was downright delicious, Pert," Miss Claggett said, stuffing her hanky back down between her world globes. She smacked her lips. "It's got a bit of a chalky aftertaste, but it's got flavor sweet as vanilla extract. You put imported vanilla in there, Pert?"

"No'm. The vanilla's just from Shriners' store up town."

"Well," Miss Claggett said, pushing her plate away from her and setting the milk glass down, "I guess you do know something about the four food groups, Pert Wilson."

I looked over at Rae Jean; her face was glowing above her pink sweater. "That's right, Miss Claggett," Rae Jean said. "I told you my Pert could cook. Now, come on in here and let's sit and talk."

Rae Jean showed Miss Claggett to the front room, and I piled the dishes by the sink and joined them.

"I really must be going," Miss Claggett was saying. "It's been lovely, Mrs. Wilson."

Rae Jean handed Miss Claggett her grade book, her pad and pen, and her gloves. I handed her the big black bag.

Rae Jean walked her to the door, and I hung a little behind. "Now you're sure my Pert will pass your class this marking period, Miss Claggett? You see how good she knows the food groups, don't you?"

Miss Claggett nodded and smiled at Rae Jean. They shook hands, and then Rae Jean opened the door.

I watched Nympha Claggett from the window. I watched the heels of her shoes sink in the mud and the polka dots sway like moving targets.

Rae Jean stood behind me and watched, too. "I was proud of you, Pert," she said. "You did a good job."

"Thanks, Rae Jean," I said, watching Miss Claggett's purse slap against her side. Rae Jean had moved away from the window. I heard two clunks that meant she had pulled off her high heels, and when I turned away from the window I saw that she sat slumped on the couch, as tired as she was after a full day of work.

"Would a glass of iced tea just about hit the spot right now?" I asked.

Rae Jean was reaching for the *Good Tidings,* and I caught her smiling at me. "Why, yes, Pert Wilson," Rae Jean said. "Hit the spot square in the polka-dot bull's-eye." Then we both busted up laughing.

I moved to the kitchen and opened the Frigidaire. Then I plopped some ice cubes in a glass and filled it to the top with tea. Before I brought it to her, I picked up the empty milk glass, holding it to my nose, sniffing the white chalky smell.

Then I screwed the lid tight on the big blue bottle, and returned it to the medicine cabinet in the bathroom.

I put Rae Jean's tea on one of the Planters peanut trays they'd been giving away at Jimmy's Texaco station; Mr. Peanut was tilting his top hat and leaning on his black cane. He seemed to be winking at me. As I set Rae Jean's glass on the end table next to the couch, I thought maybe the Planters peanut man was wondering the same thing I was: how long it took a big cold glass of milk of magnesia to work.

Ora Weevil,

TRAILER 3

Ida and me thinks that Wilson girl's got the spark of the devil in her. Ida laughed when I said the chile could come to work with Weevils when she growed up.

Missy come inside our trailer only once, and the devil is why. 'Bout five or six she are. Cain't sleep. Tosses and turns every single night. Says she saw the devil huddling in the dark. Wants to know how to get rid of him.

What Weevils knows that most peoples don't is that you cain't keep the devil away. Night is the other half of the day, and it lasts just as long, don't it? The moon has a dark side that's just as big as the light. Dark's where the devil lives. Ida and me doesn't tell peoples that. We gots to scratch out a living. What Ida and me knows is that peoples will do most anything under the sun to keep the dark and the devil away.

Missy would have believed whatever Ida told her. I hear Wife say you has to understand the devil to get rid of him, which just ain't true.

Then she wiggles her finger at Missy.

"When you talks about the devil," Ida says, "you has to *whisssper.*" I could hear the hissing sounds in the middle of that word. "If you'll come close, Missy, I'll learn you everything there is to know about the devil."

You should have seen that chile. Her shoulders is shaking, but she just throws 'em back and sticks her ear right next to Ida's mouth.

I cain't hear all of it, but I already know about the devil. How he cain't come into a place with light. How he gets a visit from the blue jay every Friday.

Then Ida asks the chile a bunch of questions.

"How does you get in and out of bed, Missy?"

Missy shrugs her shoulders. "Any which way, I reckon. Sometimes I flop on my back on top of the covers. Sometimes I crawl in from the top and slip down into the sheets. Sometimes I get in on the right. Other times on the left."

Ida scratches up under her turban while she thinks. Her eyes narrows into slits.

"That's it," she says. She slaps her hands together like a crack of thunder and Missy jumps back. "Your problem's with circles, Missy."

Ida knows that chile don't understand. She rubs her hands together and tosses back a laugh.

"You gots to make a strong circle, Missy. You gots to get into the bed on one side and get out on the same side. If you gets in or out on a different side, you breaks the circle, and the devil can get in. Devil can't come into a circle what's kept tight."

I heard Missy mouthing Ida's words like she was trying to memorize them. "Devil can't come into a circle what's kept tight," Missy repeated.

I swear but that Wilson girl'd believe anything Ida Weevil told her. She's just like the rest of our customers. Cain't they figure how the devil can go anyplace he wants? Ain't that why he's the devil?

Part Two

6

Every Sunday, Wilsons went to mass in Troy. First
Frank Alhambra would pull up in front of Gram's shop
in town; the sign on the window said Kinder Krafts, and inside Gram sold ceramics and glassware and the things she
crocheted. Then Frank would give a tiny toot with the horn.
Gram lived upstairs over the shop, and it took her a while to
come down. When Gram arrived, she'd be hauling her carpetbag and huffing. Finally Frank Alhambra would tip his
cap in Gram's direction while he held open the door. It went
like that every Sunday.

What was best about it, though, was seeing Gram. Seeing
Gram on Sunday was one of those habits I loved, like drinking coffee in the morning. Fact was, Gram was how I came
to like coffee in the first place. When Rae Jean worked the
night desk at the Sleepy Time Motel, sometimes she got
Gram to stay all night with Jimmy and me. On nights I
couldn't sleep, Gram never minded when I woke her up.
She'd make herself a pot of coffee and she'd heat me some
milk. Then she'd put a splash of her coffee in my milk while
she put a splash of my milk in her coffee. "Gram likes a little milk with her coffee, and Pert likes a little coffee with her

milk," she'd say night after night. I never wondered why I loved her for it: I just did.

Gram never had much good to say about church. Said it took a lifetime to get over being raised as a holy-rolling Baptist who turned Roman Catholic so she could up and marry Wilbur Kinder. But she came along with us to mass on Sundays because she said it was the one blessed hour of the week when you could get the whole family together. That's what she said. "Rae Jean, thank the powers that be for church. It's the one blessed hour of the week when you can get the whole family together." Gram never talked about God; she talked about "the powers that be," and when she used the term *blessed,* it sounded like swearing.

Like I said, I loved my Gram. But just because *I* loved her didn't mean Rae Jean always did. Fact was, the powers that be didn't usually have much to be thanked for on the ride to Troy most Sundays. Rae Jean and Gram often sat like two storm clouds: the little one in the front by Frank Alhambra, and the big one in the back between Jimmy and me.

Every Sunday Rae Jean and Gram had words between them. This particular September Sunday, the conversation went like this.

"Now, why don't you take an interest in a man, Rae Jean?"

Rae Jean sighed. Her rounded shoulders went up, then down. "You know why, Mama. I'm married."

"You call a man that drops an occasional note and a little spare change on you now and again a husband?" Gram heaved her carpetbag from the floor of the cab and plopped it onto her lap. She rooted around in it for some yarn and needles and then she snapped it shut and sighed extra loud.

Rae Jean stared out the window.

"Well, if you ask *me* you ought to take a look at Emerson Stamps." Gram's needles made the clicking sound of Ray Snowdon's false teeth.

"I *didn't* ask you, Mama. Besides, Catholics can't divorce and remarry. You know that."

"Wasn't talking about divorcing and remarrying. Just talking about getting up some male company. It's not right for a young woman like you to be all alone."

"I'm not alone. I've got Pert and Jimmy."

Gram was powerful stubborn. She never let things drop. "Well, that Emerson Stamps brings in that basset hound often enough," she said. "Makes me think he's sweet on you."

I shuddered. Emerson Stamps had greasy slicked-back hair the color of blue-black ink. It was crimped in waves, and when he ran his hands over it, which he did about every five seconds, I could feel shivers crawling up my spine.

"He brings the dog because it's sick, Mama. Besides, I could never like a man who treats his dog the way Mr. Stamps treats Sniffer. You learn a lot about a man by watching the way he treats his animals."

"Well, what about Duane McCracken?"

"Moves too fast, Mama. You know that." I knew it, too. So did everybody in Kinship. When Duane McCracken's Erlene died, he went into Judge Ditzel's office to sign the probate papers after breakfast, took Mabel Hardy, the judge's secretary, to lunch that same day, and married her just before Saturday supper two weeks later. "Friendship takes time to grow," Rae Jean said. "No wonder Duane's marriage to Mabel broke up so quick."

Gram was spinning yarn fast as a spider. "So what's wrong with Tommy Lee Toohey, Miss Particular?" she said. "Or don't you like a man with a thick bankbook and a big house?"

I knew Rae Jean didn't give a gum wad for a man's money. "Tommy Lee's got shady ways of getting the house and bankbook both, Mama," Rae Jean said. "He's more familiar with the Weevils than anyone ever needs to be."

I glanced at Frank Alhambra. He sat still as stone, his hands barely moving the steering wheel, his eyes fixed straight ahead on the road. It was a wonder the way coloreds made themselves invisible around white folks.

Gram changed the subject. "Don't suppose you think you ought to hire you a lawyer and get those unclaimed bank funds listed in the paper, do you, daughter?" Gram made every question sound like a statement. "You're the closest thing to a next-of-kin that Sam Wilson had."

"Not so, Mama," Rae Jean said. "He's got a *son.* I'm just the son's wife."

"And that don't count for something? And don't it count that Sam Wilson's grandchildren could stand a little bit more to eat?" Gram never gave things a rest. If there was a point she wanted to make, she'd go on and on until she wore you down. It was like arm rassling with Jimmy.

"What counts with me, Mama, is that James William is entitled to his dead father's money, however small it turns out to be. You know how James William felt about money and the lack of it."

"But did he ever bother to think about how these kids of his might have felt about money and the lack of it?"

I saw the muscles twitch on the back of Rae Jean's neck. "It wouldn't turn out to be much money, Mama," Rae Jean said. "Besides, these kids feel just fine."

I heard gravel spin under the taxi tires and felt the same: pressed down and driven over. I *didn't* feel just fine. I closed my eyes. *"If my daddy can hear or my daddy can see,"* I repeated, *"help him receive this message from me."* And then I wished my daddy back, the moving pictures across the back of my eyelids showing Horace Bertram, the banker, opening the big black safe, pulling out heavy cloth sacks of money, and dumping them out on the counter in front of my family while my daddy stuffed bill after bill into his pockets.

We was almost to St. Jude's now. I stared out the window. While the landscape flashed by, I admitted something to myself: We wasn't really doing fine. At best we was doing just okay, and on most days we was doing kinda poorly. Money was a big part of it. We always got a nickel when the need was for a dime. We was always heading off the bills by slapping five dollars over here and three dollars over there. What Wilsons had to do to make a living felt like wearing shoes held together by string instead of real laces.

But the words between Rae Jean and Gram didn't really bother me. They was like the glass of iced tea after work, or the paint-by-numbers on a Saturday night. It was all part of the Wilson family routine.

Once we got inside St. Jude's, my own Sunday routines started up. First I looked up at the stained-glass windows that made kaleidoscope reflections on the walls. Then I took my seat, in the sixth row on the right-hand side of the aisle between Jimmy and Gram, and tried to look holy. After that, I worried about kneeling.

I didn't have to worry about Rae Jean. She could kneel for hours without a squirm. But Gram and I was another story. Gram didn't even try to kneel anymore, and I was glad. I hated hearing the gasp of her breath when she lowered herself on down. Now she just sat the whole service.

I hated the kneeling, too, but it wasn't on account of comfort. I just plain hated the idea of getting down on my knees before anyone. Even if that anyone was God. I was a lot like Gram. Gram said if there was only one virtue she could hate, it would be humility. I agreed.

Still, being on my knees started up another of my habits: looking around and watching other families, especially the daddies. Looking at the daddies told me things about fatherhood. Walter Fritz looked bored with being a dad, as bored as the kids who squirmed in the pew beside him and his wife Geneva. Calvin Papp looked henpecked, nagged into fatherhood. His wife Margaret had a nose like a beak that bobbed up and down. Each bob seemed a reminder about what awaited Calvin when he got home: the sink, the muffler, the spreading crabgrass. Lonnie LeValley sat as stiff as an army sergeant. His exhausted wife Lenore sat next to him, and then Lonnie Jr., Mary, Bonnie, Stewart, Gary, and Stinky LeValley, who was known for his powerful farts. They sat like stairsteps, not a twitch or a wiggle in the group. I envied all those children in church. Whether glared at or scolded or fussed over, they all had daddies who paid attention to them. At home, whenever Rae Jean got down on her knees before her shrine to pray "Our Father," I had somebody other than God in mind.

The hardest thing for me was the wondering. What was the sound of my daddy's footfalls on the steps? How did he smell in that place behind his ear? Did his face have freckles or wrinkles or dimples? I wondered if there was things my daddy'd like to know about *me*. Would he like my hair short or long, peroxided or plain? Would he admire the way I could talk myself out of trouble? Would he care that I loved the taste of chocolate and peanuts and the feel of the wind in my hair on a ride to Troy on a summer Sunday? Would he worry that I carried the weight of the world on my shoulders? Would he offer to hold it awhile?

After mass, other routines started up. Margaret Papp always pulled her hanky from the sleeve of her dress and stuffed it back in her purse. Lonnie LeValley always tapped his foot impatiently, irritated at having to wait for Lenore to round up the kids. Jimmy loosened his tie, and Gram picked up the latest *Good Tidings* for Rae Jean. Rae Jean looked back over her shoulder at Lord Jesus up there on the cross: It was her way of saying good-bye. On the ride back home, everybody dozed off, sleepy like you get after a big meal.

I hadn't expected what happened, of course. What I expected was the familiar buck of the taxi when Frank Alhambra pulled up to the trailer court. What I expected was the familiar Sunday breakfast, Gram making pots of coffee and me scrambling a dozen eggs. What I expected was the usual Monopoly game.

Instead, I saw a tall man with a neat gray beard climbing the cinder-block steps to our trailer and rapping on the door. He had moved quickly up the steps like someone in a hurry, and the rapping was firm and demanding. When no one answered, he skipped just as quickly back down the steps. He was moving headfirst in the direction of something that looked like a bread truck painted red and covered with stickers that looked like foreign stamps on a letter. He was about to climb up into the truck when he saw us. He watched us moving across the patches of grass, and I saw

57

him blink like someone startled by a sudden light. Then one of his long arms lifted to his forehead in a partial salute.

Something about the half salute reminded me of a soldier, someone who had gone away across the ocean for a long time. To China or Siberia or Timbuktu. Perhaps the someone had gone off because he volunteered or was drafted or needed to get away from something or just couldn't think of what else to do. Perhaps the someone had been gone so long I had forgotten the color of his eyes or what it smelled like behind his earlobe or whether he had freckles or dimples or wrinkles. The someone had been gone so long that I no longer thought I would die of missing him; instead, I was already dead from the ache of wondering what had happened.

And then one day the someone showed up on the doorstep, rapping on the door in a firm and demanding way.

My brother Jimmy's mouth fell open.

My mama's lips moved up and down in motions that said, "Dear God."

My Gram blew out her breath in a short quick puff.

I was the only one to speak. I raised my hand in my own kind of half salute. I looked at him straight on and called across the dry September grass that now seemed bright with promise. *"Daddy?"*

7

I'd never seen anybody think as quick as Rae Jean Wilson.
I was about to wet my pants, but Rae Jean had said as how
we was getting ready for Sunday breakfast and wouldn't
Daddy want to stay for a cup of coffee.

She offered him the same seat she'd given Nympha
Claggett, and she took the other end of the couch by the
husband she hadn't seen for fifteen years.

Jimmy set in a kitchen chair he'd pulled into the room,
staring out the window and rearing back in his seat. Gram
set in the only other chair in the front room, her arms folded
across her chest. I set on the stool by the coffee table and saw
that nobody knew much what to say. It was like having an
itch in an embarrassing place and not being able to scratch.

I could see I was going to have to start the talking, and
fact was, Daddy and I talked the most. Rae Jean listened,
Jimmy picked up a newspaper and thumbed through the car
ads now and again, and Gram interrupted.

When I said what we did in the days of our lives that
rolled over and over, growing like balls of tumbleweed I'd
seen in Westerns at the Bijou, Daddy told about the miles
piling up on his truck after all these years.

"Then why don't you just get going and put on a few more?" Gram said.

I glared at Gram. Daddy ignored her.

When I said I worked at the movie theater at night and saw all those free movies, Daddy told me that wandering the world was the best picture show of all.

"What kind of world is worth wandering without your own family, James Wilson?"

Although Gram was mad as a boil, Daddy smiled over at her.

When I said about Jimmy's job at the Texaco station and the placemats and glasses he brought home whenever there was a special, Daddy told about how nice it was to go without placemats and eat supper from a can.

"Never did respect a person who liked can-opener cooking." That was you-know-who.

Rae Jean was irritated with Gram, too. She sent her into the kitchen to start the coffee.

While we waited for the coffee to perk, I got Daddy to talk about what he did and where he'd been. He'd always been good with his hands. He liked inventing things. He was curious. He'd moved around a lot so he could learn new things. He'd learned welding and flame cutting in Alabama. Got his electrician's license in Virginia. Picked up heating and cooling there, too. Learned cars in Tennessee.

While I tried to tell him about us, Daddy got up and looked at Rae Jean's pictures on the wall. I knew now that my daddy wasn't one to set still long.

"These your paintings, Rae Jean?"

Rae Jean nodded.

"I remember you always were good with colors."

"It's nothing special, James William," she said. "You just follow the directions is all."

I jumped in. "It is *too* special, Rae Jean," I said. "She's really good," I told Daddy. "She's done near every animal to come down the pike."

Daddy had looked at the paintings of the collie, the Pekinese, the red fox, and the white poodle. "I can see that, Pert," he said.

Then he moved to the painting over Rae Jean's shrine. "That's *The Last Supper,* isn't it, Rae Jean?"

She nodded.

"Michelangelo?" Daddy asked.

"Da Vinci."

He squinted at her, and his blue eyes nearly disappeared. Then he looked back at the painting. "That's a right nice painting, Rae Jean. Look at the way all the lines and angles and lights points to Jesus."

He laid his hand on the plastic Jesus statue on top of the shrine. "You still Catholic, Rae?"

Rae Jean turned scarlet. "Of course, James William," she said. "You don't change a religion like a pair of shoes."

Daddy frowned and fingered her rosary beads. "Still pray all the time like you used to?"

Rae Jean squirmed in her seat. She didn't answer.

"I guess you recall how being Catholic was kind of a problem for me." Daddy had turned Catholic to marry Rae Jean but, like Gram, it didn't exactly take.

"I guess I do, James."

"Too many rules," Daddy said.

Rae Jean fingered her silver cross and then took a breath. "That's why I like it," she said.

The air hung still.

Then Daddy studied the other paintings: the brown fawn, the raccoon, the basket of white kittens on a blue blanket. "Well, I can see that your mama is good with colors, Pert. What do you call that, Rae Jean?" he said, pointing to the blue blanket in the picture of the kittens.

"Cerulean," Rae Jean said.

"And that?" He had his finger on a patch of red fox fur.

"Sienna."

"And this one?"

"Ochre."

I could tell Daddy was impressed. Rae Jean knew a powerful lot about colors.

Then he pointed to the German shepherd painting.

"Ain't that Lickety?" Daddy asked.

Rae Jean blushed and nodded. "I did that one in memory of him," she said. "When Lick died, the kids helped me bury him at the edge of the woods."

"How do you know Lick?" I said.

Daddy looked over at Rae Jean and grinned. "Lick's how your mama and I met, Pert."

"You might say Lick introduced me to your daddy."

Jimmy put down his newspaper and listened.

"I'd heard tell of Wilsons, of course," Rae Jean said, "but their farm was on the opposite side of Kinship from ours, and we'd never had cause to meet before Lickety." I could see the dimple in Rae Jean's cheek now. Seeing it made me feel better.

Rae Jean said she'd been walking uptown to get stamps at the post office. She was about to go in when she saw a big dog wandering across Fenwick Street like he was dazed. His eyes looked dull and his tongue was hanging out, so she took him over to Byer's Drugs and got Cinda Samples to give him a bowl of water and a slice of meat loaf. The dog perked up after that. She walked him to the edge of town, and he seemed to understand where he was. Then he led her all the way out to the Wilson farm. Rae Jean had never been that far from Kinship before. It took an hour and a half for her to get there.

"Once I reached Wilsons'," she said, "your daddy was leaning on a fence at the end of a row of peanut bushes. Lickety's how we met."

Daddy smiled at Rae Jean. "My sister Dawn named him Lickety-Split because he could take off so fast."

Gram, her mood ugly as ever, came in with the tray of coffee things. "That dog was just like your husband over there, Rae Jean. Run off when he felt like it."

"Hush, Mama," Rae Jean said. "You're being plain rude. James William is Jimmy and Pert's daddy." Rae Jean picked up the coffee pot and started pouring.

"It's okay, Rae Jean," Daddy said. "Wilma's right. I did run off. In lots of ways I was just like Lick."

It was quiet the way it gets just before lightning flashes. Then Gram gave a big hrruumph, like a crash of thunder. There was nothing Gram liked better than being right.

"Here, Wilma," Daddy said. "Let me make it up to you. I'll bet I can remember just how you like your coffee. Will you let me fix it?"

Steam was rising off the coffee. It reminded me of Gram.

Gram didn't say anything. She just stared at Daddy. I saw that Daddy could be as calm as Rae Jean. He ignored Gram and went about his business.

"Well, first off, Wilma," he said, moving a cup of coffee in front of him, "I think I recall how you liked milk, not cream."

Gram folded her arms across her chest. "Would have liked cream if we could have afforded it. Just got used to milk is all."

"That's milk in the pitcher there, Daddy," I said.

"Thanks, Pert."

"Now, Wilma," Daddy said, lifting the tiny white pitcher, "let's see if I can remember just exactly how much milk you like in your coffee."

Gram lunged over the table and slapped her palm over the coffee cup. "No, thank you, sir," she said. "I'll pour it myself."

Rae Jean laid her hand on Gram's arm. "Mama," she said gently, "he's just funnin' with you."

"Oh, all right, daughter," Gram said, taking her hand from off the coffee cup. I was proud of Rae Jean.

Daddy lifted the pitcher over Gram's cup. The china creamer looked small in his big hands. Then Daddy gave the spout a quick tilt. He tipped the spout so quickly only a few drops of milk made it into Gram's cup. Just the way she liked it.

Then Daddy handed Gram the coffee cup. After she sipped and gave a tiny smile, everybody else grinned.

When we had finished our coffee, Daddy stood up and said, "So what'll you folks be doing the rest of the day?"

"Drinking coffee," Gram said.

"Fixing breakfast," Rae Jean said.

"Playing Monopoly," Jimmy said.

"It's what we do every Sunday, Daddy," I said. "Go to church. Eat breakfast. Drink coffee. Play Monopoly."

Daddy's lips turned down. They said that he felt sorry for us. "And tomorrow what will you do?"

"I'll be at the station by seven," Jimmy said.

"I open the ceramic shop at noon," Gram said.

"I'll be at Doc Jackson's by eight," Rae Jean said.

"School starts for me at seven-forty-five. By three-thirty I'll be managing the trailer court, and by six I'll be at the Bijou."

Daddy looked around at all of us, his eyes circling us like one of Sheriff Keiter's flashlights. "And the day after that?"

"Same thing," I said.

Daddy looked down at the toes of his boots and hooked his thumbs through his belt loops. "I was wondering," he said. "I gotta be taking off soon, but before I go, I wondered if you folks might join me for breakfast. I've got a coupon for the Lucky Buck. You game?"

Rae Jean didn't look sure. "I got a lot to do, James William," she said. "The week's laundry has piled up, and I need to go back down to Doc Jackson's this afternoon to feed a couple of the animals."

I couldn't believe Rae Jean would pass up a breakfast with Daddy to do laundry and feed a couple of dogs. Could she have wanted Daddy just to stay for coffee and then take off?

I closed my eyes. *"If my daddy can hear or my daddy can see,"* I chanted to myself, *"help him receive this message from me."*

"Come on, Rae Jean," Daddy said. "What's the harm?"

It was the only time I was ever sure my ESP had worked.

8

He had brought us here in the truck. It must have once been a bread truck, for you could still catch a whiff of yeast, and it was warm and dry inside like an oven.

Rae Jean and Gram and Daddy sat up front. Gram had pushed Rae Jean out of the way to sit in the middle of the long front seat. Her whalelike body parted the ocean between them; her carpetbag set in her lap. The front seat was draped like our couch with a blanket across the back, and something about it made me think of Daddy's bread truck as a home.

Fact was, as soon as Jimmy and me made our way to the back we could see that it *was* a home. On the driver's side was a long flat sleeping bag on top of an air mattress, and Jimmy and me set on the end of it where a pillow should have been. On the floor was a Sterno stove, and there was lots of crates filled with things like cans of beans and clothes and Duz detergent and bottles of water. On the opposite wall was a cracked mirror next to a wall calendar that showed the Rocky Mountains and said March instead of September. Beside the wall calendar was a wooden sign that said James William Wilson, Prop. It looked like one of

66

those woodburning projects we did in art class. Most of the crates was filled with tools like saws and hammers or supplies like scraps of lumber and rolls of wire. It was crowded in the back. A new-model toilet tank was shoved over to one side. A tall stack of aluminum sheets pleated like the skirts that rich girls wore took up most of the floor of the truck. There wasn't much room for Jimmy and me.

We hunched on the sleeping bag, sliding close to each other when Daddy rounded a curve. I felt dizzy. It had something to do with the ride, for my daddy drove fast, taking turns on a swerve, arriving at stop signs on a skid. Jimmy loved it: His grin was a jump rope hung from ear to ear. When we pulled up at the Lucky Buck, I felt I'd just walked off the ferris wheel.

Daddy walked quick, leading with his head. Gram hauled her carpetbag at her side and huffed to catch up. A long line of truckers was waiting just inside the front door, and Daddy cleared a path through the line like a bulldozer. "Watch. You ain't gonna have to wait," he whispered in Rae Jean's ear; she pulled away and gave a shy, quiet nod.

Daddy tugged Gram by her elbow, dragging her up to the front of the line. Then he grabbed the sleeve of the busy manager and put his bright blue eye right up next to the manager's dull brown one. "This lovely lady here," he said, glancing sadly at Gram, "has got the worst trouble with her knees. Hate to think what'll happen if she has to stand on 'em long. I'd be obliged if you could get us a table right away. I'll make it worth your while." He gave the manager a wink like a flash of dimes and passed him some dollar bills. "Got five in our party, sir."

The manager snapped his head up in a salute. "Party of five," he said, pointing to a booth. "Right this way."

It felt good to sit down. I was still dizzy. The restaurant was filled with people, and it was noisy with their talk. Dishes clattered. A busboy with pimples the color of raspberry jam rushed back and forth. Smoke curled through the air, and truckers shifted on stools. A few people waiting in line looked at the postcards on the circular rack, and it squeaked with every turn.

The waitress came with menus. She was young; her curly hair was pulled back in a ponytail, and she wore a little white half cap that looked like a sun shade. There was a swelling under her belly that said she was just fixing to have a baby or just getting over having one.

"Mornin', Janice," Daddy said. The waitress was wearing a black plastic name tag on the pocket of her blouse. JANICE, it said in white letters.

Janice dealt the menus out as fast as a hand of cards. "Be right back," she said.

I looked across the booth at Gram. She looked glad for the seat. Rae Jean set in the middle between Gram and Jimmy, and Jimmy set by the window. I set opposite from Jimmy on the window side and next to Daddy. Daddy winked at Gram and said, "Bet that's the first time those bad knees come in handy, Wilma."

Gram gave a grunt that was halfway between yes and no. I thought about what my Daddy had said to the manager: "This lovely lady here has got the worst trouble with her knees." It wasn't a half-truth; it was a whole one. I didn't see why Gram couldn't just say thank you.

"Sorry, sir," Janice said, returning to our table. She swiped at her bangs with the back of her hand and took a pencil from behind her ear. "I'm not usually this slow. We're pretty busy in here this morning, and I guess I'm more tired than usual now," she said, poking at her belly with her pencil point.

Daddy stared at her tummy. "Oh, I didn't know, honey," he said. "We won't try to rush you. When are you due?"

"Another five months. I guess I've been tired lately. I'm on my feet a lot."

"First baby?" Daddy said.

"Second. I'm hoping Jason'll go in the playpen by the time this one comes."

Daddy looked over at me and said, "This here's *my* second baby, Janice. Ain't she a beauty?"

I saw a flicker of a scowl pass across Rae Jean's face. I looked across at my handsome brother and blushed, wondering when Daddy would say something about his first baby. He was likely fixing to, but Janice cleared her throat. She was plain busy, and Daddy was jabbering.

"If you'll give me your order," Janice said, "I'll get your drinks right away."

Daddy ordered for everyone without asking what we wanted. "We'll take five biscuits with sausage gravy, five orders of hotcakes, and a plate of eggs scrambled easy. And an order of hash browns browned real good and a dozen slices of bacon fried crisp." Then he took a breath while I held mine: I'd never heard anybody order such a pile of food in my life.

"Oh, yes," he went on, "the boy over here will have a large milk. Same for the girl. And that pretty lady over there," he said, pointing to Rae Jean, "will have a glass of iced tea."

Then Daddy looked at Rae Jean and winked. "No sugar in that tea, right, honey?"

Rae Jean blushed pink and nodded.

"And that pretty lady over *there*," he said, pointing to Gram, "will have a cup of coffee."

Gram frowned. I guess she didn't like being called a pretty lady even if it got her a cup of coffee.

"Oh, and coffee for me, too. And bring us a pitcher of fresh-squeezed orange juice."

The waitress was scribbling like mad. "That it, folks?"

I tapped Daddy on the arm and whispered to him. I caught the scent of him from behind his right ear. He smelled something like iron. Daddy listened and nodded. Then I said to the waitress, "I'd like to order a fried-egg sandwich. Cook the egg over light. And pop the yolk right before you put it on the toast." I was famous for my fried-egg sandwiches when I worked the grill at Byer's Drugs.

I didn't tell Daddy that I'd been fired from Byer's Drugs for serving coloreds. Jim Wrinkle, who I worked for at the Bijou, was a lot smarter than Elmer Byer. When he saw the trouble Mr. Byer was causing for his business, Mr. Wrinkle changed his balcony-only seating policy at the theater lickety-split: Now coloreds could sit any darn place they pleased.

Daddy smiled at me. I saw that he was the kind of person who smiled more with his eyes than with his mouth. "I like a girl who knows what she wants," Daddy said. His smiling eyes made up for his calling me a girl.

Janice hurried off and came back with our drinks. Bubbles was still foaming on the lip of my milk glass. Some of the orange juice sloshed on the table when she set the pitcher down.

"Here, Pert," Daddy said, getting out of his seat and pulling me up with him. "Let's see what we can find you in that machine while we wait for our food."

The vending machine was next to the squeaky rack filled with postcards of Stone Mountain, the Okefenokee Swamp, the onion fields of Vidalia, and the golf greens of Augusta. I wished I had enough money to buy them all; Farley Ewing could have made great puzzles out of scenes like that.

The vending machine was heaped with clear plastic bubbles. Inside the bubbles was trinkets like dice and key chains and rubber balls. When you put your five cents into the machine and cranked the handle, one of the bubbles rolled out.

"Pert, I want to get you one of them rings," Daddy said. He put in a nickel and turned the crank.

I peered inside the machine and saw that my daddy had good eyes. I couldn't make out a single ring. All I could see was plastic spiders and frogs and worms.

He kept pushing in change and turning the crank. I got a slew of bubbles. They contained dice, a plastic ID bracelet, a naked baby doll, and two worms.

Daddy fished in his pocket again and got the girl at the counter to turn a quarter and a dime into change. Then he shoved more nickels in the vending machine. Out came a bubble with a jawbreaker, another one with more dice, and a third with a plastic mirror. While he put money in the machine, I saw how hard Daddy concentrated. When he turned the crank, he mumbled things like Rae Jean did when she got on her knees and prayed. Watching him, I saw how tall my daddy was, how handsome. I saw the long fingers and the black hair streaked with gray and the jaw cut square as an ax blade. I saw that my daddy spent whatever he had to get what he wanted. Finally he grabbed a plastic bubble and grinned.

"For you, Pert," he said, opening up the bubble, examining the gold ring, and then holding it up to the light. From a distance the band looked like pure gold and the stone winked like a real jewel. When my daddy took my right hand and slipped the ring on my finger, I saw that the pink stone was shaped like a heart, and when the glass chip shined in the light, I knew I'd never seen a sunset half as pretty. I twisted the ring around and around, admiring the way the pink stone set off my frosted nail polish, adjusting to the tender feeling of something new on my finger. I swore I'd never take Daddy's ring off.

"Thank you, Daddy," I said, and swallowed. My heart felt stuck somewhere up in my throat.

When we got back to our table, I laid the trinkets on the tabletop and showed Jimmy and Rae Jean and Gram the ring.

Rae Jean said, "That was right nice of your daddy to get that for you, Pert."

Then Daddy looked at Rae Jean. "I see you're still wearing your own ring, Rae Jean, honey."

Gram glared at Daddy. "She ain't your 'honey' far as I can tell."

"Shut up, Gram," I said. I surprised even myself. I didn't know where those words had come from. All I knew was they come up quick.

"Now, stop that, Pert," Rae Jean said.

"I'll stop if she will," I said.

"Don't sass your elders, Pert Wilson," Gram said.

"Then don't sass my daddy, Gram."

Jimmy stared out the window. Only thing Jimmy hates worse than fighting is when he thinks Rae Jean is upset. But Rae Jean Wilson has the stiffest upper lip you ever did see. In my whole life I'd never once seen her shed a tear. I don't cry, neither. I just put up my fists.

"Stop it. Both of you," Rae Jean said. She laid her left hand across Gram's arm, and Gram pulled her arm away. She stretched her right hand across the table to me. I refused to take it. I could be just as stubborn as Gram.

Then Rae Jean sighed and rested both her hands on the Formica, the fingers of her right hand folded over her left thumb. The plain gold band on the fourth finger of her left hand faced my daddy, and I looked down at my own new ring, shifting it back and forth against my finger. Rae Jean had never taken her wedding band off. When Gram had asked her to sell it up at the pawnshop that year she was working the day job and the night job both, Rae Jean said she had made a promise: The ring was a reminder that promises was things to be kept.

Daddy must have been thinking about Rae Jean's ring, too. "Remember when we got that ring, Rae Jean?" Daddy said.

Rae Jean nodded. Her hair fluffed around her face like yellow cotton candy. I wondered about my mama and daddy. They knew things I didn't. When they got the ring. Where. How they felt about it. Why.

My daddy reached across the tabletop to take Rae Jean's left hand. She pulled it away, and Gram looked relieved.

73

Then Daddy started talking. I saw that when my daddy talked, he was just like me: He couldn't stop. "I wanted to bring you money," he said. "Lots of money, Rae Jean." His hands flew out over his head like birds scared off. "Lots of money for you and for these babies here." His head tilted in the direction of Jimmy and me. "Heaps of money."

Daddy's words made me think of money heaped in piles like grass after it was mowed. I rubbed the gold wire around my finger while he talked.

"I wanted to bring you wheelbarrows full of money, sweetheart."

Gram drew her lips up tight at the sound of that word. I saw she felt the same way about *sweetheart* that she did about *honey*.

"Wheelbarrows, Rae Jean," Daddy said. "With dollar bills flying out the back, overflowing the sides." I pictured the piles of green grass-money heaped into a wheelbarrow and rolled to the bank.

"I wanted these babies to have a throne, Rae Jean," Daddy said. "Not a fruit crate. A throne like you always intended." I looked at the blue eyes clouding over and wondered if a man like my daddy ever allowed himself to cry.

Daddy's hands dropped for a moment on the tabletop, and Rae Jean reached over and covered them with her own. "Shhhh, James," she whispered. The sound was the same one she had made when she rocked me as a baby.

"Shhhh, James," she repeated. "Calm down. The kids are all right."

I looked across at Gram's frozen mouth. I saw that Gram didn't think we was all right, but at least she had the sense to hold her tongue.

I looked at Rae Jean's hands, pressing out Daddy's fists with her palms the way you rolled blobs of dough out into crust. I saw how small and white her hands was, how pretty. Even with the red blotches on the knuckles, Rae Jean's hands was pretty.

Jimmy and me squirmed in our seats. Then Gram coughed into her napkin loud enough to wake the dead. Rae Jean took her hands away from Daddy and passed Gram a glass of water. "You all right, Mama?"

Gram was still coughing. "I—think—so," she said. Then she took a sip.

It was dead silence.

Jimmy stared out the window, looking at the trucks pulled up at the gas pumps.

Gram stared at her paper napkin.

Rae Jean stared at Gram.

The waitress came up with our order. I shoved the trinkets aside to make room for the food.

"Thanks, Janice," Daddy said.

After she set down the food, Janice said, "Everything okay, folks?"

Everyone nodded.

Daddy poured syrup over his food and dug in. He didn't cut his pancakes; he stabbed at them. After that, he shoved scrambled eggs in his mouth. Daddy ate his food just like me: by shoveling several things into his mouth at once, all mixed up together. It was different from the way Jimmy and Rae Jean ate. They always finished one thing before going on to another. They'd finish their pancakes before going on to the eggs or the potatoes. Jimmy and Rae Jean was different from Daddy and me: They took one thing at a time.

75

When we had finished eating, Daddy signaled for the check. I knew it would be a whopper.

Janice laid the check down on the table. "That be all, sir?"

Daddy pulled something out of the pocket of his jeans. "We got a coupon, Janice," he said.

She squinted at the paper.

"It says if you come in on your birthday," Daddy said, "the birthday family eats free."

Did that mean we wouldn't have to pay for all that food? But it wasn't anybody's birthday as far as I knew. Could it be Daddy's birthday?

Somebody had put some music on the jukebox. I knew the song. It was called "Personality."

Janice looked up from the check. "So who's got the birthday?" she said. I saw her draw a big *X* through the bill and set it back down on the table.

Daddy pointed to Gram. "That lovely lady over there."

Gram looked like she'd dropped a stitch.

"Happy birthday, ma'am," Janice said.

Gram gave her a strained smile.

We slid out of the booth. I could feel the red plastic seats sticking to my sweaty legs. As I pulled my legs away, the vinyl gave a quiet sucking sound. The music was saying, "Charm. *Personality.* Style. *Personality.*"

Daddy laid a five-dollar bill on the table.

"Thanks, sir," Janice said.

"Wilma," Daddy said to Gram as she struggled with her carpetbag, "got anything finished in there?"

Gram gave him a funny look. "Like what?"

Daddy scratched his head. "Oh, I don't know. A blanket. A scarf."

Gram slammed the carpetbag on the thick vinyl seat of the booth and pushed it open. She picked out a pale blue blanket and opened it up. It looked like a diaper for a giant's son. She passed it to Daddy.

He studied it and smiled. "The blue in the blanket's the same color as Rae Jean's eyes," he said. "I like it. What would it sell for?"

Gram looked annoyed. "I'd probably ask ten dollars for it in the shop," she said. "Why?"

"Ten dollars it is," Daddy said. He handed Gram a ten-dollar bill and took the blanket out of her hands.

Gram just stared at Daddy.

Janice was passing by with another tray full of food. "By the way, Janice," Daddy said. "Good luck with the baby." Then he draped Gram's blanket across her shoulders. Janice looked about to drop her tray.

On the way out the door, Daddy grabbed me and swung me around. The song was winding down to its final words. I felt dizzy again. Daddy swung me in and out and back and forth. Then, at the end of the song, he laid me near to the floor in a final dip. No doubt about it. I felt dizzy again.

9

We high-tailed it back to Kinship, taking curves at a clip. When we made that sharp right on the Macon Highway, that turn that killed Pee Wee Hale's whole family, cartons of tools and clothes landed at my feet. The fried-egg sandwich turned somersaults in my belly.

When we got back to Happy Trails, Daddy took a last swig of cold coffee from the cup on the table and said that he'd stop by again sometime but that he had to be in Florida by Tuesday to deliver those stacks of pleated metal in the back of the truck. I couldn't believe he was fixing to leave.

Rae Jean said, "Can I heat some of that leftover coffee before you go? We can fill a Thermos for you to take on the road." I couldn't believe Rae Jean wasn't begging him to stay, wasn't telling him about Granddaddy's money.

"Thanks, Rae Jean," Daddy said. "That'd be nice."

Why wasn't Rae Jean and Jimmy and Gram trying to make him stay?

Rae Jean came in with the Thermos. She handed it to Daddy firmly and said, "Good-bye, James William." Gram and Jimmy looked relieved. Rae Jean looked ready to get started on the laundry. I think I was the only one who wanted Daddy to stay. I still had a million things to ask him.

"I'm sorry you have to go so soon, Daddy," I said. "Sure you couldn't stay awhile?" I wanted to blurt out about the money in the bank.

"No, thanks, Pert. It's a long drive."

I couldn't stand it. We had talked only about the small things. I had said nothing about my fear of the dark or Rae Jean's loneliness or Jimmy's dropping out of school. Daddy's visit felt like a long-lost friend showing up on the stoop. The visitor's return was so important that you couldn't say what was in your heart; instead, you said things like "We're out of milk, but we'll go to the store in the morning." I wondered if Daddy had left things out, too.

He held the Thermos in one big hand and moved to the door. I ran to the end table and stuffed the handprint ash-tray in my pocket. I could feel the rough ceramic scrape against the back of my ring. If he wouldn't stay, at least I could walk him to the truck, at least I could give him something to remember me by.

"Much obliged, folks," Daddy said.

Everybody wiggled their fingers in Daddy's direction. I couldn't believe how quick everybody else said good-bye. I still had about a million things to ask him.

I was the only one to follow him out the door.

Although he was in a hurry to hit the road, Daddy agreed to walk around the trailer court with me before he left. I tried to stroll casual-like, scuffing the dirt with my toes, swinging my arms at my sides. I wanted to hide the heart pounding in my chest. I had always wondered what it was to be a regular girl, a girl who took walks with a daddy every day as part of her regular life. I wondered what it would be like to stroll with a daddy hand in hand up a sidewalk at dusk; to tiptoe with him up the aisle at church and wander with him down the aisle at the grocery; to elbow through the auditorium crowds of parents at the Christmas pageant or school play, a daddy at my side.

"Howdy, Emil," I said. Emil Highwater was taking some clothes off a laundry line. Emil's underwear was gray and Myra's ruffled blouse was torn. "This here's James Wilson, Senior," I said. I wanted to say, "This here's my *daddy*," but I didn't think I could say such a tender word out loud right then. I'd wanted to say the word *daddy* for so many years, and now that I could, I was tongue-tied.

Emil dropped a pajama top into a cardboard box and shook hands. I saw the tight grip that men gave each other pass between my daddy and Emil, and it made me proud.

"Nice canoe you've got there." My daddy pointed to the Highwaters' birch canoe.

Emil grunted.

"Nothing nicer than flowing down a river in a canoe, is there, Emil?"

Emil smiled and grunted again. Wrinkles sprouted at the corners of his eyes, like crops.

"Pleased to make your acquaintance, sir," my daddy said.

"Likewise," said Emil.

We strolled off. I loved the way my daddy had said pleased-to-make-your-acquaintance. It was one of those things men said, like check-the-oil or raise-you-five.

We stood near Sophie Mulch's trailer. I saw Odette Coates, off in her corner of the court, and she waved. She was in her bedroom slippers and robe, checking the grill.

The Coateses built a barbecue pit behind Trailer 6; they made their living selling barbecue to every fund-raiser in town, and they cooked every day, including Christmas. The lights was still off in Farley Ewing's lot; he'd probably been up late working on his puzzles and decided to sleep in.

As we walked, I told Daddy about my jobs.

"I work at the Bijou in town at night, Daddy," I said. "Working at a movie theater's a swell job. You get to see every new movie to come down the pike and every soul in Kinship with a free night and a little loose change to blow."

I didn't tell him it was mostly picking up people's trash, sweating under the popcorn machine, and falling asleep during the movie you'd been waiting to see since you don't get off until eleven and you've got school the next day.

"And then I manage the trailer court for Rae Jean afternoons after school," I said. I told him how Dora and Bert Slagle owned the park. Since they'd bought a house in Kinship Acres and they liked Rae Jean, they rented their trailer out to us. Rae Jean only had to pay half the rent in exchange for managing the court. "It's really Rae Jean's job. But since she's busy at Doc Jackson's now, I help her some."

"Slagles sound rich, Pert," Daddy said.

"Rich as kings. Don't know nobody richer on this end of Kinship. Own the Sleepy Time Motel outside of town, too."

Daddy's ears lifted a tad. I didn't tell him the Sleepy Time wasn't much of a motel. Just three units and no coffee shop.

"Slagles have a hotel, too." The Kinship Hotel was one block off Fenwick Street. I didn't tell Daddy it wasn't much of a hotel, neither. Eight rooms and no bellboy.

81

Daddy said, "And then this trailer park, too. Slagles sound like Hiltons."

I didn't say how Happy Trails wasn't much of a park. Ten units and no full-time manager. I reckoned Daddy could see that for himself.

"Which job you like better, Pert?"

"The trailer court. Ain't much more than delivering mail or doing odd jobs for the residents. It's just running up to Gleason's Hardware for fishing line for the Highwaters or stamps from the P.O. for Miss Mulch. It's a lot better than shining your flashlight on people and asking them to stop kissing."

Daddy laughed. When he laughed he tipped his head back and I could see the way his beard covered his neck and chin.

I didn't tell Daddy that collecting rent made managing the trailer park powerful hard. It was due the first of every month, and nobody besides Miss Mulch ever brought it up on their own. I learned a long time ago that if you wanted rent money, you had to go get it.

"You're quite a talker, Pert," Daddy said. I could tell he was giving me a compliment. Over the years, other folks had said the same thing, but they'd meant it as an insult.

"I reckon I can talk folks to their knees, Daddy," I said, "the same way Jimmy can rassle them to the ground."

Daddy laughed again. "We'd be great partners, Pert. I believe you could polish a nickel and make it shine like a silver dollar."

I could feel my eyes shining like money, so I didn't tell Daddy that nickels was the problem. Wilsons hardly ever had two nickels to rub together. That meant we had to work night and day without breathing room for making things better. Jimmy couldn't take the time away from the station to finish his GED program. Rae Jean couldn't study animal science at the Troy Community College. I couldn't concentrate on the grades I knew I could get. Most of all, living without nickels was like living under a roof that sprung leaks in a million places; you was so busy bringing buckets that you didn't have time to climb up and patch.

As we walked, I asked Daddy about himself, watching him out of the corner of my eye, afraid to look at him directly. He'd been gone so long I could only safely look at him sideways. Staring at him straight on felt like something that might burn my eyeballs out. Like gazing at the sun during an eclipse.

He told me about the rivers he'd been down. The Rappahannock. The Suwannee. He told me about the towns he'd been in. Wheeling. Newport News. Knoxville. Chattanooga. He told me about the jobs he'd had. Plumbing. Electric. Arc welding.

"The kind of work I do, Pert," he said, "is something like flowing along, something like wandering rivers." I saw that my daddy's hair was black like mine; Jimmy and Rae Jean was blond.

"Take electric circuits, for example. They're nothing more than a kind of river, something that flows along. Only the flow's not water but electricity. Take pipes and plumbing," he went on. "It's about the same thing. I'm always wandering, exploring, thinking about something new. Life's kind of like riding a highway, ain't it, daughter?"

I was glad Miss Mulch chose that moment to peek her head out of her doorway. I thought I might faint at the sound of the word *daughter* coming from my own daddy's lips.

"Morning, Miss Pert," Sophie Mulch called. She fluttered her hand at me like a hanky.

I said, "Come on out and meet this fellow here, Miss Sophie."

Miss Mulch bustled down her steps, smoothing her hair. The gray in her curls was dusted with white like somebody had shook flour through it.

When she reached us, I took a deep breath and said, "Miss Sophie Mulch, meet Mr. James William Wilson. This is my *daddy*." It felt good to say the word. It felt good for Miss Mulch to be the first one to hear it from my lips.

I'd never seen anybody stay as collected as Sophie Mulch. It must have been the payoff of so many years of schoolteaching. She wiped her hands on her apron, and I could smell the Johnson's paste wax. Miss Mulch waxed her furniture once a week, using paste wax that came from the same kind of can as Jimmy's car polish. I'd never known anybody else in my life that waxed furniture.

"You must be so proud of your daughter, Mr. Wilson," she said, shaking his hand after she had wiped hers off.

"I reckon I am," he said.

"Well, I swannee, she's something to be proud of, sir. I taught school for over thirty years, Mr. Wilson, and there's none smarter." She beamed at me, her tiny bright bird-eyes disappearing behind her smile. "Now, I'm not so proud of this place, for sure," she said, pointing out the trailer court. "It's an eyesore if I ever saw one."

I listened to Miss Mulch point out the things about Happy Trails she was ashamed of: the barbecue smells and the planks that served for sidewalks and the broken birdbath and the hubcap collection outside Charlie Hale's trailer. Miss Mulch hated the way people scattered their ragged belongings around their rigs. Said it was like parading your messy basement in front of the entire world.

"I've got a decent teacher's retirement, Mr. Wilson," she said. "I'd gladly pay something from it to fix this place up, but nobody would be like to notice."

Daddy winked at Miss Mulch. "I've heard retired schoolteachers got money to burn, Miss Mulch."

"I swannee, Pert," she said, "your daddy's quite the kidder."

He kept it up. He was enjoying Miss Mulch. "Throwing money into this park'd be sort of like throwing pearls into a pigpen, wouldn't it, Miss Mulch?" My daddy smiled in a crooked, flirty way, his lips drawn up more on the right side than on the left. His smile pulled you in only halfway; it was like a fish you caught on the line but decided to throw back. I'd seen him flash that smile to Rae Jean and to me. Now he shared it with Miss Mulch.

"I swannee, but you do understand, Mr. Wilson," she said. When Miss Mulch laughed, her little lips drew up like a string bag. She had a *hee-hee-hee* laugh, not a *ha* or a *ho*.

I was proud that my daddy was so handsome. It added a charm that was missing from Happy Trails. Fact was, there was something about Daddy that was like a movie star, something that filled up the screen of my life. I'm sure Miss Mulch noticed it, too.

"I just get sick about it every time I think how there's no front porch to rock on, no lawns for a child like Pert to do cartwheels across," she said.

"But just think, Miss Mulch," my daddy said. "There ain't no basement to clean and no attic to insulate." He smiled, and a tooth in the back glinted like a silver fish.

"I swannee, you're a card, Mr. Wilson," she said. She gave him a quick slap with her apron strings. "I'm pleased as punch to meet you, sir." Then she gave me a wink and climbed up the steps to her trailer.

I liked it that my daddy was such a good talker. I liked it that there was something about him that crackled and sparked, something like the electric currents he worked on.

"Do you believe in ESP, Daddy?" I said.

"What's ESP, Pert?" He was fingering the side panel of Miss Mulch's trailer, pulling at the foam rubber where the vandals had slit the fake leather siding.

"It's extrasensory perception," I said. "It's a way of knowing what people's thinking without talking or nothin'."

"So it's kind of like mind reading?"

"Kind of. I think of it like invisible forces that pull on a person. It's sort of like Rae Jean and how she believes in the invisible forces of Jesus and Mary pulling on her life."

Daddy turned his eyes on me. I think they were a color that Rae Jean called Prussian. "Do you believe in Jesus and Mary, too, Pert?"

That was a hard question. "Yes, sir, Daddy," I said. "And also no. I mean I don't believe in Jesus and Mary the same way Rae Jean and Jimmy does. Rae Jean never made me get confirmed. I said I didn't want to and that was okay by her."

Daddy had pulled a few loose patches of foam rubber away from the vinyl siding. "So your mama and Jimmy are the only practicing Catholics in the family then?"

I nodded. "I believe more in stuff like ESP, Daddy. 'Course you can't prove it."

"Hmmm. Sounds interesting, Pert," he said. He was pulling the split sides of the vinyl together and pushing the foam rubber down under them. "I'm not much of a believer, but I guess I could believe in ESP if I saw it work."

"Maybe you already *did* see it work."

He wrinkled his brow; two parallel lines formed across his forehead. Daddy had finished fingering Miss Mulch's slashed vinyl and was walking off to his truck. I followed him across the bald patches of yard.

"I've been sending you messages, Daddy. Messages over all these years." I looked at his footsteps moving ahead of me in the soft dirt. "After I got that letter from you in Tennessee, the one that said you'd be back quick as a jif, I started sending you messages. ESP messages. Do you think you ever got any?" I tried stepping into his footprints like dance patterns across a floor.

Over his shoulder he said, "I don't know, Pert. What were your messages about?"

"Oh, they was things I was wondering about. Mostly just things I wanted to tell you."

I followed him into the back of his truck and watched him rooting around in the crates that held his tools.

"What kinds of things did you want to tell me?"

"Oh, when you was in Tennessee and said you'd be here in a jif, I kept saying 'hurry, hurry.' I wanted you home. Did you ever get the message?"

He pulled a paper sack across to him. He was only half listening. "Hurry," he mumbled. "Well, now, maybe I did, Pert."

"Where'd you go after Tennessee?"

"Virginia. Couldn't stand being tied down to all those cars day after day."

I thought about what he had said. "When did you go to Virginia?"

"I think it was about fifty-five."

I brightened at the thought. Nineteen fifty-five was the year Rae Jean started with Doc Jackson. I was about ten, and Jimmy was eleven. "I kept sending you a message about jobs that year, Daddy. That was the year Rae Jean got her job at the vet's."

"Well, I'll be darned," he said. I couldn't tell exactly what he was darned about. He had just pulled out a roll of dark brown tape and looked surprised to have found it. Or maybe he was surprised about my ESP message. I couldn't rightly tell.

"So what was the new job in Virginia?"

"Not just one job, Pert. First I got my electric license and did lots of electric work. Then a guy hired me to do some heating and refrigeration. I did a couple of new things in Virginia, a couple of new jobs."

"And after that?"

"Alabama."

He tossed the paper sack under the Rocky Mountain calendar. I saw that the date on the calendar was 1956, and it was now 1961. Then Daddy hopped out of the truck. "Alabama is where I took up welding. Went to school there," he said, closing the door with the toe of his boot. "Knew I needed to learn something different. Studied welding and flame cutting. First time I ever went back to school since high school."

"What year was that, Daddy?"

He frowned, thinking. "Oh, maybe about 1959."

I could feel my heart doing somersaults in my chest. "I think you was getting my ESP messages, Daddy. Nineteen fifty-nine was the year Jimmy dropped *out* of school. It was a terrible time, and I kept sending you messages about it. I was hoping you'd come back then. 'School, school,' I chanted to you. 'Jimmy's dropping out of school.' It sounds like you was thinking about school at the same time we was."

He had started back across the yard in the direction of Miss Mulch's trailer. I tagged along behind.

"After Alabama?"

"West Virginia," he said. My heart was pounding as I skipped to keep up. "Knew a guy whose uncle was big in the sheet metal trade. Got me into selling things. He saw I was a good talker, said I'd be good at sales. Got me into galvanized metal. There's money in metal, Pert. I got big stacks of pleated metal on this here truck." I nodded. I knew about the stacks of metal. I'd wondered where to put my feet when Jimmy and me rode in the back. "Taking those sheets to a fellow in Florida, Pert. I know there's money in that metal somehow. Just can't figure out how to tap into it yet."

"Do you think you might have got a message from me?" I didn't want to tell him about the money yet, about the unclaimed bank funds. I wanted to know if my ESP had worked. Ever since I found out about my granddaddy's bank funds I'd been sending Daddy messages. The messages said "Come home. Come home, Daddy. Come on *home.*"

He looked at me then. There was something electric about the connection that ran between us. He was lightning and I was the rod.

89

"I can't really say, Pert. I don't know much about your ESP." His eyes was so deep and blue, I thought I might drown in them. "But I will say that something was pulling on me. Maybe that metal in my truck connected somehow to the magnet of your messages. I'm not sure why I stopped off in Kinship. I do remember feeling pulled, Pert."

He had reached Miss Mulch's trailer then walked up her steps and knocked at her door.

Miss Mulch came to the door, and Farley Ewing was behind her.

"Sorry to disturb you, Miss Mulch," my daddy said. "But I'd like your permission to repair that siding of yours if it's all right by you."

Miss Sophie's face sparked like a firecracker. "Oh, Mr. Ewing," she said, looking at Farley. "Pert's daddy is offering to fix up that awful spot on my trailer." She clapped her hands like a young girl. Farley Ewing held a cup of tea in his hand and blinked with each clap. Miss Mulch always called him Mr. Ewing, never Farley.

My daddy flashed Miss Mulch a smile and moved down the steps and across the side of the trailer to the slashed vinyl. "Here, Pert," he said. "Mash that there foam down for me." I mashed the foam down good, and Daddy pulled the slashed vinyl together real tight. It felt good to be working like a team.

Then my daddy pulled out his pocketknife and sliced off pieces of tape. As he taped down the vinyl, I saw how good the dark brown colors matched.

Miss Mulch tripped down her stairs, and Farley Ewing stood at the door. "Oh, thank you, Mr. Wilson," she said. "What do I owe you for the favor?"

"No charge, Miss Mulch," Daddy said. The fake leather on the side of the trailer looked good as new.

"Yoo-hoo, Odette," Miss Mulch called. "Come on over here. Emil, Myra," she said, "come see what Pert's sweet daddy's done."

They all came to look, and my daddy shook hands all around. "Well, I've gotta be shoving off," he said. "Nice to meet you folks. Good luck to you." Then he moved off in the direction of his truck.

My shoulder muscles worked like an accordion, squeezing tight. Daddy couldn't go just yet. I couldn't let him.

"Daddy," I said, watching him open the truck door, hoist himself up on the running board, and climb into the cab. "I got some news for you."

"News, Pert? I didn't think nothing ever happened in Kinship." He stuck his key in the ignition.

"It's news about *you*, Daddy."

"About me?" He squinted at me.

I nodded. I was thinking fast. The handprint ashtray felt heavy in my pocket, and I remembered how the print was of my right hand, the same hand that now wore Daddy's ring.

"Fact is," I said, taking in a deep breath, "your news came to me in a dream. A beautiful dream."

He stuck his key in the ignition and then leaned back against the seat. "A beautiful dream," he said. "With good news," he said, crossing his arms. "About me." He cocked his handsome head. I could see why Rae Jean had fallen in love with him. "Tell me about it, Pert."

I hopped up on the running board and stuck my head through his window. Then I sucked in air, loading up for a whopper. "Well, it was a dream about eggs, Daddy."

He busted out laughing so hard I could feel drops of spit like rain. "Eggs?" he said. The broad shoulders under his white shirt shook.

"Uh-huh," I said. "There was this chicken, see." I looked over at him out of the corner of my eyes. He had stopped laughing so hard. He looked interested. "A great big fat ol' hen. Settin' up in the sky on a fluffy white cloud." I held tight to the window ledge as I talked.

I saw the half smile that was becoming familiar.

"The cloud, see," I went on, "was the chicken's nest. And the chicken was up there settin' for a long time. Hatching."

Daddy snapped his fingers. He had big thick fingers. They made a big thick snap. "I know what happened next, Pert. Then it rained."

"Nope," I said. I loved the look on his face. It said he was curious. "Guess again."

"I can't guess again, Pert."

"Here, Daddy," I said. "I'll give you a hint."

He smiled over at me.

"What does chickens lay, Daddy?"

"Well, of course, they lay eggs, Pert."

"That's right!" I said, snapping my own fingers. They was thin and long. They made a thin long snap. "And so did this chicken. In the dream the eggs fell one after another from the cloud. Only the eggs wasn't eggs. And they wasn't white, neither."

"Well, if they wasn't white eggs, what was they?"

"I'll give you a hint. Think of something that's silver and round."

"A flying saucer."

"Too big."

"Hubcaps."

"Smaller." Hubcaps reminded me of Charlie Hale. A fellow once drove all the way from Arkansas to look over Charlie Hale's collection and pick up a hubcap for his 1936 Dodge pickup. Charlie didn't charge him. Said if it meant so much to drive that far, he could have it for free.

"Here, Daddy," I said. "I'll give you another hint. It's something that jingles in your pocket, something you used to buy this ring for me." I lifted my ring to his face, and the heart-shaped stone glowed pink.

"Money," Daddy said. "Change. Coins." Something in his voice chimed like dimes dropped into a cash register. There was a happy ring to Daddy's voice when he said those three words.

"Good, Daddy," I said. I hugged the truck door with my left hand now.

"You mean the chicken laid silver coins?"

I nodded. "That's a true fact, Daddy. Coins as silver as your beard."

It was then that I told him about the money. About the notice in the *Troy Tribune*. About the unclaimed funds setting in the bank like a chicken on a nest. About Daddy's daddy, laying a giant egg filled with money for his son to collect.

I'd never talked so much in my life. Or so fast. It felt like talking a gorilla out of a banana. Or a bone from a hound dog's mouth. I said he should wait at least until the bank opened tomorrow morning. Then he could leave after that if he wanted. He'd still have time to make it to Florida by Tuesday.

"What happened to the silver coins?" he asked, interrupting me.

"What?" I had near forgot about the chicken and the nest and the eggs. Fact was, I didn't much care about the dream anymore. I just wanted Daddy to stay, collect his money, and find out that he loved us all so much that he could never leave again.

"*You* know, Pert—the silver eggs. What happened to the coins when they fell from the sky?"

I was pooped. I couldn't hardly think straight anymore. Telling whoppers was like getting lost in one of Farley Ewing's puzzles. Sometimes you couldn't find any more matching pieces.

"Tell you what, Daddy," I said. "If you stay over till tomorrow I'll let you know."

Then my daddy reached over and rubbed the top of my head. I could tell he had messed up my spit curls. But I didn't care.

Part Three

Alice Potter,

My bottles is all kinds of colors, don'tcha know. Blue and green and gold and pink. When Pert Wilson were small, she's bringin' me dabs of color from her mama's old paint-by-numbers sets, and we's settin' on the rusty metal chairs shaped like tulips and brushin' color on the bottles to perk 'em up. I can't paint like I used to. I's gots the shakes real *b-b-bad* now.

Sometimes I's thinkin' of colors for people. That pink one's for Rae Jean Wilson. Reminds me what the granny woman say: *Dimple on the cheek, Soul mild and meek.*

Been thinkin' on that feller what showed up in that truck. I's wonderin' who the feller were. Never seed him before. Tall. Gray beard. Movin' *q-q-quick.*

Feller sets me to wonderin' about Pert. The *l-l-look* on her face is sayin' he were somebody important, don'tcha know. That gal is hangin' on to his truck for dear life when he were fixin' to go. I 'spect Pert Wilson was talkin' a blue streak to *m-m-make* him stay. When he reaches over and rubs her *h-h-head,* I 'spect he's stayin'.

10

Jimmy went on to work like it was any old Monday, but when I begged, Rae Jean said I could be late to school so I could make Daddy breakfast and tell him good-bye. Daddy had slept in his truck on the sleeping bag in that narrow rectangle next to the pile of metal sheets. I tossed all night like I often did, but when I came over early to check on Daddy and see how he slept, he yawned and stretched like one of the Weevils' peacocks, spreading his arms out like feather fans. "Slept like a baby, Pert," he said.

I cooked him hash browns for breakfast, making sure they was extra crispy and had lots of salt. After that he went up to the bank, and after that he told us that Granddaddy Sam Wilson's unclaimed funds amounted to a hundred dollars, and after that he got ready to leave.

Now he was saying his good-byes.

The whole trailer park turned out to see him off. Odette Coates handed him a paper plate of barbecue wrapped in newspaper. Farley Ewing gave him a nervous handshake, and Emil Highwater passed him a paper sack full of fishing flies. Miss Mulch went right up and chucked his cheek as if my daddy was no more'n one of her schoolkids.

Daddy brushed Rae Jean's forehead with his lips and she blushed purple. Then he slid onto the front seat of the truck. He was in a hurry to get on the road, so I didn't have time to give him the handprint ashtray. He had already started the engine.

It was then that Mayor Cherry showed up. His black Lincoln convertible blocked Daddy's path. It was the only time in my life I'd been glad to see a politician.

It surprised me to see Mayor Cherry at Happy Trails. Usually he just showed up at Kinship events like the Hayes County Little Miss Pageant or the tractor pull at the county fair. Mostly he showed up places where there was lots of people fixing to vote.

When he walked, Mayor Howard Cherry came belly first like a penguin. He waved a piece of paper like it was a campaign flier or something.

"Dora or Bert Slagle here?" he asked.

Everybody shook their head.

"Order from the zoning commission."

Everybody wrinkled their foreheads.

Rae Jean stepped forward. "I'm the manager here," she said. "I'll see that they get it."

Everybody stepped closer to Rae Jean, trying to figure what the paper was about.

Rae Jean took the sheet, opened it up, and shook it out. She read the words quick. I looked over her shoulder. The words was too big for me to understand. They sounded official, though. They was words like *dismantle, ordinance, governance.* And a *whereas* about every other sentence.

"What does this mean?" Rae Jean said.

"Means you folks is set to go before the zoning commission. This area's being zoned for family homes. Permanent housing. These mobile homes ain't family homes, folks. They're tin cans on wheels. They're going to be in violation of the zoning regs." Mayor Cherry rocked back and forth on feet that spread out like forks in the road. "You're going to have to get out."

Rae Jean's face got dark. "What do you mean, Howard Cherry? Of *course* these are homes. Been our homes for years, and you know it. They're a roof over our head same as anybody else's." I liked the way Rae Jean called him Howard Cherry instead of Mayor.

"Mobile homes ain't the same thing as permanent family dwellings, Mrs. Wilson." I heard the way Mayor Cherry said *mobile*. He was an idiot. I knew that *mobile* rhymes with *global*. Mayor Cherry said it sort of like the city in Alabama. "*Mo*-beel," he said. Mayor Cherry was an idiot. No wonder he was mayor.

"They're permanent to us," Sophie Mulch said. "*Laws,* we're not going anywhere, Mayor."

"But can't you up and move 'em when you like?"

"Well, yes. I guess we could," Miss Sophie said. Then she stuck out her tiny bottom lip. "But we won't."

Miss Mulch was right. Nobody was like to pull up stakes. Only Gene Nugent and the Highwaters and Charlie Hale had cars. Gene's was a Fleetwood Cadillac big as a boat. The Highwaters' station wagon was rusted out, but they kept the tailgate down all summer so they could sell tomatoes and pole beans from it. Charlie Hale had a pickup he drove to whatever construction job he was working on. Anybody else in the court who wanted to go anywhere had to walk.

"*Won't* and *could*'s two different things," Mayor Cherry

100

said. "So you admit, Miss Sophie, that you *could* up and move these trailers?"

"Y-Y-Yes," she said.

"I rest my case. If you can up and move 'em, then a trailer's not a permanent family home." I couldn't wait until I was old enough to vote for anyone *except* Howard Cherry.

"But they're permanent family homes to us," Rae Jean said. "We're settled in here. Been here for years. This is permanent to us. This is *home*."

Mayor Cherry took to strutting. He crossed back and forth across the dirt. Then he swung his arm around like a lawyer in a courtroom. "Tell me, Mrs. Wilson," he said, "does this really look like home to you?" He began to point. "All this stuff laying around these trailer rigs?" He pointed to the birdbath, to the rusty buckets of rainwater, to the old truck tires and hubcaps around Charlie Hale's trailer, to the pile of trash with the old gold carpet outside Alice Potter's lot. Across the way, the Weevils' chickens fluttered and squawked, and the rooster pecked at an old hen.

Rae Jean said, " 'Course it does, Mayor. 'Course it looks like home. It *is* home. What's it look like to you?"

I hoped Mayor Cherry wouldn't answer Rae Jean's question. I looked around at the cracked flowerpots and the green snakes of garden hoses twisted up in knots and the dried-up marigolds and Sarge's dog chain and the cigarette butts all over everywhere like paper snow.

Mayor Cherry's fat lips turned down like the hoses Jimmy replaced in cars. "Looks like a run-down old place in violation of Kinship's zoning regulations to me." As I heard his words, a familiar fire began to blaze in my belly.

It was then that my daddy turned off his truck. Mayor

Cherry's Lincoln had blocked Daddy's way, and Daddy had been letting the engine idle while he waited for the mayor to go away. He had been listening to Mayor Cherry blab, and when he hopped out of the truck, there was something electric in his step, something charged.

"I'm James William Wilson, Mayor," he said. My daddy shook the mayor's grubby paw with his own strong hand. I hoped Daddy hadn't picked up any of the mayor's cooties.

Daddy looked back across the park and then around at the gathered faces. "How much time we got here, Mayor?" he said. There was a glint in my daddy's eyes. Reminded me of the Fourth of July and the way a sparkler suddenly bursts into silver pinwheels once the match catches hold.

"You got until the zoning board meets a week from Tuesday," Mayor Cherry said.

I thought back to that rhyme Gram had taught me when she'd stayed with Jimmy and me all those nights. *Ladybug, ladybug, fly away home. Your house is on fire, your children all gone.*

A look fast as a June bug's wings passed between Daddy and me. Even though it moved quick as a jif, the look gave me hope, hope that somehow my daddy would save me from a burning house. From the feeling of being on fire. From the feeling of being all gone.

Iris Breeding,

TRAILER 1

I could have *daah'd* the way this trailer court looked when the mayor showed up. Laundry was hanging all over. On lawn chairs. From antennas. Across Alice Potter's birdbath. Emil Highwater's red suspenders hung on a *ta-may-tah* stake. The place looked like a hobo camp.

Pert's daddy was the only one to see it straight and get down to business. James Wilson took charge like a general. I never saw a man as calm *in this world*.

After the mayor left, everybody was fuming about that resolution.

"It ain't fair," Alvin Coates said.

"They can't do that to us," said Myra Highwater.

"We got our rights," Farley Ewing said.

While they were whining, James Wilson had hauled rectangles of sheet metal off his truck. They looked like a big bale of metal hay. He pulled out a tape measure and got Charlie Hale to help him measure the side of Miss Mulch's trailer.

"They *can* do it," he called over to the group of trailerites. They were still squawking like *hayuns*.

"You think you've got your rights," he said. "*I* think you've only got till a week from *tahmahrah*."

I'd never seen so many jaws drop at the same time *in my life*.

11

Miss Mulch stepped out from the group. "Mayor Cherry was right," she said. "Just *look* at this place, people." She swept the court with her arm like Mayor Cherry had. "What did he say these trailers looked like?"

Nobody answered.

Then Rae Jean said, "The mayor called them tin cans on wheels."

"The mayor is right," my daddy said. "They do look like tin cans. Shoeboxes. Gypsy wagons."

Daddy paused, and everybody looked at each other while his words sunk in. Alvin Coates took a hanky from his pocket and wiped his brow. Farley Ewing gave Miss Mulch a puzzled look. Emil Highwater grunted, and Myra stroked the feathers on her fishing flies.

"I reckon ever'body thinks of these trailers as home, folks, but you want these places to *look* like homes if you ever hope to keep them," Daddy said. He strutted in front of the group, and I saw for the first time that his boots might have been expensive. The leather was carved and tooled, and the heels was made of a metal like brass. "You want to get these here trailers to look like loaves of bread pulled from the

104

oven," he said. "Warm. Inviting." When Daddy talked, energy flowed from him. "Way I see it, folks," he said, "I reckon you got you till a week from Tuesday to make this place look like home."

I thought about that word. *Home.* What was a home? What made a place look like it? Was it the columns on the porches of the houses lining the hills north of town? Was it the neat rows of azaleas in the side yards? Did it mean attached garages like the people had out in Fenwick Acres? Did it mean fences marching around property lines, or chimneys puffing smoke like pipes between the teeth of bankers?

Home didn't mean any of those things to me. For me, home meant Rae Jean rubbing her stockings after a day of work. For me, home was Jimmy making coffee from the hot-water tap in the kitchen and boxing with me in the front room. Home was going yarn fishing with Gram: sitting for hours while she crocheted, the long strings of yarn hooked on her needles like worms. Home was clipping coupons with Sophie Mulch, sorting feathers with the Highwaters, fetching the newspaper for Gene Nugent.

I looked at the faces around me. They was startled and blank. I wondered if the folks in the trailer court was thinking as hard as I was about what was meant by *home.*

My daddy looked frustrated by the blank faces. "Here, folks," he said, using his index finger as a pointer. "Let's start with this here stack of sheeting. Let's just measure us a bit and cut off what we need. Let's wrap it around the bottom of Miss Mulch's trailer here. Then maybe we could hide us some of that junk behind it and see what we think."

Light dawned on the faces around me.

Daddy went on. "If we wrap this here sheet metal around the bed of your trailers, you can hide your old tires and your broken birdbaths behind it, and you'll have you a sight as pretty as a lady's skirt."

There was no question about it. Energy flowed from my daddy like a turned-on switch. One by one the faces in front of him lit up like bulbs.

Miss Mulch stepped right over to him. "Well, now," she said. "You got your first customer, sir. I see you just measured the side of my rig. What do I owe you?"

"Only one dollar a foot," my daddy said.

"Sold," said Miss Mulch.

Daddy worked all day, measuring, cutting, screwing, hammering. Jimmy and Charlie Hale helped him, and everybody else watched. I liked hearing what they said about Daddy's idea. Alvin Coates noticed that Miss Mulch's trailer skirt would block the wind. Farley Ewing predicted that it would make her floor warmer. Odette Coates begged Alvin to buy her a skirt, and Iris Breeding said she'd like one, too.

It was amazing what I learned about the folks in the court. I found out how hard my brother could work. Jimmy worked steady without a break all day long, driving Charlie Hale's truck to town now and again for more supplies. I found out how strong Charlie Hale really was. He picked up sheets of metal and slung them across his back like they was nothing more than squares of tin foil. And I found out how generous the Coateses really was. They laid a pig across their spit and said folks could have all the barbecue they could eat all day long.

In the late afternoon, Dora and Bert Slagle showed up.

106

They had read the resolution by then, and they was hopping mad. Their faces was pinched as tight as gathered seams, but when they looked around and saw what my daddy had done to Miss Mulch's trailer, the seams loosened up a tad.

Miss Mulch still had reservations. "Maybe it doesn't look as much like a junkyard, people. But this court still doesn't look like home, and it's nothing like a neighborhood." I heard the way Miss Mulch always said *people*. I bet it was a habit left over from teaching school. I could picture her saying to her fifth-graders, "Now quiet down, people. *People*, will you quiet *down*?"

Dora Slagle fiddled with her sweater guard. It linked the two halves of the thin white sweater that draped her own thin white shoulders. "What do you think it would take, folks, to make it look like a neighborhood?"

I looked around. It felt like staring into the empty Frigidaire, wondering what you could fix for supper.

"Well, Mrs. Slagle," I said, stepping up to her, "a neighborhood usually has grass. And trees."

Mrs. Slagle nodded. "Grass and trees sounds nice, Pert," she said.

Miss Mulch was thinking. I could always tell when she was thinking because she took one of her quick short breaths and fell silent. It was what she always did when she went through her magazines and tried to decide whether she'd clip a coupon for something like toilet-bowl cleaner that she didn't buy regular. While Miss Mulch thought, Farley Ewing scratched his chin, Emil Highwater folded his arms across his chest, and Alvin Coates wiped his brow.

Bert Slagle got out his checkbook. "How much would it cost for grass and trees, you figure?"

My daddy took his notepad from his pocket and wrote down some numbers with a pencil. "I reckon it'll cost you more'n you want to pay, sir," Daddy said.

Bert Slagle looked over at the notepad and frowned.

While they talked, I glanced over at the sign that Pee Wee Hale and me had made when we was kids. It was cheap plywood slung on sticks. HAPPY TRAILS TRAILER COURT, it said.

"If you don't mind, Mr. Slagle," I said, "it might make sense to put up a nice sign, too, while you're at it."

Bert Slagle smiled at me cautious-like from under his glasses.

"And maybe we could give the court a new name." I felt like I did when I made a meal out of nothing. "*Happy Trails* sounds like somebody getting on a horse and riding off into the sunset. It's not a good name for someone set on permanent housing in a nice neighborhood."

I could tell from the faces around me that I had not only made a meal out of nothing: I was feeding a bunch of folks with it as well.

The face I liked best, though, was Daddy's. Bert Slagle had written his name across the bottom of a check and passed it to him.

"Would a blank check do you, sir?" Bert Slagle asked.

The look on Daddy's face said he thought he'd dropped his drawers.

Charlie Hale,

TRAILER 10

Tonight everybody was in the mood to set and talk. Most nights it's just Rae Jean and Sophie Mulch outside on their lawn chairs. If it was nice out, I'd come by and bring iced tea. I'd rigged up poles so that Rae Jean could string her Christmas-tree lights outside, and they lit up the darkness like colored fireflies. I confess there's nothin' prettier than Rae Jean's pink skin and yellow hair under those blinking lights.

Everybody wanted a skirt like Miss Mulch. Odette Coates drove Alvin near to death with her begging. She wanted a skirt painted yellow to match their trailer. Iris Breeding wanted a skirt bad, too. Tonight her husband Carter stayed inside studying. Iris said they were planning on moving to Kinship Acres as soon as they could, and Carter thought pouring money in the trailer didn't make good sense. But she said she had her ways.

I wondered about good sense. James Wilson charged one dollar a foot for those sheets, and people signed up without blinking an eye. I told folks that I could get the same thing in Troy for fifty cents or less, but they didn't seem to hear. I confess I always thought it strange the way a big fellow like me has such a time being heard.

It's different with James Wilson. When he speaks, folks listen. It doesn't seem to matter what he's saying. Everybody pays admission to hear his one-man band.

Tonight near everyone had pulled up a chair to talk. Alvin

Coates brought over the stool he kept out by the barbecue pit, and Myra Highwater sat on top of a stepladder with a pot between her knees, snapping beans. Rae Jean's lawn chair was busted out in the seat, so I offered to replace the webbing. I unscrewed each old web, crisscrossed the new, and then tightened up the screw again.

I always listen while I work. I *b'lieve* I learn a lot that way.

Everybody was trying out names for the court. Alvin Coates said he liked *Moving Inn*. 'Course you'd spell it *i-n-n* instead of *i-n*," he said.

"That ain't no good, Alvin," Pert said. "Can't have a name with *moving* in it. Got to show those commissioners that we're permanent, we're planning to stay."

Farley Ewing said, "What about *Shady Court* or *Shady Oaks*?"

"Ain't got no shade," Pert said.

"Ain't got no oaks, neither," Alvin Coates said.

Everybody laughed. I heard Gene Nugent out walking Sarge. I *b'lieve* he wanted to overhear what we were saying. But he didn't actually want to join the group.

"Besides," Myra Highwater said, "*Shady Court* puts folks in mind about shady doings."

"We got enough shady doings going on already with those Weevils over there," Odette said.

"What about something with *Kinship* in it?" Alvin said.

Everybody thought about it. I wove one last strip of webbing across Rae Jean's lawn chair.

"What about *Kinship Court*?" It was Myra Highwater. Her beans snapped like cracking knuckles.

Pert said, "No, Myra. That'd make folks think we was marrying cousins like they do up in the hills."

"Well, what about *Kinship View?*"

"Put folks in mind of Peeping Toms, nosing into their neighbors' windows."

"Pert's right," Alvin said. "We got to make the name sound homey. We got to make it sound clean as a whistle. What about *Homey Acres?*"

"Ain't no acres here," Pert said. "Just ten plots."

I screwed the last screw through the webbing and helped Rae Jean up from the stoop. "Thank you, Charlie," she said. I confess her voice is soft as sweet peas on the vine.

She was just settling into her chair when James William came over. He'd been at the Weevils'. I confess he was only trying to get them interested in cleaning up their place, too. The look on his face said he hadn't had much luck.

"What about something with *homestead* in it?" James William said. "I reckon you're all something like home-steaders—settling down, staking a claim. What about *Homestead Court?*"

People looked over at James William Wilson like he was Moses come down with a tablet.

I confess I don't know what it is about sweet-talkers. But I *b'lieve* folks can be either talkers or workers. I can always tell which is which.

12

It was amazing what a small bunch of folks could do in a week. Daddy had called the fellow in Florida with an order for a hundred more sheets of metal. He collected money from Farley Ewing and the Coateses right away, and Iris Breeding borrowed money from her aunt Olive. I tried to talk Gene Nugent and Alice Potter into signing up for metal skirts, but they wasn't sure. Gene was afraid the metal would mess up his radio signals and Alice was afraid it would attract lightning. The Highwaters signed up straight off but told Daddy he would have to wait for his money. Now Daddy knew how I felt when I had to collect rent.

Gram was the only sour grape in the whole bunch. She said a slattern's petticoat's not the same thing as a lady's skirt.

Everybody was mad at the Weevils. Daddy had gone over to sell them sheeting, and Ida Weevil shooed him off like he was a fly. Ida said one dollar a foot was too much to pay for something she didn't need. She made me mad: She and Ora was the only folks in the court able to fork over money without a second thought about their bank account. Gram said that Weevils wasn't fools when it came to money and that Charlie Hale could get the same sheeting in Troy for fifty cents a foot. 'Course when Miss Mulch marched over and volunteered to pay for the Weevils' skirting, Ida finally nodded her agreement. Gram shrugged and said penny-pinchers like Sophie Mulch was some of the biggest spenders there was.

Daddy ordered the grass sod and bushes from the nursery in Troy, and he sent Jimmy up and down the back roads picking up and delivering the orders whenever he could get away from the station. Jimmy liked driving the bread truck, and sometimes I went along, loving the feel of the wind in my hair and the thought of work done for my daddy. Everybody in the trailer court now had dirt under their nails from laying sod. Except for Gene Nugent and the Weevils.

The hundred new sheets of metal almost didn't come. Daddy's partner in Florida was hard to get ahold of. Near every day Daddy walked up to the phone booth in front of Byer's Drugs and called places like Apalachicola and Melbourne and Ocala to check on the order. Daddy was worried because his partner needed all the money up front, and Daddy wasn't sure he could get it all; some of the trailer folks just didn't have it to give. When Miss Mulch offered to make up the difference, Daddy mixed Miss Mulch's contribution with the Slagles' blank check and wired the money straight off.

The sheets came just two days before the zoning commission meeting, and everybody in the court worked night and day to fix things up. When Alice Potter and Gene Nugent put up skirts and the Highwaters finally paid for theirs in full, everybody in the park celebrated. They raised toasts to Daddy, clinking glasses of iced tea and slapping him on the back.

The zoning commission meeting was on Tuesday afternoon. The commissioners had come out to the park to take what Mayor Cherry called a look-see. Daddy shook hands all around and answered all their dumb questions as nice as pie. The commissioners rooted around the park like pigs, peeking behind the new bushes set outside the trailers and digging their heels into the soft new turf. Then they stood in a group and eyed the new sign that marked the entrance to the court.

The sign was my idea. The Slagles had decided on Daddy's name, *Homestead Court,* but I talked them into one bitty change. I thought *park* was better than *court.* I figured *park* would set better with the commissioners. Daddy agreed. He said *court* reminded folks of tourist camps, those dingy little sleeping places you found along the road to anywhere else, where the beds was nothing more than cots with bugs. When Daddy said that *park* put people in mind of weeping willows and crape myrtle and that I was a clever girl, I beamed like headlights.

The best part of the sign was the extra line I put in under the name. It now read: HOMESTEAD PARK: WHERE THE NEIGHBORS IS JUST LIKE KIN. Jimmy had bought some particleboard special from the lumber yard in Troy, and Pee Wee Hale and I had used one of Miss Mulch's old stencil kits. We'd written the letters in Old English script just to be fancy, and we'd measured and penciled in the letters before we painted them. I loved the curling *H* and *K* the best. I figured we'd hit about everything those zoning commissioners wanted with *homestead, park, neighbors,* and *kin.*

Everybody came out to watch the commissioners, and as I looked at my daddy escorting them around the park, I felt plain proud. Iris Breeding had put a cute little picket fence around her trailer hitch, and Charlie Hale had painted the Coateses' skirt yellow to make Odette happy. Farley Ewing had walked every step of the court picking up cigarette butts, then had given them to Emil Highwater to add to the coffee grounds in his night-crawler mulch.

After the commissioners had roamed their fill and went home, the trailerites all cheered for Daddy and sang "For He's a Jolly Good Fellow" over and over. Emil Highwater came over with something he'd brought from his Seminole tribe. It was a huge headdress, full of red and yellow and blue feathers on a leather band, the tails of the feathers tipped in white. It took Myra and Emil both to lift it onto Daddy's head, but once they did, everybody danced, beating their hands on their mouths in war whoops. Even Rae Jean was dancing. First time I'd ever seen my mama dance. I wondered if Lucinda Adkins up on the hill had ever had this much fun. I hoped she had. As I watched the dozens of feet carving circles in the dirt, I hoped the dancing was keeping the devil out, the devil that drove a black Lincoln and pretended to be a politician.

Gram kept her arms crossed flat across her chest like Princess Tiger Lily's father in *Peter Pan*. She was red-faced and scowling, too. Said it would take a lot more than a metal skirt to get commissioners to dance in public with the folks in Happy Trails.

Sophie Mulch,

TRAILER 4

Oh, *laws,* but Pert's daddy's just as clever as she is! I swannee, my new metal skirt is a stroke of genius. Of course, after James Wilson put it on, near everybody in the court except Weevils wanted one. I ended up paying for Weevils' skirt and putting up money for those who didn't quite have it in full. I don't mind a bit. It was my pleasure. Been wanting to fix this place up for years.

Laws, but the place looked nice for those commissioners! Alice Potter had spread Sarge's droppings around the bases of the new hydrangea shrubs Jimmy brought over from Troy. Emil Highwater had scrubbed down the old picnic table and closed up the back of his station wagon. Charlie Hale and Pee Wee had put waistbands up on everyone's skirt and painted the Coateses' skirt yellow. Odette Coates pranced around like the queen of the ball, and Pert Wilson, bless her sweet heart, told those commissioners that everybody was fixing on painting their skirt and that once they got through, Homestead Park was going to look sweet as a roll of Necco wafers.

I swannee, I hated the way those commissioners nosed around. They poked their snouts behind the bushes and dug their toes into the grass. Lucille Beauchamp, that new real estate agent who came along, left holes in the sod with her spike heels. Dora and Bert Slagle paced back and forth with worry while the commissioners minded everybody else's business.

I was glad Rae Jean had insisted on a few flowering trees. She said no picture was prettier than a flowering tree against green pines. *Laws,* but she's got an artist's eye! Everybody liked the idea of crape myrtles, and Rae Jean said if they were pinched back now, they might give a second bloom by winter.

After Jimmy bought the crape myrtles, Pert's daddy, bless his heart, surprised Rae Jean with a passionflower vine. I don't think she'd ever heard the story about it before. James Wilson told her how the flower was supposed to be about the passion of Christ with the center standing for the crown of thorns and the five stamens like the five wounds. Carter Breeding heard them talking. He got out his notebook when James Wilson said how the ten petals stood for the faithful apostles and how there wasn't twelve since you couldn't count Judas and Peter. Rae Jean said she didn't think James Wilson knew that much about religion. *Laws,* but I thought he was romancing her all over again!

It was near evening by the time those commissioners left, and the people in the court didn't seem to want to go back inside, bless their hearts. Pert brought out iced tea, and as the sun went down, they sang and danced and carried on. Farley Ewing strummed his ukulele. People groaned about their backs aching from hauling sod, and they picked the half-moons of dirt out from under their fingernails. People complained right and left about all the hard work, but they reminded me of those kids I had back in 1949: whining to beat the band but working like beavers.

I swannee, those commissioners couldn't make a decision. Maybe they'd think faster if *their* lives depended on it, but since it was *our* lives, they just took their sweet old time.

13

Daddy had been here for ten days now. He'd found out that there was money in sheeting, and he knew his Florida partner'd be itching to make some more with him. But he'd promised me one thing. He'd promised that he wouldn't leave Kinship until we'd heard from the commissioners.

Even though Daddy slept through breakfast, I cooked for him every single morning. Usually I'd leave a plate he could warm in the stove, but sometimes I'd sneak back home from school near around eleven o'clock to prepare something fresh. Daddy'd stumble through the door, rubbing the sleep from his eyes, giving that big deep groan like he always did, asking me the same hungry question: "What you got cooking, daughter?" It almost got to seem like one of our routines.

I was always proud of what I fixed. I'd do French toast with powdered sugar on top the way he liked it. I'd do eggs over light, rolling them over gentle like a baby in a crib. I'd fix grits fried up in bacon grease, crusty and brown.

Money was easier now that Daddy was around. We'd stopped using powdered milk, and I didn't have to use potatoes that was sprouting eyes. I used as many eggs as I wanted in the French toast, not worrying about stretching one egg with a pile of water. Now we used cream for Gram's coffee instead of milk.

Sometimes while I cooked, I saw Daddy wink at Rae Jean. When he did that, she ducked her head. Daddy just kept trying to spread looks across Rae Jean like butter on warm toast, but Rae Jean never seemed to have much appetite for them.

Jimmy didn't have a lot to do with Daddy. He'd been leaving every spare chance he got, which wasn't much between his job and the work he was doing for the trailer park. When Jimmy took off, it was always to see his girlfriend, Sue Ellen Jenkins.

Rae Jean encouraged me to spend as much time as I needed with my daddy, and I did. One day Rae Jean even let me take a whole day off school during the middle of the week.

My daddy took time out for me. We went to the Thom McAn in Troy, and he made fun of the kind of school shoes that Miss Mulch bought me there. He said a girl like me needed good boots. I told him I already had some boots; got them two years ago at the rummage sale the Presbyterians have. They was white with fringe that shook when I walked. But Daddy said they wasn't grown-up boots: They was boots for little ladies playing cowgirl. I felt a catch of shame for all the times I had worn those boots so proud.

The boots Daddy bought me was just like his, and he paid for them by laying a fifty-dollar bill on the counter with a slap. When I walked, the heels made clicking sounds like my old Keds with thumbtacks in them. When we left the store, Daddy and me went tapping down the sidewalk together, laughing like fools.

After that, I took my daddy to the movies. I loved it that I could give him a free pass, and we watched *Psycho* together. I grabbed his hand during the scary scenes; it was big and warm and strong, and it made me feel safe.

Best of all, I loved driving with Daddy in the bread truck. I liked it when he revved the engines or shifted the gears with a lurch. When he laid a patch of rubber, the way the tires squealed ran a current up my spine.

One time when he backed up too fast, Daddy smashed into the new bushes outside Farley Ewing's trailer, and he frowned at the tiny scratches on the back panel. When I ran inside and found red nail polish to fix them up, he laughed so hard he had to hold his sides. After that was when he told me how much he liked how wild I was. "Clever and wild" was how he put it, and then he said that was the problem with Jimmy: Jimmy played life too safe. I didn't know what Daddy meant. Hadn't he seen the way Jimmy picked up speed out on County Line Road?

Sometimes after supper Daddy and I walked at the edge of the piney woods together. Often Daddy invited Rae Jean to join us, but she usually said, "You two go on. I think it'd be nice for you and Pert to spend some more time together." Rae Jean would sit on the chaise lounge with Mittens on her tummy and wave to us as we walked off.

After we'd left, Rae Jean'd get out her paints. She seemed to be bored by her paint-by-numbers now. She'd bought a scrap of muslin and stretched it across slats, painting her own scene of the piney woods. She used every shade of green she had: lime green, forest green, apple green, spring green. She decided where each color needed to go her own self.

And then Daddy had brought us the wheelbarrow. He

sent Jimmy up to Gleason's Hardware in town to buy it. We didn't really need a wheelbarrow, since we'd already laid all that grass, but Daddy bought it anyway. While Jimmy was picking one out at Gleason's, Daddy took me with him to the bank and laid a laundry sack across the teller's counter. At first I thought he was fixing on robbing the place, but then I saw him pass the teller a five-hundred-dollar bill and heard him say he'd take the whole amount in singles, if she didn't mind. The teller's eyes liked to pop out of her head.

When we got home, Daddy asked Rae Jean to come out and set on the stoop with her eyes closed. He took the wheelbarrow out of the truck and held the laundry bag over it. Dollar bills floated into it like piles of green dirt, and some of the bills scattered away in the air like dandelion fluff. Then Daddy pushed the wheelbarrow across the grass, dollar bills flying every which way. When Rae Jean opened her eyes, she near fell off the stoop. Then Daddy told me to go on inside the trailer and bring out the fruit crate, the one they had laid me in when I was a baby.

I brought the fruit crate out to the stoop, and Daddy held it high, dumping out all my underwear beside the trailer; it arced and fell like cotton fireworks in pinks and blues and greens. Then Daddy lifted the wheelbarrow by its handles and dumped the dollar bills into the fruit crate. Now my crate was heaped with dollar bills, and my daddy's chest puffed out with pride.

I saw the look that passed between Rae Jean and Daddy. It said something about how they had felt about that baby in the fruit crate, something about how they felt about the daughter that was me.

Part Four

Odette Coates,

TRAILER 6

Well, now, I been worryin' less about Pert Wilson but missin' her more.

Like I say to Alvin, there's nothing to ease a hungry heart like a full belly. I like seein' Pert gettin' three squares a day. One Saturday I saw her with her daddy and Rae Jean out on the stoop, gobblin' up a big sack of peaches. I liked seein' Pert lickin' the peach juice off'n her fingers. Made me think that young gal's finally got some happiness in her life.

Pert's daddy's been buyin' up stuff faster than po' folks at an auction, and payin' top dollar for it, too. Emil Highwater said James Wilson shelled out for one of them rotary lawn mowers so Jimmy could mow the new grass in the park. Farley Ewing said Pert's daddy bought her a leather jacket and one of them big motorcycle belts. Like I say to Alvin, every young pig's entitled to a tit. And Pert Wilson ain't had nothin' to latch on to for years.

Got to admit I miss her, though. Pert don't come around much anymore. Sophie Mulch misses her, too. Said Pert wasn't comin' by to watch TV afternoons. But Miss Mulch said Pert's grades was goin' up, and the fact of that made us both happy.

Well, now, like I say to Alvin, if you expect things to stay the same, you a fool.

14

Daddy bought me things. A Revlon lipstick that looked like a gold bullet. A fancy notebook for my schoolwork and a whole box of pencils. When he came home with the Hula Hoop, he sat on the stoop and laughed while I tried to keep it spinning around my waist. I felt like a drunken sailor walking on a rolling deck. The best thing Daddy bought was a record player and three 45's: "Mack the Knife," "Put Your Head on My Shoulder," and "The Twist." Rae Jean went outside now to read her *Good Tidings.* Said it was the only place she could get peace and quiet.

It had been two weeks and four days, and we still hadn't heard from the commissioners. That meant my daddy would keep on staying—at least until we'd got word from them. It was the only time in my life I'd liked how slow things went. While we waited, Daddy took me off in the truck with him. We was partners, Daddy and me. Business partners. Rae Jean wasn't happy about it, so I didn't tell her when I skipped school to go. Daddy helped me keep that secret from Rae Jean, and he said clever people was too smart for school.

Daddy and me was going around to trailer parks all over

the state of Georgia selling metal skirting. Since it didn't make sense to ship skirting all the way from Florida, Daddy had the name of Charlie Hale's supplier in Troy. When I asked Daddy how he could charge folks the same amount he'd charged our trailer folks now that he got sheets for less, he winked and said one word: "Capitalism."

Daddy was proud of the way he'd settled his debts and had enough left over to help out our family. From what he'd made on these new jobs, he'd paid Miss Mulch in full for buying the Weevils' trailer skirt. She said she hadn't expected to be paid back, but Daddy insisted. And after he'd ordered the grass and bushes and trees, Daddy'd given Slagles an itemized bill, and it matched the amount on their blank check to the penny.

Somehow I could look at things different when I rode off on jobs with my daddy. As we drove east, the columns on rich folks' porches looked like white arms holding up the gray clouds, keeping off the rain; farther out, as we drove near the nice rows of new houses called Fenwick Acres, the antennas on the rooftops looked like direct lines to heaven. And from the front seat of the red bread truck, I felt like I was joyriding with God.

Fact was, the drives in Daddy's truck helped me breathe free and leave Kinship, Georgia, behind. I felt plugged up by all the things packed close together in my life: the trailer with its coffee table banging your shins; the high school with its teachers like Nympha Claggett whispering about your family; the vet's office with its wet fur smells lingering in your nose; Mama stuck in the ruts of her own ways. My life in Kinship was a stuffed-up head cold; the drive in Daddy's truck was a welcome sneeze.

Daddy said I was a key part of his business operation because I knew trailer courts.

I'd first find either the manager's trailer or the nicest rig in the park. Then I'd up and introduce myself. "Howdy-do," I'd say. It tickled Daddy.

I knew trailer folks inside and out and could talk a blue streak about what they needed. The trailerites would gather around scratching their stomachs after a meal or stretching from their naps. "Life in your little court here, folks, is nice, ain't it?" They'd all nod.

Then I'd say how life in the courts was good but a little shameful, too. I talked about how folks sometimes looked down on trailer people because their courts needed sprucing up a bit. I'd point out the broken flowerpots and the tangled weeds and the cigarette butts just like we had over in Happy Trails. I'd flash them a smile. Daddy said my smile was a lightning rod: It drew folks in.

Then I'd tell 'em about what happened in Kinship. About Mayor Cherry and the zoning commission and the fact that we could lose our homes. Folks' eyes got big as marbles when I told that story, and they woke full up from their naps. They looked at each other like you did when you played Clue. Who had the answer? Was it Miss Scarlet or Colonel Mustard? And was it with the rope or the lead pipe?

After that Daddy made his pitch for the skirting, and I'd help seal the sales. Folks always seemed to like it that they was buying things from a kid.

On the rides back home across the red hills of Georgia, Daddy drove so fast it was like the roller coaster at the county fair. When my stomach sank on the downside of the hills, it felt like love-in-the-belly. Daddy said someone as clever and wild as me was bound to be good at business, and fact was, business was good.

When we'd made a sale and had pockets stuffed with money, we always stopped at model trailer lots to gawk. I liked the names of the models: Wrangler, Conestoga, Prairie Schooner. They reminded me of lighting out, heading West, moving into new territory. Daddy liked what they had inside: built-in radios, card tables, birch paneling. He said how he was saving up to buy Rae Jean her own house trailer. When he said things like that, I could feel my heart leap. Things like that gave me hope that my daddy might stay.

But sometimes when we got back home, things felt a little torn. I wasn't sure what it was, but it had something to do with Rae Jean and Daddy. The space between them felt rough somehow: a ragged fingernail scraping on the edges of their talk.

"I'm not sure I like Pert wearing that black leather jacket, James William," Rae Jean would say.

"Why not?"

"Puts folks in mind of motorcycle gangs."

"And what does it put folks in mind of when she wears that there blue pajama top, Rae Jean?"

Most of the time conversations ended like that: with Daddy having the last word. It was just like Rae Jean. "If somebody cares about having the last word that much," she'd say with a shrug, "what's the harm in letting them have it?" Rae Jean was nothing like Gram or me. Or Daddy.

Sometimes Daddy and Rae Jean had words about church.

"So why don't you come along to mass with us on a Sunday, James William?" Rae Jean'd ask. I thought it'd be swell, too, Daddy up front driving and no taxi.

129

"Reckon you know I ain't much of a believer in all that church stuff, Rae."

Rae Jean frowned. "You said you believed it when you married me."

Daddy winked at her. "People say lots of crazy things when they're in love."

Or they'd snap about simple things like waking up. Rae Jean got up early in the morning; Daddy slept in his truck till near noon.

Sometimes they'd spark about work. Daddy claimed selling sheeting was a full-time job; Rae Jean said working for Doc Jackson every single day was what passed for full-time in Kinship.

Or they'd snarl over Jimmy. Rae Jean said he didn't need to work at a station all day and keep up the trailer park property both. When Daddy said there was nothing better for a young man than learning responsibility, Rae Jean asked a question: "Same for older men, too?" That time, Daddy didn't answer back.

After their spats, Daddy would come home with things for Rae Jean, but she never seemed to appreciate them like I thought she should. Most of the time she passed them on to me. I was beginning to think my mama was a stubborn old ingrate.

One time Daddy bought her a new griddle. She handed it to me. "You're really the cook in the family, Pert," she said. "This will help you keep your daddy's hash browns crispy."

Another time Daddy brought a bottle of perfume called Tabu. I'd seen the ads for it in the magazines up at Byer's Drugs. They showed a longhair piano composer and a lady in a satin gown; the player must have been bored as nails with writing tunes, for he had rose up from his piano stool to plant a big one on the lady's lips. It reminded me of folks in the Bijou. They'd rather kiss than watch the show.

Rae Jean unscrewed the perfume bottle and sniffed. "Smells good, James William," she said. "Thanks. I'll bet Pert will love this."

"But it's for you, Rae," Daddy said.

Rae Jean smiled. Her dimple dug a hole in her right cheek. "I'm on my way to work, James Wilson. Work with animals all day, remember? Last thing Doc Jackson's place needs is another smell."

My mama didn't seem to give a red hot for the little things Daddy bought. But I wondered how she'd feel about the big thing, the biggest gift of all that he was working and saving for. I knew how much Rae Jean loved home. I couldn't wait for the day when Daddy gave her the best present of all: a big long mobile home from which our family could travel the cotton-pickin' world.

Pee Wee Hale,

TRAILER 10

I've known Pert Wilson since we were kids. I'm the only other kid in the court besides Jimmy and Pert. Pert and I made the park sign out front years ago. I wasn't 'zactly proud of it, but Pert didn't much care. When we decided to make it, I wanted to plan it out. Pert wanted to just paint it up any which way. Doing it my way would have made a better sign. Doing it Pert's way was more fun.

Ever since her daddy came back, Pert Wilson has been downright happy. Not just on the outside like she always was, clowning and fooling around. But on the inside. Down deep.

I know about how hard it is to be happy down deep. When I was five, my whole family was killed out on the Macon Highway. Mother. Daddy. Sisters Ellen and Joann. Brother Tommy. The last thing I remember is twisted steel and arms all tangled up together. I don't know what I would have done without my uncle Charlie. He took me in. Uncle Charlie was my dad's favorite brother, and I'd been named for him. In a way, I'm luckier than Pert. Folks give you more respect when your family's dead than when they've run off.

I like seeing Pert happy. I give her rides to school on mornings when she isn't late and when Uncle Charlie doesn't need the truck. We have fun on the drive. Can't nobody make you laugh like Pert Wilson. I've never seen a girl who can talk like she does, swinging between trailers like a monkey, dropping out one door and in the other. She's a social critter.

15

I hadn't gone to anything ever at school. I'd missed pep rallies, band concerts, 4-H club meetings. I always said I couldn't go because of work, and that was half true. The whole truth was the shame I felt.

I was different from the other girls at school. Other girls came from families that drove to church in their own cars and didn't have to hire a cab. Other girls came from families with fathers who worked at regular jobs and had life insurance, not dreamlike daddies who disappeared into the mists of Tennessee to work on tires with wings. Other girls came from families who stopped at Shriner's Grocery to pick up ice cream, not families who stopped there to trade empty pop bottles for milk money.

Fact was, the other girls had mothers and fathers who lived together and made a living easy as flipping pancakes. I didn't go to things at school because I didn't want to call attention to the fact that Wilsons was always waiting on their dough to rise.

But things was getting better for me now that my daddy was home. I had new boots and a leather jacket. My grades was going up, and best of all, in two Saturdays Daddy was taking me to the father-daughter dance.

For the first time ever, I signed up for something at school. I put my name on the sheet that said you would help with the dance decorations at lunch hour.

When I came up to Julie Nolan and Cissy Simmons and Linda Lumpkin at the cafeteria table, they had already started working. Rolls of crepe paper was spread all over the tabletops.

"Hey," I said.

"Hey, Pert," Julie Nolan said. "What're you doing here?"

"I come to help with the dance decorations. Didn't you see my name on the sign-up sheet?"

Linda Lumpkin looked over at the list. "I guess we did, Pert. But we thought someone had written it down as a joke."

I was steamed. "Ain't no joke, Linda," I said. "My daddy's taking me to the dance, and I'd like to help with the decorations."

The girls all looked at each other. Then they giggled.

Julie Nolan said, "Well, the theme is Hawaiian Islands Fantasy Cruise. We've decided to hang crepe-paper streamers and blow up balloons in tropical colors. What colors should we use, girls?" Julie asked the other girls. She didn't ask me.

"Yellow," Linda said.

"Pink," Cissy said.

"Maybe we can use a few colors like orange and yellow and red," Julie said.

I frowned. Nobody had asked me what I thought. "Those colors are right pretty and all, ladies," I said, "but don't they put up crepe-paper streamers and balloons at just about every pep rally and dance to come down the pike?"

The girls looked at each other and winked. Then they looked back at me, and I kept talking.

"You could think about using empty refrigerator boxes from the appliance store in Troy. Maybe you could paint a cruise ship with portholes and railings."

Julie looked over at Linda.

"Then you could cut out cardboard palm trees and co-conuts, and prop them on stands."

Linda looked at Cissy.

"Maybe you could have a hula dance and a limbo con-test."

Cissy looked at Julie. While I talked, those girls stared and blinked, dumb as mules. They reminded me of our trail-erites when you was trying to talk about something that they hadn't thought of before.

"It might be really fun to make tropical flowers like hi-biscus and orchids out of all this crepe paper." I pointed to the colored coils. Then I twisted a few lengths of crepe paper into a flower shape and placed the flower next to Julie Nolan's ear. She pulled away and gave a wavery smile.

"You could even make leis to drape over the necks of every girl at the dance. They could be your souvenirs."

I could tell by how hard they was trying not to look in-terested that the girls liked my ideas. Especially about the paper-flower leis.

Linda Lumpkin was tapping her finger on the tabletop. "You know, my older sister Violet works at the garden cen-ter in Troy," she said. "Violet might be able to get us real flowers at cost. I think she even knows your father, Pert. Helped him out on a big sale."

I had forgotten about that. We'd got our trees and shrubs

135

for the trailer park at the garden center in Troy. Daddy said their prices was hard to beat.

"I think your daddy took her to lunch at the Lucky Buck for being so helpful," Linda said. "I remember Violet saying how she'd given him good prices on some crape myrtles. Mother wasn't too pleased that Violet had lunch with him."

"Come to think of it, Pert, my brother Stanley saw your daddy in the five-and-dime over in Troy, too." Julie Nolan said my daddy was with that young waitress from the Lucky Buck and a friend of hers. "They was looking over the layette sets. Your mama's not expecting a baby, is she?"

I could feel my cheeks getting hot. Stanley Nolan wore glasses as thick as soda bottles. How could he know what he was seeing at a five-and-dime in Troy?

Cissy Simmons said, "I heard my own daddy saying he figured that the skirts on trailers weren't the only skirts James Wilson was interested in." She giggled, and the other girls did, too.

I hated Cissy Simmons. I had hated her since third grade. She thought she was somebody just because she had a daddy who owned the pecan plant.

"Well, I guess I heard tell that *your* daddy's worked with *nuts* so long that he's finally turned *into* one!"

I took a red roll of crepe paper and threw it at Cissy. It shot forward like one of those coiled snakes that pops out of a can.

Then the lunch bell rang, and I stomped off to Business English. I swore to goodness I'd never help with another school project again.

Every time I went to Business English, it made me mad to see Jimmy's girlfriend, Sue Ellen Jenkins, setting behind her typewriter at the desk right next to mine. I had to set the whole period beside her pig chops and her pig fingers and her head of pig's-tail curls.

Every single day Sue Ellen said, "Hey, Pert. Now you tell that sweet brother of yours I said hey to him, too."

And every single day I said, "Why don't you tell him yourself?"

Today I was even madder to see Linda Lumpkin sitting at the front of the room behind her typewriter. I knew what Linda's older sister looked like. Violet Lumpkin looked just like Linda. The Lumpkin girls had tiny eyes and big ears. Whenever they pulled their hair back into ponytails, they looked just like Dumbo.

We was finishing up our letter of inquiry from yesterday. Mr. Mandell was having us type letters requesting career information from any company that interested us. They was due at the end of the class. I didn't like typing; tapping on the keys ruined my fingernails. I was still smoking from what had happened in the cafeteria, but I looked over what I had wrote so far:

September 22, 1961

President
Coca-Cola Bottling Company
Atlanta, Georgia

Dear Mr. President of Coca-Cola,

I've been wanting to be a receptionist at a big company like Coca-Cola in a big city like Atlanta ever since I was old enough to whistle. I can't think of anything more swell than answering the telephone for important folks like you and wearing a different color of nail polish every day.

Now about me. I'm 15 and a sophomore at Hayes County High (school colors: red and black). I can type 35 words per minute, and I can spell like a teacher. I got an A on my last Business English assignment. We had to write a letter of complaint. I wrote to the Prell shampoo folks because their shampoo was the exact same stuff that Rae Jean and I use to wash dishes. It's hard to rinse off of dishes and hair both. They wrote back to say they was sorry, and they sent a box of free samples to boot.

I'm a good worker. I've walked the Steigers' Doberman, stuffed credit notices in First National Bank of Kinship envelopes, washed the Matlacks' third-story windows from a ladder, fed Jell-O to the old men up at the VA, swept the curls off the floor in Millie's Curly Q Salon, and put on a clown suit to flag folks down for a car wash. Right now I'm working at the Bijou, helping Rae Jean manage the trailer park, and learning trailer sales from my Daddy.

I'll need to move to Atlanta to be a receptionist. You see, there ain't a single receptionist in Kinship. Everywhere you go, folks just walks on in. The beauty parlor. The doctor's office. I'd love to have a job where you get to wear high heels.

Thanks for the information, sir.

Sincerely Yours,

Perty Wilson

My hands was still shaking after I read my letter, and I decided that I wanted to add some new stuff. I looked ahead at Linda Lumpkin. I could see the back of her head and her Dumbo ears. I typed in new information in my "good worker" paragraph. I added "baby-sat the Lumpkin brats."

"Pssst, Pert."

Sue Ellen Jenkins was poking my arm.

"Pssst, yourself," I said, pulling my arm away.

"Don't be upset, Pert," she said.

"I ain't upset," I said.

"You are."

"I ain't."

"Yes, you are, Pert Wilson. I can tell by the way you're banging your typewriter keys."

I was sick of these girls who thought they was so smart. Cissy Simmons who thought she could say whatever she wanted about my family. Julie Nolan who thought her brother Stanley knew what was in front of his crossed eyes. Linda Lumpkin whose mother wasn't pleased about a lunch that was just a thank-you. Sue Ellen Jenkins who thought she could tell when I was mad.

I stared at my letter. I never could figure out about business letters. Wasn't you supposed to indent the paragraphs different? Did you capitalize "Sincerely" *and* "Yours"? How many spaces was you supposed to skip between the closing and the signature?

"Pssst."

I felt her fat fingers on my arm again. I glared at her.

"Pert," she said, "I heard what those girls said about your daddy. They don't know what they're talking about. Your daddy's helped everybody in Happy Trails, and he's helped out you and Rae Jean and Jimmy, too. Don't pay any mind to them. You know how hateful folks can be."

Sue Ellen's eyes was wet. There was a smudge under her eyelids where her black mascara had started to run. I turned away from Sue Ellen. There's nothin' I hate worse than fake tears.

I put my fingers on the typewriter keys.

I banged away. "P.S.," I typed. "One question: Is it true what my Business English teacher Mr. Mandell says? He says a receptionist has to keep her fingernails short to type and dial the phone. If this is true, could you refer me to another department where fingernails can be as long as you want?"

Then I frowned at the *Sincerely Yours.* I aimed my eraser at the paper. I rubbed at the *Y* in *Yours.* I wanted to rub out more than that letter *Y.* I wanted to rub out hateful girls who said ugly things about my daddy. I wanted to rub out chubby girls who said things to get in good with my brother. I rubbed so hard I wore a hole in the paper. When I retyped the capital *Y,* replacing it with a small *y,* the ink went right through the paper and onto the platen.

I ripped my letter out of the typewriter and balled it into a circle. When Mr. Mandell turned to the blackboard and picked up the chalk, I took aim and hurled it to the front of the room. It hit the stick-out Dumbo ear to the left of the ponytail dead on, and I grinned like a goat for the rest of the day.

Alice Potter,

TRAILER 2

Carter Breeding come by to look at my bottle tree, don'tcha know, when I was rearrangin' the bottles. Says my bottle tree's just like the kinship tree he done made up for that college what's up North.

I sets to laughin'.

"No, it ain't, Mr. Perfesser," I says. "Bottle trees ain't like kinship trees. Not one bit." I tells Carter Breeding he's gots it *c-c-cross-eyed* and *w-w-whomper-jawed*.

I tells Carter Breeding what the granny woman says about kinship trees: *Kinship trees is all the same, Kinship trees just bears the name.* I's tryin' to explain that a bottle tree's different, don'tcha know. Bottle trees is about stories. I tells Mr. Breeding the other granny-woman saying: *Every bottle tree has stories. Pride or shame, sin or glory.*

Finally I's sayin' to him, "Don'tcha know the difference tween bottle trees and kinship trees?"

The way Carter Breeding *w-w-walks* away, scratchin' his head. I 'spect he ain't understandin'. Nothin' dumber than a smart perfesser, don'tcha know.

16

One Friday afternoon Daddy came home with the biggest gift of all. He had it in the back of the truck in a big cardboard carton, and he asked Rae Jean and me to stay inside while he got Charlie Hale and Jimmy to haul it in for him.

They'd almost got to the stoop when Mayor Cherry showed up. This time he'd brought Gladys Rowley with him. She was the zoning commission secretary and treated Howard Cherry like he was President of the United States instead of head of a bunch of lowlife commissioners in a dumb little town in Georgia.

Mayor Cherry'd stood outside our trailer and called for Rae Jean. I could see him out the window, taking his hanky from his pocket, polishing his Lincoln with it, and then using the dusty hanky to wipe his brow.

Rae Jean rushed out, a dishrag slung over her shoulder. "You made your decision, Mayor?" she said. "Can we stay?"

"Well, commission's made a decision, Mrs. Wilson. But we got something else to think about." He pulled a paper out of his pocket. "Another notice for the Slagles."

Rae Jean looked at him hard and put her hands on her hips. "We're finished with your notices, Howard Cherry."

"I don't think you are yet, Mrs. Wilson."

Howard Cherry gave Gladys a knowing look. Gladys Rowley had a poodle haircut that would only have looked good if she'd been pretty.

"We've answered your commissioners, Howard, and we've cleaned up this place just as you liked. Now it's the neighborhood you said you wanted."

"Not exactly," he said, shifting on his heavy flat feet; I wondered what store stocked shoes that big. "What we'd said was that we wanted permanent housing. This may be cleaned up, Mrs. Wilson. But it ain't permanent."

Gladys Rowley nodded agreement with him.

Mayor Cherry handed the notice over to Rae Jean. "Just see that the Slagles get it," he said.

I was surprised when Rae Jean grabbed the notice out of his hand: Rae Jean wasn't a grabber. Fact was, Rae Jean'd been doing a lot of things different lately: grabbing things, speaking her mind, having the last word now and again.

While Mayor Cherry walked away, she shook the paper open then read it. "They want us to clear out of the park. They say this isn't permanent housing. Say it's been zoned for permanent residential. They want permanent family homes here. They'll listen to us at a hearing in two weeks."

Then Rae Jean stomped off and knocked on every single door in the trailer park, telling everybody the news. After that she got Jimmy to drive her to Slagles' in Daddy's truck.

While she was gone, I went door-to-door with Charlie

Hale, trying to calm the park folks. Finally they gathered outside our trailer like a swarm of ants.

Alice Potter got the shakes straight off. Her body trembled just like the branches in her bottle tree when the wind blew through them. "I don't know where to *g-g-go*," she said. "Don't have a living soul in this *w-w-world*!"

"Those commissioners can't make us go," Emil Highwater grunted. Poor Emil! White folks been pushing his Indian folk around for centuries.

Odette Coates wailed, "Alvin and me's put good money into that barbecue pit. Ain't a brick barbecue sign enough of something permanent?"

Miss Mulch got all fired up. "I'm not going to put up with it! Not for a single minute! I taught school for near forty years, and I know what to do with bullies!"

Farley Ewing said we needed a good lawyer. Charlie Hale asked where we was going to get that kind of money.

It was bad enough listening to the neighbors raging. Worse was hearing what was said in our own trailer after Rae Jean got home.

Daddy said the wrong thing right off. "Think about it, Rae. Moving might not be such a bad idea. Don't you reckon that's what trailer life's about? Moving? Change?"

Rae Jean stood still as her Jesus statue.

Daddy just kept talking. "Trailer life makes sense, Rae Jean. We could travel the world. You could see you some cathedrals and art museums. The kids could see them the Statue of Liberty. We could all see us the wheat fields." He moved closer to her. "Ever seen a wheat field, Rae Jean?"

She backed away. "I've seen plenty of fields in my day, James William. Peanut fields. Soybean fields. Cotton."

"Ain't the same thing as a wheat field," Daddy said. "A wheat field's miles and miles of grain waving in the wind, all golden and yellow and brown. It's just like an ocean only on land. A wheat field's what folks mean by peaceful."

"Don't need to go to a wheat field to get peaceful," Rae Jean said. "All I have to do to get peaceful is stay right here."

Then Daddy asked Rae Jean what I'd often wondered: "Do you really think you can keep things from changing, Rae Jean?"

Rae Jean's face went blank.

"Ain't you ever thought that maybe you're going to *have* to move?" Daddy said. "Whether you like it or not? Ain't you ever thought them commissioners might just have their way?"

I could tell Rae Jean never *had* thought those things before. She fingered her silver cross as she turned to Daddy. "How do you know?"

"They got ever'thing on their side, Rae," he said.

"Like what?" Rae Jean could be stubborn. Just as stubborn as Gram. Gram didn't like anyone trying to change her beliefs about things.

"Time. Money. Power. Votes," Daddy said. "You need any more reasons?"

I saw the corner of Rae Jean's mouth twitch, and she swallowed hard. "Where are we supposed to go, James? This is the Slagles' trailer. We're just squatting here."

He came across the room to her, headfirst like he always did. My daddy wasn't afraid of the future; he moved into it full speed ahead. "Pert and me have been making good money selling them trailer skirts. We've been looking at mobile homes. Rae, they've got a Pioneer Voyage with one of

145

them bay windows and a double sink. There's a little corner off the front room where you can set up your paints." I remembered the mobile home, but I didn't remember the corner off the front room. If Daddy had just made that part up, it was for a good cause. A place for Rae Jean's paints would be a good selling point.

Rae Jean didn't say anything, and in that quiet space I thought about what Daddy was telling her. About a home. On wheels. For all of us. To go anywhere in the cotton-pickin' world. Together.

"Think about it, Rae," Daddy said. "A trailer's a good life. Especially for a person who likes change, who finds it hard to stay in one place."

Then Rae Jean's shoulders tightened and her words dripped icicles. *I don't find it hard to stay, James William.*

He heard the shiver in her voice, and he tried to warm her up in a blanket of words. "Well, think about it, honey. In a trailer you can have you the best of both worlds. You can put down roots and pull 'em up. Anytime you want to. In a trailer you can sail from place to place or you can drop anchor anytime you got you a mind to. In a trailer you can see the world without ever leaving home."

I liked the pictures Daddy's words made. I liked thinking of a trailer as a boat, sailing over the wheat fields, dropping anchor when you wanted to rest a spell, casting off when you was ready to go.

"But Jimmy's got his job and Pert's got school and Mama's here and Miss Mulch and Mr. Ewing, and Doc Jackson needs me to take care of the animals."

I had to admit Rae Jean was good at details like that; Daddy and me was happier leaving details to others.

146

"Now, don't you start your fretting, Rae. Ain't got to worry about things right yet. Just think about what I've said. Thinking about it's all you have to do right now." I saw that when Daddy didn't know what to say, he talked more. Fact was, I was the same way.

"Besides," Daddy went on, "I've got something else for you to think about. I've got you a big surprise, remember? Did you forget about that, Rae Jean? It's setting right outside by the stoop. Come on, gal. Cheer up. Don't spoil James William's surprise."

"I've had enough surprises for one day," Rae Jean said.

"Well, this one will cheer you up. Guaranteed."

Daddy went back outside and called for Charlie and Jimmy. Together they hauled the big cardboard box into the living room.

Daddy took out a pocketknife and slit the sides of the box. They fell open like a stripper dropping her robe. I couldn't hardly believe it. My daddy had bought us a TV!

My heart jumped into my eyeballs. I couldn't wait to see *Dinah Shore* and *I Love Lucy* and *American Bandstand*.

Then I looked over at Rae Jean. She was frowning. "It's blocking the shrine, James William," she said.

"Shoot, Rae," Daddy said. "You can move that there shrine anyplace you like. It don't take up that much room. Looks to me like that corner over there's the only place big enough for the TV."

Daddy was right. Rae Jean could move her shrine anywhere: the coffee table, the bookcase, the windowsill. It was only a statue, a candle, and a Bible; she could stack both the candle and the statue on top of the Bible and stash it most anywhere in the trailer. Fact was, that corner where she kept her shrine was the only free spot in the place.

Rae Jean stomped her foot. Her soft cloud of hair shook. "I'm not moving that shrine. And I'd like to know how people get to tell me what I need in *my own home!*" The blood was rushing to her cheeks.

Jimmy looked nervous. Charlie Hale shuffled his feet and said, "Well, now, I *b'lieve* I'd best be going, folks." He had to duck his big head as he went out the door.

"I thought you'd like the TV, Rae Jean," Daddy said. His voice was mild. "I was just trying to surprise you. You haven't had many surprises in your life, Rae Jean. Never was much money for surprises, you know?" I heard a sweetness in my daddy's voice, like the music of silver coins falling from clouds.

I saw Rae Jean soften as she looked at him. The red color faded from her cheeks.

"I'm grateful, James William. Truly I am. You're right. We barely had enough money for what we needed. Didn't have time to even *think* of what we might want." She touched her silver cross quickly.

"Now that you do have time to think about it, ain't a TV the kind of surprise you might want?"

I couldn't see why Rae Jean couldn't just blurt out yes.

Instead, she put her index finger to her mouth like she did when she was thinking hard and said, "Don't rightly know. You have to be careful about wanting things, James William. There's a difference between wants and needs. Taking care of needs doesn't carry much of a price. Taking care of wants does. My mama always said 'Be careful what you wish for.' "

Daddy looked mad now. His eyes turned navy and the

muscles in his neck bunched together. "You just don't ap-preciate a man's hard-earned money." The ax blade of his chin sliced upwards.

Rae Jean snapped at him. "Don't know where you're get-tin' it, James William, but it don't look especially *hard*-earned to me."

I wished Rae Jean would shut up.

"It *is* hard-earned, Rae. I've been out on the road almost every day, making sales. It ain't easy getting folks to buy stuff. Don't see *you* bringing in fistfuls working with them mutts all day."

Rae Jean's eyes squinted into slits. I was glad Daddy hadn't mentioned me. On days I skipped school, we made sales to-gether. On other days, Daddy went back by himself and hammered up the skirts.

"I'm just bringing it in like most folks. In a steady pay-check. One week at a time." Then Rae Jean opened her eyes wide, looking calm as air after a rain.

Daddy was getting ready to tear out. His brass heels clicked against the linoleum as he crossed the floor.

He had his hand on the door when he said, "That Jesus statue ain't nothin' but a piece of plastic on a little lace hanky anyway." Then Daddy tried to slam the door behind him, but the metal latch was busted, and the door gave only a hollow click.

I lunged at Rae Jean, grabbing her shoulders and shaking them. They felt fragile under my fingers: wishbones easily snapped.

In an instant, Jimmy had pulled me off of Rae Jean while I wailed, "He was just trying to be nice to you, Rae Jean! He was just trying to help out this poor, dull, stuck-in-the-mud ball of people we call a family." I could feel the pressure of Jimmy's big fingers on my arms and knew I'd have bruises in the morning.

I hollered at Rae Jean, "Can't you appreciate what he's done for this clump of folks who's had their pockets empty most every day of their life?" I was screaming so loud I thought my eyeballs would bust out of my skull.

Rae Jean's own eyes drew back into her head and filled up with something damp.

"Can't you see that he's just trying to bring some *fun* into your life?" I yelled. "To make you *happy*?"

I used the back of my heels to kick at Jimmy, but he held on tight.

Rae Jean's hair was wild like a tangled ball of yarn after the cat played with it. "People make their own happiness, Pert." she said quietly. "It doesn't come out of a TV."

The flames was so hot my eyeballs was melting. I was so mad I was blind.

Rae Jean was dull as dishwater.

She couldn't change.

She was stuck.

As Jimmy pulled me down on the couch, I screeched, "What in tarnation's wrong with a TV?"

I don't know how Rae Jean managed to stay so calm in the face of all my yelling. It was hard to hear with Jimmy on top of me and all, but she whispered something like, "It just won't be the same anymore, Pert. It'll change things. You'll see. It just won't be the same *home*."

Then Rae Jean walked back into the bedroom.

Home. I heard the groaning sound in the middle of that word. *Home*. It was a sound like a moan.

Sophie Mulch,

TRAILER 4

I swannee, Rae Jean came to call more often since James Wilson arrived; her daughter Pert called less. Lately when Rae Jean came by, she'd weep cups, bowls, and buckets. Wouldn't let herself cry in front of her kids. I don't think her tears would have hurt those kids one bit. Bless her heart, Rae Jean's eyes turned the prettiest shade of blue gray when she cried.

I'd pass her the plate of pecan tarts or set a few pieces of fudge at her elbow, but Rae Jean never took the first bite. She'd just dab at her eyes and start talking. Should she stay? Should she go? What was best for Jimmy, Pert, Wilma, James William, her? How much money did you need, and how much money could you want? Did you have to go away to change, or could you change by staying just where you were? Was it kinship that made you family, or was family something different from kin? I swannee, Rae Jean Wilson was just a pack of worry.

It seemed to help Rae Jean when I got out my Bible. I always liked Second Corinthians. "We walk by faith, not by sight" it says in 5:7.

I swannee, it near broke my heart to look at her. I'd remind her that you can't always see where you're going while you're going there. It's like steering a ship on a stormy night. You navigate by faith, Rae Jean. Not sight.

17

I hadn't realized how much I had missed my brother. He'd been spending more and more time with Sue Ellen, and I hadn't thought about just why until today.

Jimmy had asked me to meet him at Matlack's Used Cars when he got off work, and of course I said "fine."

The sky had just turned dark when I got to Matlack's. The ring of yellow lights that circled the lot was dancing against the night. Since the lot was in back of Peter Matlack's new-car Ford dealership, you had to pass the new-car display window on the way there. That was a clever business gimmick, clever as the sign that called Matlack's used clunkers *pre-owned* cars.

I saw Jimmy before he saw me. He had his nose to the showroom window like a kid outside a pet store. Jimmy would have died to have a new car with a warranty, a fresh carpet smell, and no gum stuck up under the driver's seat. For a minute, my heart swelled up.

He was drooling over the boxy fins and the leather seats as I approached. "Hey, Jimmy Wilson," I said.

Jimmy jumped. I had startled him. "Hey, Pert Wilson."

"It's like one of those naked girls in your magazines, Jimmy," I said, pointing to the T-bird.

"Whadda you mean, Pert?" His big face turned to me.

"You can't really have one. All you can do is look."

Then Jimmy grinned and started play-boxing with me like he always did. He'd ball up his fists and mock punch and dance around and then I'd try to match him fist for fist, always ending up in bear slaps since I never was as quick.

When I'd finally given up and he'd held his hands over his head in the championship sign, he said, "Glad a loser like you agreed to help a winner like me pick out a car, sis."

It was Jimmy's way of saying thanks. Fact was, we both knew that Jimmy needed me.

"You gonna go on in and write out a check for that one, champ?" I said.

"Naw," he said. "All they do is start depreciating once they leave the showroom. The future of a new car once it's driven off the lot's like the future of Christmas on December twenty-sixth."

"Jimmy," I said, "picking out a car ain't the same as buying, is it?"

"Sure is, Pert," Jimmy said, patting the back pocket of his jeans, where he kept his wallet. "I got two hundred dollars saved up." Then he pulled out a wad of ten-dollar bills.

I gave a long whistle. "My word, Jimmy," I said, looking up at him, "how'd you do that?"

Jimmy looked back down at me, and I saw again how big he was. Big and strong in a soft and gentle kind of way. "Did it the same way most people does, Pert. Opened a savings account and put in one deposit at a time."

I beamed, proud as the devil of my big brother.

He strolled over to a Buick, running his hand along the side panel and moving to the front hood. "I like the low beltline on this Skylark, Pert," he said, stopping at the front end and peering down at the shiny silver ornament that looked like a bomb sight. "What do you think?"

"Nice, Jimmy," I said, but the shiny front grille had more teeth than a shark and I wondered what kind of bite it would take out of Jimmy's savings account.

Then Jimmy gave a low whistle and moved to a black-and-red Chevrolet a few cars down from the Skylark. "What a deal," he said, his eyes fixed on the sticker tag.

He gave me the rundown. A 1957 Chevy Bel Air. Convertible. Black exterior. Red vinyl seats. Whitewalls. Half a foot longer than most other cars. Only four years old. I had to admit I was impressed with those tail fins. They was long and angled like wings. That car looked as if it could fly.

"Don't seem like there's a thing wrong with it, Pert," Jimmy said. "At five hundred dollars, it's a steal." His eyes had a glazed look.

"Hold on a minute now, Jimmy," I said. I peered over the dashboard. Then I laid down on my back on the ground, slid under the car, and looked up. Next I crawled out, brushed off my hands, and opened the door on the passenger side, running my hands up and down the door frame.

"You're right, Jimmy. Ain't a thing wrong with it. Just a hundred sixty thousand miles, a rusted-out engine, and a crack-up somewhere. Buttermilk Pike'd be my guess."

Jimmy's handsome face dropped.

"Why don't you look at this one over here," I said, pointing to a sky-blue model that looked like some kind of Oldsmobile.

"It's got that Rocket V-eight, Pert," he said quietly.

Now I was sorry I had mentioned that Olds. "Don't a larger engine burn up more gas?" I asked.

"Yeah, but the power's worth it," Jimmy said.

"But don't more power mean more spark plugs and more oil? It costs money for those things, Jimmy."

"Yes, Pert, but the Olds Eighty-eight'll make up for that in quick acceleration." He had stopped listening to me. All of a sudden he was throwing away every common-sense notion he ever had about a car: It was all coming down to how fast the car could snap your neck when the light turned green.

I hadn't seen her coming, but all of a sudden there was Sue Ellen behind Jimmy, her arms stretched around his waist, her cheek nuzzling up to the valley between his shoulder blades. "Sorry I'm late, sweetie. Mother'd come back from the hairdresser fit to be tied. That new girl just doesn't know how to hold a set. Mother made me rewash and reset it." About the only thing in this world Sue Ellen Jenkins could do right was hair. She always nagged me about cutting my own hair in short layers, but I'd never in a million years let her lay one finger on me.

"That's okay, baby," Jimmy said, wrapping his big hands around hers. "Pert here was helping me till you came."

I wanted to spit. I wasn't Jimmy Wilson's temporary help. And Sue Ellen Jenkins wouldn't know a dipstick if she tripped over one.

"What do you think, Sue, baby?" Jimmy said. "I'm about sold on this Olds Eighty-eight."

"Well, now," Sue Ellen said, loosening her grip on Jimmy and moving over to the tires. "Aren't you 'sposed to kick the tires? Daddy says that's one of the things you do when you're picking out a car."

She stuck out her foot and gave the tires a tiny tap. I could see Jimmy's eyes moving up her leg from her ankle to her knee. Sue Ellen was wearing red flats, and the flesh at the place above the instep was rounded and puffy. It made me feel good to think that when Sue Ellen got old she'd have problems with swolled-up feet.

"That ain't the way to do it, Sue Ellen," I said, shoving her aside. I took my heel and reared back on that tire something fierce. "You got to wallop it good." I had to admit that the tire did seem solid against the pressure of my heel. "Then you got to think about the gas mileage and the handling and the engine. Not to mention the cost."

Jimmy frowned. "Pert's right. We forgot to think about the price." He looked at the tag hanging from the rearview mirror. It said $700.00. Jimmy's face dropped to the basement. "That's five hundred more'n I got saved."

"Why don't you just ask Mr. Hanks for an advance?" Sue Ellen said, lifting her eyebrows to Jimmy. "You've been a good employee. Mr. Hanks knows you'd pay him back."

"An advance like that would last into the next decade," Jimmy said.

"Why don't you ask your daddy?" Sue Ellen said.

"Already did. Asked if he'd spring me a few hundred bucks if I needed it. He said no."

I looked at the worry lines on Jimmy's forehead and wondered why my daddy had refused him. "Do you think maybe you asked for too much money, Jimmy?"

156

"Maybe so," Jimmy said. "But I don't see why he had to jump to a flat-out *no*. He spends money like a sailor on leave. Besides, *he's* always asking *me* for dough. Half the time he doesn't pay it back."

"If Daddy owes you money, Jimmy," I said, "why don't you just ask him for it?"

"I can't, Pert. Somehow I feel like it's my duty as his son to help him out. It's sort of a man-to-man thing."

I looked down at the ring on my finger. The pink stone winked. I thought about how fathers and daughters was different from fathers and sons.

"What really sticks in my craw," Jimmy said, "is the thing with the wheelbarrow." He looked down while he said those words. There was something soft and tender about him, like something bruised.

I raised my eyebrows. "The wheelbarrow?"

"I paid for that wheelbarrow, Pert. Sent me to Gleason's Hardware for it. And then he made the fancy presentation and all. He's never offered to pay me back one dime. What do Wilsons need a wheelbarrow for? But I'd feel like I'd let you all down if I tried to take it back to Gleason's and get my money."

Jimmy was right; we didn't need a wheelbarrow. But I had to admit I'd be sorry if he took it back. That wheelbarrow was a family memory now.

Jimmy shuffled his feet and then he looked straight at me. "Besides, Pert," he said, "James William Wilson doesn't think I'm clever like you. I'm not a talker. I'm not that smart. I'm big and slow."

I held my tongue. I noticed the way Jimmy never called him *Daddy*. He always said *James William Wilson*.

Now Sue Ellen jumped in. She was always having to add her two cents. "There's nothing wrong with *big,* Jimmy." Sue Ellen never got the point.

She slipped her hand in his. "Don't your mama have any money?" she said.

I felt like throwing fists. Of course Rae Jean didn't have any money. Leastways not any money that was due Sue Ellen Jenkins. Rae Jean wasn't like Sue Ellen's parents. Don Jenkins was the pharmacist at Byer's Drugs and acted like he was the same as a doctor. Jenkinses was the ones with money.

"Not much," Jimmy said. "Unless you count that two hundred dollars Mama has stashed in the teapot."

"Jimmy," I said, feeling my cheeks burn, "you know that money's just for emergencies. If it was for anything else, we'd have the hole in the roof fixed or the couch reupholstered."

Sue Ellen folded her arms and leaned against the car. "But Jimmy," she said, "this *is* an emergency. Your family's needed a car for years." Then she gave a little pout.

Jimmy moved to her and put his arm around her shoulder. "No, it ain't. Pert's right, Sue-E."

I thought I would be sick. Sometimes Jimmy called Sue Ellen Sue-E as a nickname. When he said it, it reminded me of calling pigs. Fact was, Sue-E fit her just fine. Everything about her was round and pink.

Sue Ellen uncrossed her arms and glared at me. Then she lifted her eyes to Jimmy. I saw the way her mascara stuck together in big clumps. "Well, now, I guess Jimmy and me got other things about this car to think on besides money," she said, opening the car door and slipping into the front seat. Then she patted the driver's seat for Jimmy to set down.

He got in beside her, settling his big frame behind the steering wheel. I could hear her whispering things to him.

"I like the fact that this is an automatic transmission, Jimmy."

"Why's that, Sue, sugar?"

"With an automatic transmission you've got room to keep one arm around me when you drive."

Jimmy grinned and turned to kiss her.

Then Sue Ellen was pushing him out of the car. "Go on, Jimmy," she said, shoving him out the door. Sue Ellen Jenkins was about the bossiest girl in Kinship.

"Hold on, Sue," he said, staggering.

Then she was out, too, and pushing him into the backseat. "Come on, now," she said, shoving on his overgrown frame.

"Why you want me back here, baby?" I heard him say.

"You ain't going to buy a car, Jimmy Wilson, without us trying out the backseat." Then she slid her arms around his neck, pushed him down, and snuggled up next to him. She gave him a couple of long wet kisses, and then she came up for air, remembering me.

I was fuming so bad that smoke was coming out my ears. When I saw her give me a little wave, I was on fire. I shoved my fists in my pockets and stormed off, kicking my heels on the black asphalt. I was hopping mad. Not for myself. But for my brother. Jimmy Wilson had come here looking for something sleek, reliable, and easy to handle. And all he had to show for it was Sue Ellen Jenkins.

Pee Wee Hale,

TRAILER 10

Pert surprised me on the ride to school today. Talked to me about hiccups.

"You troubled by the hiccups much, Pee Wee?" she says.

"The hiccups? Why should I be troubled with the *hiccups*?"

"Just wondering. Folks who've been too serious too long have a lot of trouble with hiccups."

I thought about that. I didn't know what Pert was getting at 'zactly. I knew I could be downright serious. I work hard at school and then I work hard at the sawmill after that. I gotta get out more. Don't have many friends beside Pert and maybe Jimmy.

Then Pert elbows me in the ribs and tells me she'll give me four free movie passes if I promise to ask out Sue Ellen Jenkins. Told me if I didn't get out more, I'd wake up one morning an old man who'd never had any fun. She's right about that.

Sue Ellen sits across from me in Business Math. She's downright smart and tries not to show it. Sue Ellen's good with hair. She won a beauty school scholarship. The beauty school's in Albany, and Sue Ellen's parents are setting her up in an apartment there as soon as she graduates.

Sue Ellen's downright cute, too. She has curls like black wood shavings all over her head. Pert said she thought Sue

Ellen would go for me. Said she liked guys with cars. I told Pert I'd think about it. I didn't 'zactly know if Sue Ellen liked guys with pickups that their uncle let them drive now and then, or just guys with their *own* cars.

I was sure surprised, too, by what Pert said about Jimmy and Sue Ellen. I didn't know they had broke up.

18

Today we was heading over to Claxton to see a man. Claxton was on the other side of Vidalia, a far piece from Kinship. It was where Gene Nugent would go if he made the state bowling championships and where they was famous for their fruitcake. The man we was going to see was going to help us branch out. He was a fellow Daddy knew through his business partner in Florida.

Daddy was getting tired of skirting. Said it had got too predictable. We'd been selling skirting for a few weeks now, and Daddy said the routine of it was making him feel dull around the edges. He needed to branch out to sharpen up. Daddy said he always knew when he needed to move on. I was proud of his business sense.

Daddy and me was branching into concrete. We was branching into concrete because of Mayor Cherry. And because of me, too.

The trailerites'd had a meeting at Miss Mulch's to talk about what to do. Farley Ewing was there. So was the Coateses and the Highwaters and Charlie Hale and Pee Wee. Mayor Cherry had said the court was zoned for permanent residential housing. There was a lot of talk about how the commissioners couldn't do that, could they? But most of us knew that proving it would take time and money and a heap of lawyers. So I simply said, "What's more permanent than concrete?"

Miss Mulch's living room fell silent.

Everybody looked at me.

I don't know what made me think of the idea. It was like that story about the silver-egg dream: It just flashed into my mind, and then it poured right out of my mouth.

"Daddy and I saw a trailer park just the other day," I said. "Outside of Milledgeville, I think it was. It was a park just like ours, only it had a big ol' trailer with the wheels gone and the trailer hitch off, and the whole thing was setting on a solid block of concrete like a whale on ice." Then I swallowed. "Set me to wondering what's more permanent than concrete."

The looks that passed around Miss Mulch's living room reminded me of the faces of folks that don't want to show their poker hands.

Then Charlie Hale stood up and shuffled his feet. Like Jimmy and my daddy, he was so tall he couldn't stand full up in a trailer but had to crook his head. I saw for the first time how shy Charlie Hale was. When he finally talked he acted as nervous as if he was making a speech.

Even though he fumbled for words, Charlie talked slow and steady. He said I had a good idea. He'd worked in concrete all his life. If we wanted to make the trailer rigs into permanent residences, it was a simple matter of pouring a foundation under them.

Charlie Hale's big feet scraped the floor, and the room fell quiet. Then he set down.

Emil Highwater spoke up. "What if you don't *want* to make your rig permanent?"

"Then you just up and leave before things get *made* permanent," Myra Highwater answered her own husband.

Emil looked puzzled. I could tell he hadn't thought much about upping and leaving. He didn't look like he knew what he wanted to do.

"And just exactly how does this work and how much will this concrete cost?" Farley Ewing said. "Seems folks here have just barely had enough to pay for their skirts. Now they might need to pay for concrete, too." Farley was always concerned about just *exactly* how you was going to work things out. He looked on things like puzzles to solve.

"Well, now," Charlie Hale said, his big body leaning forward, "you take the wheels off the trailer, pour the foundation, get rid of the hitches, and set the trailer back down on the concrete slab. You'll need some special moving equipment and all, and it takes time to let the concrete set, but concrete's not all that costly, and, *b'lieve* me, the job's not all that complicated."

I saw my daddy's eyes go bright. "I know a fellow over in Claxton," he said. "Deals in concrete."

Charlie Hale cleared his throat. "Been working in masonry all my life, Mr. Wilson," he said. "Got contacts right here in Hayes County that can give you good prices."

"I'm sure you can, Hale," Daddy said. "But my contacts will swear to beat your prices cold."

Charlie Hale hung his head. You could *tell* he'd worked in masonry all his life; he was big and solid and stiff as a concrete block himself.

People was interested in Daddy's ideas, for sure. At least

some people was. Miss Mulch, naturally, and Farley Ewing. Coateses was interested, too. Highwaters wasn't sure. They might want to move where there's better fishing, although I'd never known them to fish anywhere but Pearl Lake for years. Breedings and Alice Potter hadn't come to the meeting; we'd have to check with them. We reckoned how we couldn't count on Gene Nugent. He never wanted to do anything that everyone else was doing. He hadn't come to the meeting, neither. And Weevils. You knew for sure you couldn't count on them.

You should have seen Miss Mulch. "People," she said, "you have less than two weeks to make up your mind." When she offered to float them loans from her retirement fund, everybody perked up. "Would five hundred dollars about do it, people?" I swear to goodness I never saw any-one more generous than Sophie Mulch.

So that's why we was in Claxton meeting a man called Earl Shivers. Daddy and I was making a deal for concrete.

I loved watching my daddy make a deal.

Earl Shivers was a partner of Daddy's business partner in Florida. He had an office in a shack beside the insurance agency in Claxton. He had on a T-shirt smeared with grease, and when Daddy came in, he tucked it into his pants and buttoned his pants at the waist.

They talked back and forth about prices and delivery dates and moving equipment and up-front money. Then Daddy passed Earl Shivers a wad of cash, and Mr. Shivers stuck out a fat hand covered with hair. Daddy took the hand and shook.

On the way back to Kinship in the truck, Daddy had the same kind of look I'd seen on Jimmy when he flipped through his girlie mags. Daddy told me how much fun it was cutting deals.

Earl Shivers and his crew was coming the Monday morning after next weekend. Mr. Ewing and Miss Mulch and Coateses and Highwaters and Charlie Hale and Breedings and Alice Potter and even Weevils was signed up to set their trailers into permanent concrete. Weevils said they'd been looking for a way to say their business was legitimate, and pouring concrete all around it was the best way they knew how. It helped that Miss Mulch was acting as banker, of course, floating loans until everyone could pay her back. Gene Nugent wasn't signed up for anything, of course.

But there was one thing I hadn't counted on. Us Wilsons. Seems that Wilsons wasn't signed up for concrete yet, neither.

Fact was, Slagles came by the next day and told Rae Jean and Daddy they was thinking about getting rid of their trailer—the one we lived in. The commissioners had near drove them wild with their demands, and Slagles was even thinking about selling the trailer park itself and getting out from under the whole blessed business.

I saw Rae Jean's lips squeeze together.

But Slagles wasn't sure yet. Dora Slagle said it depended on how things turned out with the commissioners. Maybe Rae Jean could go ahead and order the concrete to make Slagles' trailer permanent if she'd agree to manage the park for them until they made up their mind. Of course, Slagles wouldn't be footing the bill for the concrete; Rae Jean would have to come up with that money herself. Rae Jean mumbled something about a little rainy-day money stashed away in the teapot and something about not expecting to have to use it on concrete in a place that might be sold. I watched Dora Slagle fiddle with her sweater guards. They looked like two gold alligator snouts that could either eat you or swim away.

After Slagles left, I could tell what Rae Jean needed. She needed to get quiet. She needed to sit out on the stoop awhile and stroke the cat. She needed to read her *Good Tidings* until she settled down.

I was beginning to see another way in which Daddy was just like me: He started talking when he should have shut up.

I watched them out the window and opened my ears wide. Daddy was saying about how he'd finally found a trailer for himself, in one of those nice new mobile-home showrooms we saw last week in Lawrenceville. It was smaller than the one in Crawfordville, but it was better for a starter home. He'd even put a down payment on it. " 'Course you and Pert and Jimmy's welcome to come."

I pushed my ear right up to the window and held my breath. Daddy was talking about a home for all of us. A home that would let us see the whole wide world. Together.

Rae Jean brushed Mittens's back, running the fur up and down like you did when you stroked the nap on velvet. "Don't want to come. Want to stay."

Rae Jean opened her little book. Her eyes gobbled up the type like it was food.

My knees quivered, and I gripped the window ledge.

"I'm thinking about taking off right soon," Daddy said. "Told Pert I'd stay long enough to hear what them commissioners had decided. Sounds like commissioners has made up their minds." Daddy talked, but he didn't try to sit down.

I didn't agree with Daddy. It didn't sound like that to me at all. I knew politicians never decided anything for sure. Even when they made decisions, they gave themselves plenty of wiggle room.

Daddy cleared his throat. Again he said, "I'm thinking about taking off, Rae. Right soon."

"Heard you the first time." She didn't look up. I wondered if her eyes was blue or gray; I was pretty sure I knew. "I'm staying. No matter what."

Daddy balled up his fist and started punching the air with it. "How can you be so stubborn, Rae Jean? You're about to lose your home, gal. I'm offering you another one."

"Don't want another home," she said. "Want this one. I like things permanent, James William." I was starting to see that Rae Jean was Gram's true daughter. She was stubborn as stains.

Daddy moved closer to her. Mittens flinched. Rae Jean drew her book up closer to her eyes. She wouldn't look at him.

"Ever'thing is only temporary," Daddy said. "Ever'thing in this world is only temporary, Rae Jean." I couldn't see her face, only his. "Don't you know that?"

"Only thing I know for sure is that my foundation's built on God. That's not temporary, James William," Rae Jean said. I wondered what she was reading in her *Good Tidings*. I reckoned it was about vines or branches. Seemed like every Bible passage was about vines or roots or branches.

"You can't avoid changes, Rae." I knew Daddy was right.

"I can try," she said.

He stomped off then, and I saw her look up and watch his back moving off to his truck. She closed her book with one hand and stroked Mittens with the other.

I hated it when they had words like this: one of them pushing, the other one pulling; one of them wanting to set down roots, the other one wanting to pull them up; one wanting to go, the other wanting to stay.

Usually when their voices got loud, I turned up the TV. Daddy'd set it on wheels in the corner in front of the shrine, and when Rae Jean wanted to pray, she wheeled the TV out of the way.

When Daddy and Rae Jean pushed and pulled at each other like that, I tried to concentrate on the laughter of the studio audience as I watched *I Love Lucy*. I tried to keep my eyes on the flying pins in the hands of the jugglers on *The Ed Sullivan Show*. But I always snapped the TV off before I got to the end of *Dinah Shore*. At the very end, Dinah Shore always sang, *"See the U.S.A. in your Chevrolet,"* and then she blew the studio audience a great big kiss. I couldn't stand to watch her do that. I didn't want to think about Chevrolets rolling across the U.S.A. I didn't want to think about blowing kisses. I didn't want to think about how people ever said good-bye.

I heard Daddy's truck door slam; the noise startled Mittens, and she jumped off Rae Jean's lap and hid under the new hydrangea bush. Then I heard Daddy gun the engine and take off.

I reckoned that was the difference between the two of them: Daddy liked to gun the engine; Rae Jean couldn't even put a key in the starter.

Ida Weevil,

TRAILER 3

Folks is tryin' to run Weevils out of the court right now, but that fool husband of mine and I ain't budgin'. We's as much a right to stay as anyone else what's here. Police is been tryin' to run us out of this here trailer court for years. They's always pullin' up in the middle of the night with them red lights flashin'. Sends my customers right out the back door and into the woods. Ain't gonna arrest someone for strollin' around in the woods, is you? Police never finds nothin'. Folks in the park been mumblin' about gettin' us out too. Says they's tryin' to keep the neighborhood nice. "Permanent residential" is what they calls it. Says Weevils is got a commercial business goin' here and this here neighborhood ain't zoned for that. Let 'em prove it. Ora Weevil and I ain't budgin'.

Little Missy come on by yesterday afternoon. Wants to know how to make love stay. Wonders if Weevils has a love potion for it. I covers my mouth quick. Doesn't want her to see me smile.

Only fools believes in love potions, but I tole her one anyways. You gets a fat ripe tomato. You gets a pile of sewing pins. Then you sticks the pins in the tomato. You uses the same number of pins as they's letters in the name of the person you's wantin' to stay.

Doesn't charge her for the potion. Why should I? Ain't

like to work and she ain't got no money nohow. Doesn't tell Missy that for some folks love potions never takes. They's the same folks what never finds they family, never knows they home. Some folks just gots too much of the devil in 'em for that.

19

I twirled in front of the mirror. The white crinolines rolled and tossed like surf. I stuck my face right next to the silver glass. I had stopped peroxiding my hair, and I saw that the dark color at the roots was the same color as my daddy's. I spit on my fingers, smoothing my curls into place. I lifted the eyebrows that I had plucked into round arches, and I peered at my own face. I saw the nose and cheeks with freckles thrown across them like sand, and the crooked mouth that had got me into trouble and out again.

My dress was pink satin on the underskirt and top; a layer of pink net floated on top of the underskirt as I twirled.

At the dress shop in Troy, Daddy had liked the black dress with the bare back. He said my cameo on the black velvet band would look just right with it. Rae Jean had insisted on this pink dress with the line of paper roses across the neck. She stomped her foot and said, "Pert's had enough darkness in her life, James William. She'll take the pink one." It was one of those times Rae Jean had the last word.

But Rae Jean let Daddy buy me the shoes I wanted. They was a pair of spike heels sitting in the window of the Thom McAn. They was pink, too, and three inches high. When I first put them on, I wobbled like a skyscraper in an earth-quake, and Rae Jean clapped her tiny hands and laughed. After I practiced walking slower and more careful, I didn't shake so much. For the first time in my life I felt like a grown-up woman, not a gawky young girl.

I felt a big arm around my waist and saw the big face in the mirror behind me.

"I've got a prediction, Pert Wilson," the big face said. "You're gonna be the prettiest girl at the dance."

I wanted to smile; instead I gave my brother a punch in the stomach.

Jimmy had borrowed Charlie Hale's pickup to drive me to the dance. Daddy was over in Claxton, doing some last-minute business with Earl Shivers, making sure everything would be right on Monday morning. Jimmy would drop me at the dance, and Daddy would meet me at the door to the gym by eight.

On the way to the school, I thought how I'd never rode in a fancy dress before. Fact was, there was lots of things in my life now that had never been there before: real milk every day, good grades in math, a school dance to go to, a daddy.

Jimmy dropped me at the door to the high school. I was nervous going in all alone. Loud music was playing as I went inside, and I saw that they had made everything over to fit the Hawaiian Islands theme. The dance was in the down-stairs gym, and the steps to get there had been turned into a gangplank. I teetered carefully down the slanted board, grip-ping the banister.

I could see lights flashing from inside the dark gym; wig-gling shapes floated across the floor.

"Evening, Pert," a voice said. "Good to see you here." It was Mr. Stewart, our principal. He'd never in his life said it was good to see me before. Every time I'd ever seen him, something not-so-good had happened.

"Thanks, Mr. Stewart," I said.

Mr. Stewart was wearing a white suit and a captain's hat. He was standing next to Mr. Foley, the phys ed teacher. Mr. Foley was wearing a sailor suit. It looked pretty tight on him and a bit worn: like something he had just pulled out of an attic trunk.

Daughters on the arms of fathers entered the gym through a door that was dripping with tropical flowers cut from crepe paper. I grinned when I saw those decorations; I knew whose idea they'd been. As couples passed by me, moving into the gym, Mrs. Parello, my last year's English teacher, slipped a flowered lei over each of their heads. Violet Lumpkin must have got a good deal on real flowers. You could smell them all the way into the hall.

I stood at the door and peered in. Julie Nolan and Linda Lumpkin was dancing with their daddies. I fluffed the pink net on my skirt and swolled up with satisfaction: Neither one of their crinolines fanned out as stiff as mine. Cissy Simmons swirled by on her daddy's arm, and I felt a secret pride that I hugged to my own self. Russell Simmons had a belly the size of a barrel, and I couldn't wait for Cissy to see me on the arm of my tall, thin, handsome daddy.

Mrs. Parello said, "Won't you come in, Pert?" She was wearing a blue sarong with purple flowers on it; she had pulled her dark hair up into a twist anchored by a lavender orchid. I had never noticed how pretty Mrs. Parello was before.

174

"No, thanks," I said. "I'm waiting for my daddy. He'll be here soon. He's coming in from Claxton on business."

Inside the gym a foghorn blew. Linda Lumpkin's daddy grabbed the mike and announced another special event: the limbo contest. This was a contest where you tried to dance under the rack as the rack was lowered closer and closer to the floor. If you were a daddy, your biggest problem was getting under the rack without falling. If you were a daughter, your biggest problem was keeping folks from seeing up your skirt. I liked it that the limbo had been my idea.

I glanced at the clock in the hallway. I usually looked up at it when I changed classes between English and phys ed. Now it was draped with crepe-paper hibiscus, and the white banner under it said, WELCOME TO THE HAWAIIAN ISLANDS FANTASY CRUISE. DEPARTING SAN FRANCISCO AT 8 P.M. DOCKING HONOLULU AT 11 P.M.

Behind me I heard the gangplank groaning. Nympha Claggett was crashing down toward me, a red muu-muu draping her body like a tent. She hurried right over and put her fat fingers on my arm. "I've been hearing about those good grades this year, Pert Wilson," she said. A dark smear of lipstick stained her left front tooth. "I hear you can lay it all to your daddy. Why don't you introduce me to him?"

"He's not here yet, Miss Claggett," I said. "He'll be here in a sec." I could see the sweat balls on her upper lip and smell her Juicy Fruit breath.

"Well, now, you just bring him right over as soon as he gets here," she said, rolling to the door of the gym. The last two contestants was dancing under the limbo rack.

I was getting fidgety standing outside the door. Looking

into the shadowy gym at the dancing bodies was like staring into a fish tank in the dark, the colorful forms darting and swishing, circling round and back through damp, thick air.

My feet was tired from pacing in my heels. Mr. Foley, the phys ed teacher, sat at the ticket table counting money. He motioned for me to take a seat on a vacant metal chair. I sat down, the cold metal pressing against the back of my knees. I took off my heels and rubbed my arches. I twisted the band on Daddy's ring. I looked up: 9:00, the clock said.

I picked at my fingernail polish. It was pink, the same color as my dress and shoes. I looked at the pink stone in the ring on my finger; in the dim light it was hard to see it sparkle. I twisted the gold band round and round. Now the clock said 9:15.

The foghorn blew, a groaning sound like the word *lonesome*. They was announcing the twist contest. I'd give anything to join in. I'd been twisting every night outside our stoop; it was some of Daddy's and my best times. We'd twist together, our hands flying off in the opposite direction of our hips, our knees lowering ourselves down and up again like screwdrivers. I could feel my hips just busting to move.

And then I heard heavy footsteps on the gangplank.

I looked up.

I saw the leather shoes first and then the cuffed pants. The right hand held something shaped like a box.

My heart leaped up until I recognized who it was. Then it dropped like an elevator.

"Jimmy Wilson!" I said. "What are you doing here?"

"I predicted you'd be the prettiest girl at the dance. Came

to see if I was right. Turn around, sis." He made a circle with his index finger.

I twirled around, my crinolines lifting and falling like wings.

Jimmy gave a low whistle. It was the same sound he made when he turned his girlie calendar over to a new month. "I was sure right about that. Wish I'd bet money on my hunch. I'd be the richest fool in Kinship."

I slugged my brother in the stomach and felt his belly like dough. He hadn't had time to make it flat and hard.

"Brought something from your daddy," he said, handing me the thin white box.

I felt my spirits lift. I was happy to see Jimmy, but the truth was I'd been happier if he was my daddy. The box meant Daddy was in some way here.

"Where *is* Daddy?" I said, lifting the flap on the box.

"He hasn't got back from Claxton yet."

I sifted through the soft green tissue paper. It rustled like leaves.

"Guess he got tied up," Jimmy said. "Something probably happened with that fellow and the concrete order. After all, they're going to have to start pouring on Monday."

"Oh, Jimmy," I said, lifting the pink bouquet from the green tissue. "They're beautiful." The flowers was tiny pink roses gathered onto an elastic band. "Isn't this just like Daddy?" The roses was romantic. They was like something out of the movies.

Jimmy nodded. "It's called a wrist corsage, Pert," he said. "Daddy figured a wrist corsage would be easier for dancing."

My disappointment faded. It was just like Daddy to do

177

something like this. It was the kind of fancy gesture that made me crazy about him.

I slipped the elastic over my right hand. The roses looked as sweet as pink gumdrops.

"They're called sweetheart roses," Jimmy said. "Daddy said he wanted sweethearts for his sweetheart."

I grinned and felt something like sunburn flushing my cheeks.

"So why'd *you* get all dressed up and come over here?"

"I told you, Pert," Jimmy said. "I had to see if you was the prettiest girl at the dance."

Jimmy looked into the gym. "Hey, Pert," he said. "Stop flapping your jaw and start dancing. The twist contest is going on, sis. Let's get moving."

He took my hand and pulled me onto the dance floor. We twisted up a storm. All the girls eyed my brother. Fact was, he was the handsomest fellow at the dance, and the looks on the faces of the other girls told me they couldn't quite place him. Julie Nolan's eyes said she'd seen him before but just wasn't sure where. Jimmy had likely filled Simon Nolan's gas tank at the Texaco station, but that uniform with the red star was a dern sight different from his church suit, and the light brown hair that lay slicked back against his strong head tonight was different from the sun-streaked strands that fell across his forehead when he leaned over to check the oil. Jimmy's shirt looked pressed neat, and something tender crawled up my neck at the thought of Rae Jean on her knees, running the hot iron across the cotton fabric.

"I thought you was going out with Sue Ellen tonight." I had to shout to make myself heard, and my words came out in puffs between twists.

"Already did, sis. Took her home early. She wasn't feeling so good," Jimmy shouted back.

Bodies flew back and forth, feet shuffling to the beat. Lights circled through the dark like the emergency lights on the top of Sheriff Keiter's police cruiser. I saw Nympha Claggett's red muu-muu billowing out like sheets in a breeze. Most of the daddies was sweating and most of the daughters was smiling. When the music stopped, Jimmy and me crashed into each other to slow down. Then Jimmy wrapped his big arms around me and hugged.

"Hey, sis," he said, pointing to a line of people standing by a fake ship backdrop. "Want to get our pictures took?"

We waited in line behind two posts with a velvet rope like they had at the Bijou. When it was our turn, we stood in front of the fake cardboard portholes and the ship railing. I wondered if Julie and Cissy and Linda had got the cardboard from a refrigerator box like I suggested.

Mr. Foley was taking the pictures, and he had us push our heads through two life preservers that had S.S. FATHER-DAUGHTER, 1961 wrote on them. Jimmy and me grinned, and then the hot bulb flashed, and my big brother took my hand and led me over to the refreshment table.

Jimmy poured me a fruit punch first, and then he took one for himself.

"I want you to give me a toast, Pert," Jimmy said. "For good luck."

I'd do about anything in this world for Jimmy Wilson. Especially tonight. I couldn't have asked for a better brother.

"Sure, Jimmy," I said. "Anything you'd like."

I held the paper Dixie cup in my hand. I was happy to toast my brother. There was lots of things Jimmy Wilson needed good luck about. It would take luck to get him a better job, luck to get him a better education, luck to get him a better girlfriend. But I figured he deserved all the luck in the world.

I held my cup high. He held his high, too. Then I pressed my Dixie cup against his. "A toast for good luck," I said.

We gulped down our tropical fruit punch. The smell of it reminded me of Nympha Claggett.

When I had finished, I said, "So what you need luck about, Jimmy?"

"Sue Ellen," he said.

I felt a grin creeping onto my lips, but I forced my mouth still. I was hopeful. Maybe Pee Wee Hale had done good work. Maybe he had moved in on Sue Ellen. Maybe he had used some of those free movie passes on her.

"You guys having problems, Jimmy?" I said. I could see why. Sue Ellen bossed Jimmy around something fierce. Maybe Jimmy had finally gotten sick of it.

Jimmy filled up our cups again.

"No, Pert," he said. "No problems." He drank his punch straight down. "In fact, I love Sue Ellen more than ever."

I swore I didn't care how late it was when I got home. I was going to rap on Charlie Hale's trailer and have him send out that nephew of his. I was going to have to tell Pee Wee Hale to get down to business.

I looked over at Jimmy. His brown eyes was soft and glowing. "So what you need good luck for, Jimmy?" I said.

"I'm going to ask Sue Ellen to marry me."

I dropped my Dixie cup on the floor. The red punch spilled down the front of my dress, beading up on the net of my skirt. The juice splattered across the toe of my shoes, staining my pink heels.

A crowd of fathers and daughters stared at me in my clumsiness, and I stared at the back of Jimmy Wilson; he was moving to the table to get some towels.

I knew it would take more than a couple of towels to clean up the mess Jimmy would make if he married Sue Ellen Jenkins. How could I *ever* have Sue Ellen for a sister-in-law? How could I stand to hold her hand over grace at our kitchen table? How could I ever ride next to her in Frank Alhambra's taxi or kneel beside her during mass at St. Jude's?

Jimmy brought the towels, and I snatched them out of his hand. I was so mad I could hardly breathe. I dabbed at my skirt and realized something powerful wrong had happened. Maybe Ida Weevil had got the message backwards. Maybe Ida had given me the wrong instructions. When I had asked Ida Weevil about how to make love stay, I had meant something else. I didn't mean between Jimmy Wilson and Sue Ellen Jenkins.

Part Five

20

Sunday morning Rae Jean didn't go to mass. Said she'd been up all night, pacing the floor. Said she was worried. About where Daddy'd been and what it meant for me.

Frank Alhambra showed up at the door like he always did, and Rae Jean said, "Sorry, Frank. We won't be needing your services today." Her face looked set in stone. Frank tipped his hat and said, "See you next week, then?" Rae Jean nodded. Then she tightened her robe, poured herself another glass of tea, set down on the couch, and stared at the blank TV screen.

She was still staring when Gram walked in. Gram had got suspicious when Frank Alhambra didn't show up in his taxi, so she ordered a taxi for herself and talked Frank into driving her over to our trailer. She wanted to find out "why the daughter who never missed mass was missing today."

I hadn't slept much. I was sad that Daddy hadn't made it to the dance and mad that Jimmy was thinking about marrying Sue Ellen. Fact was, I'd been so restless my heart felt sore. I had tossed all night long, waking up with the sheets coiled around me like the shell of a snail. I figured how a snail was a lot better off than Pert Wilson: At least it had a permanent home.

Somebody had taken the knobs off the TV. The shafts stuck out like sticks without Popsicles. You couldn't turn the TV on or off, couldn't adjust the volume, couldn't change channels. Gram said it was just as well. We hadn't done anything as a family for a while. It might be nice to set and talk.

When Daddy stopped by to explain why he didn't make the dance, I was grateful for a little noise in the place. Daddy looked tired, too. The droops hanging under his eyes looked like tiny black curtain swags. But once Daddy started talking, he picked up steam. He'd had to look all over Claxton for Earl Shivers, and by the time he found him, lollygagging in the local tavern, it was too late to make it home to the dance in time.

"I'm truly sorry, daughter," my daddy said, hanging his head. "I'll make it up to you, you hear?"

I said, "I understand, Daddy." I know I was *trying* to.

Anger set in the middle of our front room. It was like somebody'd let gas. Everyone was mad, only no one wanted to say how bad things stunk. Gram tried to be cheerful. She said maybe we could play Monopoly like we used to on Sunday afternoons. Nobody much wanted to play Monopoly, but since we all knew how Gram could nag until she finally got her way, and since Daddy felt bad about missing my dance, we all gave in.

It started out bad and got worse.

We set up the game at the kitchen table. Jimmy took the car, of course, for his playing piece, and Gram took the thimble.

"Here, Rae Jean," Daddy said, passing her the silver wheelbarrow. "You can be the wheelbarrow, honey."

"Don't want the wheelbarrow, James William," Rae Jean said. There was an edge to her voice like a sharpened knife.

"You don't want the *wheelbarrow?*" Daddy said. He folded his arms across the tabletop and stared at her.

She stared right back. "Don't want the wheelbarrow. Want the dog." Rae Jean reached across the board and picked up the silver dog.

I didn't know why Rae Jean had to be that way. "*I'll* take the wheelbarrow, Daddy," I said, reaching for the piece. "I think wheelbarrows is swell."

He looked at me, sighed, and gave me his crooked grin.

I put my wheelbarrow next to Rae Jean's dog. Daddy picked up the man on horseback. The horse was rearing up, its front legs pawing the air. I swallowed hard. The horse and rider looked like they was fixing on galloping off.

It went on from there. Daddy and Gram argued about who was going to be banker.

"*I'll* be the banker, James Wilson," Gram said, straightening the piles of tens and fives. "Everybody can trust me to keep my personal funds separate from the bank's."

Daddy gave her a look like a gunshot. "Now what's *that* supposed to mean, Wilma?"

Gram was passing out money. Everybody got fifteen hundred dollars to start. "Means anything you think it means, son," Gram said. The way she said *son* sounded like a slap.

Daddy wanted to go first. He said he'd start, and then everybody to the right of him would take their turn. He had picked up the dice and started to shake them.

"Hold up a minute, bud," Gram said. She had reached for the instruction book. "You gotta play Monopoly by the

187

rules." I could tell by the look on Daddy's face that he didn't much like being called *bud*.

Gram flipped to the part in the manual that she wanted. "It says right here that you roll the dice to see who goes first. The player with the highest number starts."

Daddy pushed up from the table and poured himself a cup of coffee while we rolled dice. Then he sat back down. Jimmy was the high roller, so he started. Gram was the low roller, and I think that cheered up Daddy.

It went like it always did when we played Monopoly. Jimmy and Rae Jean was happy to keep going around and collecting their two hundred dollars. But Daddy played like me. We bought up everything in sight as fast as we could. Gram always bought property when she had money and traded or sold it when she didn't.

I don't know why Daddy had to get on Rae Jean like that. She'd bought both Baltic Avenue and Mediterranean Avenue. They was cheap properties that Rae Jean thought she could afford because they came up right next to the GO square. When you passed the GO square, you automatically got two hundred dollars from the bank, so Rae Jean felt safe in buying Baltic and Mediterranean.

"You ought to put you a couple of houses up on your purple properties there, Rae Jean," Daddy said. "You could make you a bundle."

"A house costs fifty dollars, James, and if somebody lands on it, I only get a few dollars more in rent. It's not like what you get when Pert puts a house on Park Place."

"She can't put a house up on Park Place unless she somehow gets Boardwalk from me." I kept trying to get Daddy to sell me Boardwalk so I could make a killing with houses and hotels, but he was having fun holding me off.

Daddy kept going. "Ain't you able to see you're the only one who can put up houses and hotels yet, Rae Jean? You're the only one out of ever'body with the hope of making money right now."

It was true. Gram had a couple of railroads and Jimmy had the electric company. The rest of the properties was divided up every which way. Only Rae Jean owned all the properties in a set. She could have made a killing.

Rae Jean arranged her money into neat piles. She set the blue fifties right next to the yellow hundreds. "No, thank you. Think I'll just stay where I am, James."

Daddy pushed his face across the board at her. "What do you plan to do with all this here money, Rae Jean? Just sit and *look* at it?"

Gram stuck her nose in. "She can look at it if she wants. She can stare at it all day long if she wants to, buster. It's her money."

I wished Gram would shut up. *Bud* was bad enough. *Buster* was even worse.

Daddy pushed up from the table, and the wobbly legs shook. Our kitchen table wasn't much sturdier than a card table, and you had to be careful about moving too quick.

"Can't you ever take a *risk*, Rae Jean? Can't you ever let yourself have some fun in your life? Can't you see that money is something to be played with? It's like *life*, Rae Jean. It's all just a game."

"It's not a game, James William," Rae Jean said. "It has consequences. Especially when there are children involved."

"What does *children* have to do with it?"

I agreed with Daddy. I didn't see how children got into this conversation. They was talking about money and risks and fun and games, and now Rae Jean was talking about children. I'd been learning lately that sometimes when Rae Jean and Daddy talked, the real subject was things they hadn't even mentioned.

"There are consequences when you let children down." She shook the dice hard, and they slammed against the board. "Like when you tell them you'll take them to a dance and then don't show up." Rae Jean banged her dog across six squares and landed on Community Chest. She read her card and then put seventy-five dollars into Free Parking.

Daddy sighed and scratched his head. "I said I was sorry to Pert, Rae. That's why I'm already up and here on a Sunday morning. You know I like to sleep in. I was dead tired when I got back from Claxton last night. Got up and came over here early just to say I'm sorry."

I could see the two of them wouldn't quit their picking unless I changed the subject to *make* them stop.

I jumped up from the table and ran to the Frigidaire. Over my shoulder, I said, "And your roses was beautiful, Daddy. Thank you." I pulled my corsage from the top shelf. I stuck my nose into the roses to smell them again. The petals was cool and damp against my cheek.

When I got back to the board, it was still as the grave. Everybody was looking at everybody else kind of funny.

I sat down and slipped the corsage over my wrist.

Daddy gave a whistle. "Those are beauties, Pert. As beautiful as my daughter."

Jimmy looked over at me and winked. "Sweethearts for a sweetheart," he said.

I grinned at Jimmy and said, "Thanks, Daddy."

Gram cleared her throat and told us to get back to playing.

It was quiet; nobody talked. I heard the tap-tap-tapping of the pieces as they rounded the board. I heard the clinking of Daddy's coffee cup as he set it back in his saucer. I heard Mittens lapping at the bowl of milk Rae Jean had set out for her.

Jimmy rolled doubles three times, and Gram got a get-out-of-jail-free card.

When Rae Jean passed GO, Daddy told her again to buy a couple of houses.

Rae Jean clamped her teeth over her bottom lip. "Playing with money is for people that has it, James," she said. "Playing isn't for folks like Wilsons."

"What do you mean?" Daddy slapped his arm across the board. "I *know* what it is to be poor as dirt. You know that about me, Rae Jean. It don't mean I can't have any fun in my life."

Jimmy tried to look busy. He straightened up the board while Daddy talked.

"Don't you think Sam Wilson taught me about being poor when he lost that thumb of his and started drinking? Don't you remember that I know what it's like to watch somebody lose ever'thing—his talent, his skills, his sanity, his money?"

When Rae Jean turned her eyes to Daddy, I saw that something in them was wet and glassy and sparkling like the colors in a prism. "And his *family*," she said. "Did you forget about that? Did you forget that he also lost his *family*?" Rae Jean was right about that. Not one of my grandpa's kids ever said anything nice about him.

I tried to understand what all this had to do with our Monopoly game.

Daddy wasn't done. He got up from the table again and paced the floor. "Don't you see how much I know about the lack of money? The shame of it? The fear? Know so much about the lack of money, Rae Jean, I'd leave my family—my wife and my little kids—to get money for them. Don't you remember that the fact of leaving them was less painful than the fact of watching them kids there starve, watching them grow up just like me? Don't you know that I never wanted to come back to Kinship until I could bring you wheelbarrows full of money?"

Rae Jean's eyes floated with colors. Gram's mouth was set. Jimmy stared at the board.

I closed my eyes like I did at the scariest parts of the movies.

"If you know so much about being poor, James William," I heard Rae Jean say, "then don't deny me the privilege of keeping safe against it in *my* own way." I heard a crack in her voice like a tree branch broken in a storm. "I've kept this little family together for years without your help. Did it by scraping things together one day at a time. Didn't play with my money, James. Tried to keep it for the things I needed, for the food to go into our mouths."

I opened my eyes. Rae Jean's lips was shaking and her voice cracked, but she wasn't crying. The wet pools in her eyes was filled to their banks, but they didn't spill over. I'd never seen Rae Jean's eyes spill over and cry in my life. I knew she got sad sometimes. And lonely. But I'd never seen her cry. I don't think anybody in this world had ever seen Rae Jean Wilson cry. Not even Gram.

Rae Jean stood up and threw her head back. She picked up one of the green plastic houses. "Don't talk to me about taking *risks*," she said, the word *risks* coming out like a hiss. "Risks are for people who are already safe. I'm not like you, James. I'm not fancy like you. I don't talk fast and I don't have boots and wheelbarrows. I can't buy my daughter a pretty dance dress. But I keep my family safe, James. I keep them safe by staying, James William Wilson. That doesn't leave much room for taking risks."

She threw the green house across the kitchen, and then she turned over the board and ran to the bedroom. The playing pieces went every which way. The houses and hotels slid across the table. The piles of money fluttered in pinks and greens and blues and yellows that was the same colors I'd seen in the prism pieces floating in Rae Jean's eyes.

Jimmy got up and brushed by Daddy. He went back to the bedroom to see about Rae Jean. I noticed for the first time that he was taller and bigger than Daddy.

When she ran out of the kitchen, Rae Jean had flung some things from her pocket. They made a hollow ringing sound against the linoleum and a twanging metal sound against the tabletop.

I followed the noises and bent to pick the somethings up. Then I stared down the hall toward the bedroom, holding the TV knobs in my hands.

Farley Ewing

Just yesterday Pert said, "Mr. Ewing, would you believe in a potion for making love stay?"

"Hmmph," I said. "Well, now, Miss Wilson, the answer to that question sure is a puzzle, isn't it?"

She gave me a funny look like she expected an answer, not another question. Said she was desperate. Said she'd got up the nerve to go see the Weevils. Said they'd given her a spell for making love stay, but she thought it wasn't taking.

"Do you think the spell will work, Mr. Ewing?" Pert said.

Hmmph. I didn't like the idea of that young girl spending time with the Weevils, see. They run gambling over there or something. Sophie Mulch and I have been worrying about it for years. Funny thing of it is, nobody much knows what's going on. Prefer to look the other way.

I said to Pert, "Well, now, can't know if it'll work if I don't know what the spell is."

I listened to her tell about the love potion while I stalled for time. Seems you were supposed to take a big red tomato and stick pins in it. It was a puzzle to me how folks could believe things like that. Come to think of it, it was contrary to science. I worked in aeronautics at the air force base all my life, see. Been a retired project development engineer a number of years now. It's physics that makes things happen, see. Not vegetables.

Because I'd worked in aeronautics so long, I'd learned that

making things fly was a lot harder than sticking pins in tomatoes, but I didn't say anything. Pert had a puppy-dog look in her eyes, see, that made me want to pet her. "Hmmph," I said. "Well, now, I don't know. That's kind of a puzzle, isn't it, Miss Wilson?"

I was sorry that she stormed off. Funny thing of it is, that's how people usually act when they're faced with puzzles. Don't have the patience to sit still long enough to figure them out, see. Don't like to stare questions in the face.

Hmmph. Right now the park's a puzzle for everybody around here. Figuring out whether they'll stay or go. I'm staying. Trailer life's a perfect solution for me. One person. Not much upkeep. Nothing too complicated to fix.

Funny thing of it is, I'm finally getting over my Alma. She's been gone six years now. Hmmph. I wish those Weevils were right. Wish you *could* make love stay. But it's been my experience, see, that figuring how to make love stay is the biggest puzzle of all.

21

On Monday morning everybody in the trailer park was waiting outside at the crack of dawn for Mr. Shivers's big white concrete truck. The air was gray and the sky was pink and Miss Mulch had made a Thermos of black coffee to share. Highwaters had decided to stay; Gene Nugent had decided to leave, and I think I was the only one who was going to miss him.

Even Ora Weevil stumbled by, sleep in his eyes and dust in his beard. Folks had been muttering about getting Weevils out of the park, but Odette Coates brought it up right to his face. Said Weevils was like to ruin the neighborhood with what they did in that trailer. But Ora Weevil yawned and picked at his beard and said he wasn't budging. That went for Ida, too. They was setting their trailer in concrete, same as everyone else.

We had planned to work and pour all day long and then go to the zoning commission on Thursday to explain about the concrete as a way to make things permanent residential. Every time a big truck went by on the highway, folks held their breath. We was just *sure* it was Mr. Shivers this time. But instead it was a flat rectangular truck hauling logs or a square refrigerated van delivering milk. All we wanted to see was the round white concrete truck twisting like a gyroscope, the letters on the side of the cab reading EARL SHIVERS, CONTRACTS IN CONCRETE.

At about nine o'clock Rae Jean slapped her hands together and shrugged her shoulders. "He's not showing up," she said. "I'm going on over to work."

I don't know how Rae Jean knew that, but she did. The rest of us waited until lunchtime. Mr. Shivers never came.

It was awful to watch my daddy. He talked like a one-man band, and nobody much appreciated the noises he was trying to pass off as music. He'd been over there Saturday night, he said, checking up on things in Claxton. He'd been working so hard, he'd even missed his own daughter's dance.

I knew what it was to run off at the mouth like that. I'd done it lots of times. As I watched my daddy throwing smoke out the tailpipe of his mouth, I wondered if *I'd* ever looked that way.

"Shut up, James Wilson." It was Farley Ewing. I'd never heard Mr. Ewing talk like that before.

When Farley put an arm over Miss Mulch's shoulder, I noticed then that she was trembling.

"You'd best be heading up to the bank and putting a stop payment to that check you wrote for Mr. Shivers," Farley said.

Daddy hung his head. "Didn't write a check," he said.

I saw Miss Mulch's jaw drop open.

"You don't mean you paid the man *cash,* do you?" Mr. Ewing said. The lines on his forehead looked broke up into a hundred puzzle pieces.

Daddy nodded. I remembered the wad of bills he had

shoved into Mr. Shivers's hairy paw before they shook hands. Miss Mulch's jaw dropped some more.

"Well, then," Mr. Ewing said. "Did you get a receipt or an IOU?"

"No," Daddy said. "We was business partners. A handshake's as good as a receipt between business partners."

I could see folks getting mad, their anger gathering up like a funnel cloud. Emil Highwater paced in the dirt. Alvin Coates pounded a clenched fist into an open palm. I began to wonder what kind of businessman my daddy was, why he wandered from job to job and place to place and never sent much money. Even Rae Jean kept every last receipt. You could trip over the box of them if I hadn't shoved it under the bed.

Farley Ewing led Miss Mulch back to her trailer. "It was near all I had," she mumbled. "Near all my retirement savings, Mr. Ewing."

I closed my eyelids and saw Earl Shivers against the black theater screen. He was wiping his hands on his greasy shirt and hiking up his waistband to button his pants. Then he cracked a bullwhip and sent caravans of trailers rolling across dark fields. Sophie Mulch and Farley Ewing and Coateses and Wilsons. And then the trailers turned into covered wagons and the dark fields turned into fields of wheat, and the line of rolling vehicles looked like homesteaders heading across wild prairies.

I opened my eyes. I could see things wasn't going to be permanent residential around here. Folks would be out of a place to live. Fact was, there wasn't going to be much in the way of homes for any of us for very much longer.

Home. I wondered about the pioneers. Their wagons was

the original mobile homes. Those settlers was the first trailer folks. And it wasn't a simple matter of just staking a claim. After that came winter, Indians, wolves, zoning commissioners, Howard Cherry, and Earl Shivers. No wonder they huddled into circles, setting up camp, keeping the devil out. It was a struggle to make things permanent residential. Always had been. It was hard work making a permanent residential *home.*

Iris Breeding,

TRAILER 1

I'd never seen such commotion *in my life.* First, that Mr. Shivers doesn't show up, and then Sophie Mulch takes to her bed, and finally I hear Rae Jean's having an open house in her trailer: Sue Ellen Jenkins and Jimmy Wilson are engaged!

After Rae Jean's open house, Verna Jenkins stopped by to order a few aprons for her husband's pharmacy reps. She brought the photo album of Sue Ellen and Jimmy's engagement party. Whoever took the pictures didn't know a thing *in this world* about photographs. The pictures were fuzzy and a little sad. Some of them made the wrong kind of memories. One of the snapshots showed the damp stains under Verna Jenkins's armpits that reminded you there was more tension at that party than you've ever seen *in your life.* If this was just the engagement party, you can imagine what that *ma'dge* will be like.

I admired how clever Rae Jean was about entertaining. Her trailer was small, so she called the party an "open house"; that way, folks could drop in and out when they wanted to instead of crowding the place up all at once. I heard Verna Jenkins tell Rae Jean that it was nice of her to offer her home "even though it was too small for a decent party." I thought Verna was rude.

Jenkinses claimed to live in Fenwick Acres, the suburb on the east end of town that says your husband makes money.

But they actually live on the *ay-edge* of Fenwick Acres. The way it was growing, the suburb might expand to include them one day, but they didn't really live there right now: They just said they did.

My Carter couldn't make the open house because he had to work, but he'd been excited about what the trailerites did the night they got Rae Jean's invitations for Jimmy and Sue Ellen's party.

He said, "Iris, darlin', get out here quick." My Carter'd never moved so fast one day *in his life*.

We heard them coming across the grass toward the Wilsons' trailer. They were rattling paper sacks of dried beans and scraping graters with forks. Miss Mulch was rapping on a colander like a drum, and Farley Ewing was shaking a box of rice. The Coateses were waving leather straps of jingle bells left over from the Tabernacle Baptist Christmas pageant. Emil Highwater was playing a comb wrapped with tissue paper, and Alice Potter was blowing on the lip of an empty Coke bottle filled with water. Pee Wee Hale and his uncle Charlie had taken a couple of hubcaps from their collection and were banging on them with soup spoons.

My Carter got out his notepad and scribbled on it like mad. I threw my yellow baby afghan over my nightie and ran outside to join him.

"What are they doing, Carter?" I asked.

"It's a shivaree, Iris, darlin'."

"What's a shivaree?"

"It's a celebration. It's a custom of locals in places all over the world. Folks in a kinship unit will shivaree a young couple getting engaged or a baby who's just been born. They get together and bang homemade noisemakers and hoot and howl."

At the engagement shower, the folks from the trailer park came with presents. They didn't have as much as a dime *in this world*, but they still brought *gee-iffs*. Alice Potter brought a pink glass bottle painted with purple flowers, and the Highwaters brought their best boning knife. Coateses brought free tickets to the Mount Zion Baptist family picnic, where they're selling barbecue in a couple of weeks, and Charlie and Pee Wee Hale brought matching white terrycloth robes that made Jimmy and Sue Ellen blush. I brought Sue Ellen a calico apron.

You can see that Sue Ellen's got a baby on the way, and Rae Jean doesn't make a fuss about it, but I guess I said the wrong thing to Verna Jenkins. I told her that Carter and I wanted a baby more than anything *in this world*. We wanted one so bad we were even thinking of adopting. If Verna ever knew of someone who wanted a good home for a baby, I said, she should call us.

I've never seen anybody *in this world* as rude as Verna Jenkins. I didn't even get to show her our baby's hope chest or my yellow baby afghan. Verna just slammed her photo album and left in a rush. It was another thing I could tell Carter about *Suuth-anuhs*. They're sweet as pie, and then one day they get mad about something, and—*blam!*—they up and shoot you in the face.

22

I was surprised when Sue Ellen showed up at the Bijou. I was huddled in the corner of the balcony, eating popcorn and watching the part of *The Parent Trap* where Hayley Mills meets her twin sister at camp for the first time. I figured Sue Ellen had come to chew me out for the way I treated her at the engagement party.

Since the party the only Jenkins I'd seen was Verna Jenkins, who brought over the photo album for us to look at. She'd decorated the cover in white wrapping paper and put a pink heart in the middle of it with the words *Jimmy* and *Sue Ellen* written in Elmer's glue and silver glitter. The glitter made globby clumps across the cover. The album didn't fool me. It was a happy-occasion album for an unhappy occasion.

I flipped through the pictures quick. I scanned the group shots of both families just before their frozen smiles turned back into scowls. I skimmed over the one of Sue Ellen's father, Don Jenkins, slapping his brother Delbert on the back. Don Jenkins acted as if the party'd been thrown for him, not his daughter.

My daddy hated parties. He said happy times was something that just happened. You couldn't plan for them in advance and expect things to go good. Fact was, what he said came true: The party didn't go very good at all.

First Gram was late with the cake. She'd made it up special with vanilla cream frosting, the kind with the Crisco in it, and she'd had to run to the store for extra powdered sugar. Then the bride's head on the bride-and-groom decoration had fell off, and Rae Jean had to find some glue to stick it back on. Next Gram couldn't find the cake cutter. And the last straw was when Rae Jean realized she hadn't bought enough ginger ale. She was making punch in Miss Mulch's glass punch bowl. You put rainbow sherbet in the bottom of the bowl and dump ginger ale all over it.

Rae Jean asked Daddy to run to the store for more ginger ale. He was out of cash, so Rae Jean opened the lid to the teapot where she stashed her rainy-day funds, then fished around inside the pot. The line of her mouth grew tighter and tighter as her fingers came up empty. Daddy ended up borrowing some money from Jimmy for the ginger ale, and he didn't get back until the party'd been going on for near an hour. When Rae Jean saw he'd brought back Coca-Cola instead of ginger ale, she dabbed at the corner of her eye with a napkin. I sent Farley Ewing back to his trailer for a six-pack of Vernors, wondering all the while where Rae Jean's money had gone.

It wasn't until I looked at the picture of Jimmy slipping the engagement ring on Sue Ellen's finger that I figured it out. Where in the world had Jimmy Wilson got the kind of money for a ring? He was planning on buying a car, wasn't he? When it dawned on me, I hated it that Jimmy now needed a ring *and* a car and that he had to take Rae Jean's money to do it. I hated it that Jimmy was getting married, baby or no. Marriage, especially one with babies, put a lot of pressure on a man. It mattered about his job and money and where he lived now. No wonder Jimmy needed that money.

Flipping through the pictures in the photo album re-minded me about how a part-truth is the same thing as a whole lie. Fact was, the only true picture in that album was the one of the toast. All the family members was in the pic-ture: Verna and Don Jenkins and Verna's sister Coochie and her husband Mel and their kids and then Don's brother Del-bert and his wife Marvella and their son Del, Junior. And then Gram and Rae Jean and me. Daddy didn't want to be in the picture, so he offered to take it for us. Jimmy and Sue Ellen was standing off to the side, with Jimmy gazing down at Sue Ellen while she gazed up at him. They looked like two mules that didn't have a lick of sense between them.

In the photo everybody is raising their punch cups except for me. I had tossed my punch at Sue Ellen just as Daddy snapped the camera. There's a turned-down look to Sue Ellen's mouth that matches the turned-up look of my own. We was like the tragedy and comedy masks they put on the programs for the senior play every year. After the party, Rae Jean said she'd never been ashamed of me in my whole life until then.

On account of all that, I wouldn't be expecting Sue Ellen to look for me in the movie theater and tell me the things she told me, would I?

I could hardly make out her ring of black curls in the dark, but her white face shone up at me like the moon. On the movie screen, Hayley Mills and her twin was plotting to get their parents back together. The Hayley Mills twins was separated when their parents got divorced; one of the Hayleys went with the father and the other Hayley went with the mother.

"Pert," Sue Ellen whispered, "I want you to help me throw the baby."

I had been making regular chomping noises on my popcorn. When I heard those words, I felt a popcorn husk catch in my throat, and I coughed.

Sue Ellen patted my back with her small fat fingers.

"Don't touch me," I said.

She stopped patting.

"I don't want to marry Jimmy," she said. "I want to throw the baby."

I looked at the screen and felt split in two like the two Hayleys. Had Sue Ellen just told me two things I was sad about or glad about? Or did one thing make me sad and the other glad? And which was which?

"I thought you loved my brother," I said. The sounds that came out of my mouth reminded me of the growling noises Lickety used to make if you tried to touch him while he fed.

"Pert, I do love Jimmy," she said. "He's sweet."

I nodded over my popcorn tub. She was right. Other than taking Rae Jean's rainy-day money, my brother was about as sweet as a boy could be.

"He's good to me, Pert."

I nodded again.

She clutched my arm. I could see her engagement ring winking in the darkness and I liked to spit.

"Pert, I can see how hard it's going to be. We're not going to have any money. We'll be living with my folks."

206

I had stuck my nose in Sue Ellen's room one time when Jimmy had stopped by to give her the schoolbooks she had left at our house. It made me shiver to think of her pep-club pompoms lying next to Jimmy's Texaco uniform, to think of the teddy bears on top of the pink bedcovers and Jimmy Wilson under them.

"It's no way to start," she said. "He's not ever going to amount to much without an education. I'm not, either. I was hoping to go to beauty school once I graduated. Mama and Daddy had it all worked out."

"Hmmph," I said. I didn't give a lick for her lost chances at an education. Fact was, I didn't give a lick for anything about Sue Ellen Jenkins. All I cared about was Jimmy.

"But what about the baby?" I said. I stared into the pop-corn tub. The white round kernels reminded me of the hundreds of eggs inside the ovaries in *A Baby Is Born*. We'd watched that movie in Miss Claggett's home ec class. I tried to picture Jimmy's tiny sperm swimming in to howdy one of Sue Ellen's eggs.

"I don't want the baby," she said. Her voice was flat.

I must have jumped a little, for some of the kernels of popcorn went flying out of the tub. Without Sue Ellen Jenkins's fat dumb whining baby, things could go back the way they was for Jimmy and Rae Jean and Daddy and me.

"No baby deserves to be born to parents too young to know how to take care of it. It'll be so hard on this baby, Pert. Babies should only be born to people who *want* to love them and *can*."

Then she stuck her fingernail between her front teeth, thinking. "Besides," she said, "I don't want to turn out like Rae Jean, Pert. She's got about the hardest life I know. Rae

Jean had you babies and never enough money and no husband to give her a hand all these years."

I felt like I'd been punched in the stomach.

Sue Ellen kept talking, chattering on about Rae Jean. Her kids. Her trailer. Her husband gone for most of her life. I watched her lips move in the dark; they made motions halfway between whispering and spitting.

"*Shut up,* Sue Ellen!" I yelled. I threw my popcorn tub smack on the floor. "That's your problem. You never learned when to shut up!" The tub made a hollow thwacking sound, and the kernels flew everywhere.

The people in the front of the balcony turned around and started hushing us.

I could tell Sue Ellen was mad. Her lips pursed, closing tight against each other like a kewpie-doll mouth. She kept her eyes fixed on the screen.

The picture had split in two. One Hayley Mills was on one half of the screen; the other Hayley Mills was on the other. They was talking on the phone, plotting about how to get their parents back together.

Then Sue Ellen turned to me. I could see a gleam like reflecting water in her eyes. "I think I'm going to go crazy, Pert," she said. "I think I'm going to lose my mind. I want you to help me. I need you to help me get rid of this baby."

I couldn't see what was so dern special about Sue Ellen's mind when my *own* mind was troubled enough.

Sophie Mulch,

TRAILER 4

I swannee, I took to the couch with a sick headache for a whole day after Earl Shivers didn't show up. Swallowed Anacin every four hours. I was so tired I slept with my shoes on. I've never felt so old in my life.

Don't know what I would have done without Mr. Ewing, bless his sweet heart. He borrowed Odette's collection of church fans and sat by my couch and fanned me all afternoon. At night he read to me from *The Search for Bridey Murphy.* It was about a housewife who was put in a trance and came to find out she wasn't really a housewife but a nineteenth-century Irish woman. I slept through most of it. I don't hold much truck with people trying to figure out their past lives. I swannee, I got enough to do to figure out just this one.

The thing that helped me recover was that visit from James Wilson. *Laws,* I was so mad at that man I could have cussed, but I let him sit down and say what he came to say, and I asked Mr. Ewing to leave while he said it. Mr. Ewing looked ready to punch the man in the nose.

At first James Wilson tried to drown me in a flood of words. He'd gone to Mayor Cherry and got a two-week extension on the hearing. He'd figured a way to get my money back, offering excuse after excuse that I didn't care to hear. After a bit I raised up from the couch and laid my hand on his arm and said, "Mr. Wilson, sir, actions speak louder than words."

I'd never seen a grown man's ears turn so red, but he told me I was right, and he promised to make good on my money. Every penny of the five hundred dollars he'd lost. He'd write me an IOU, he said, and he wrote it on the spot. The piece of paper said, "I.O.U. $500. James William Wilson." I said, "Thank you very much, Mr. Wilson. Good day."

Oh, *laws,* but I perked up right quick after that. When I heard Jimmy was getting married, I called him over and told him I wanted him to have something of mine. After all, Hugh Mulligan stood me up at the altar near forty years ago, and what's an old woman going to do with a diamond engagement ring from a man who up and married her twin sister?

Jimmy seemed pleased as punch with the ring. I like giving the Wilson kids things they need. *Laws,* but I miss my sweet Pert. Saw her out the window the night she left for the father-daughter dance. She looked sweet as strawberry shortcake in her pink dress and pink shoes. It was about time that girl had some regular fun. Sometimes that brother of hers can't tell split beans from coffee, but he's also about as good as they come. Think of him going off to that dance for her when her daddy didn't show! I swannee, Jimmy Wilson's welcome to that old ring. It's my pleasure.

23

I pulled on the door to Doc Jackson's office. It was at the front part of the building, where the people came in. On the door hung a Halloween decoration of a witch on a broom.

I signed in on the sheet Doc Jackson had taped to the window. After I wrote my name, I shivered. I took a seat and waited. An old man was nodding off in the chair across from me. I picked up a magazine and hoped Rae Jean wouldn't come in. She rarely entered the front of the house; she stayed on her side with the animals. But sometimes she needed to ask Doc Jackson for help.

When it was my turn, I jumped up too sudden, and I dropped the magazine back onto the coffee table with a loud slap.

"Hey there, Pert," Doc Jackson said when he came into the examining room. "What can I do for you today?"

I was sitting up on the examining table. I felt like a car up on blocks. The white paper underneath me rustled whenever I moved.

"I've got trouble with my ear here, Doc," I said. Before he came in, I had been rubbing my left ear hard to make it red. I had covered it up with my left hand.

Doc Jackson's eyebrows turned down in a frown and he moved closer. "Let's take a look there, Pert," he said.

I removed my hand.

"Been out in the sun too long lately, Pert?" he asked. "Looks like a powerful case of sunburn."

"No, sir," I said. "It hurts down deep. Inside. I couldn't hardly sleep a wink last night. It throbs kind of. I can hear my pulse beating in my ear."

Doc picked up a shiny silver instrument and pressed on something that made a tiny light appear on the tip. Doc's face was so close I could see the gray and white hairs growing out of his ears and nostrils. I'd never seen anyone that was such a mess of hair in funny places.

Then Doc put his eye up against the instrument and slipped the instrument into my left ear. He looked and looked. Then he switched to my right ear.

Finally he put out the light on the tip of the instrument and asked me questions. He wanted to know if my ear had been hurting longer than twenty-four hours, whether I was finding it difficult to swallow, when I'd started having trouble sleeping, and if I had had a bad cold lately.

Then Doc Jackson said, "I'm not finding anything wrong, Pert. Will you come again if it continues to hurt?"

I nodded. He motioned me off the table, and then I gathered my breath and said, "By the way, Doc, how do you throw a baby?"

I saw the hair in his nostrils move as he exhaled. "*What* baby?" Doc Jackson said. "*Whose?*"

I swallowed hard. "Oh, well, maybe not a baby. Maybe just a puppy," I said, waving my fingers like a rich lady with diamond rings on more than one finger. "You know how

Old Gal is always coming around with litter after litter."
Old Gal was a stray that came to the vet's office whenever
she was fixing to give birth. "And you know how Rae Jean is
taking up collections to have stray animals fixed. And you
know how the collection isn't going too well. Isn't there
some cheaper way for Old Gal to get rid of her babies?"

Doc Jackson's bushy eyebrows turned down again. "Well,
yes," he said. "Yes, I suppose there is. We have abortion
agents we can use on a bitch after she mates. The best treat-
ment, however, is prevention. What your mother is trying to
do is best. Spaying the females. Neutering the males."

"These abortion agents, Doc," I said, "do they work for
humans, too?"

"Sit back up on that table, Pert," Doc said. His voice was
firm. "You need to listen." Then he folded his hands across
his chest while I climbed on the table. "These agents," he
said. "You wouldn't want to try them. People have been trying to abort unwanted babies for centuries. There are hundreds of old wives' remedies and folklore methods. There's
danger in every one of those remedies."

"What kind of remedies? What kind of folklore methods?" My feet dangled down the side of the table, and I
could feel their nervous tapping. I was a foot tapper; I tried
like the devil to get my feet to stay still.

Doc Jackson gave a tiny cough. "Why, Pert?" he said.
"Why would you want to know?"

"Just wondering," I said. I stopped kicking my heels
against the table. "Just curious, is all."

Doc Jackson frowned and then moved with purpose to
the sink in the corner. He rolled up his sleeves and began
washing his hands with a liquid soap from a green bottle.

"You ever had a pelvic exam, Pert?" he said, scrubbing his lower arms. "I think you should lie down and let me take a closer look at you."

"No way, Doc," I said, leaping off the table. "Never had one and never will. Thanks so much, Doc, but I'll just keep my private parts private. I'll just keep my pelvis to myself if it's all the same to you, sir."

He picked up the terry-cloth towel from the towel rack, dried his hands, and slung the towel over his shoulder. His voice got gruff. "Get back up on that table, Pert Wilson."

I jumped back on the table again. The white paper crinkled up under me. Then Doc Jackson came over and put his eye right next to mine. "Pert," he said, "have you missed a period? Do you think you might be pregnant?"

We stared eye to eye for a minute. I was the first one to blink. "Heck, no, Doc. You know how I am about boys. Never let 'em touch a thing. I promise."

"So why do you want to know about how to end a pregnancy?"

"I don't know, Doc. I'm just curious. It's my age is all. We had this film in home ec class about having babies, and I've been watching Rae Jean help with the whelping of Old Gal and such. You know, at my age, it's on my mind. All those new words and things. *Testes* and *menses* and all that stuff. It's hard to shake the thought of it."

I saw Doc's mind working behind his black-and-gray eyebrows. They fanned out from the bridge of his nose and lifted gently like gulls' wings. He was considering what I had said. "Then let's be truthful, Pert. Let me tell you everything I know. The first thing is that abortion—what you call 'throwing a baby'—is illegal." The way he said the words *throwing a baby* felt like a slap.

"If it's illegal," I said, my heart sinking, "then there's no way you can get rid of a baby you don't want?"

"There's no *legal* way," he said. He hesitated before he went on. "Well, perhaps, if your life was in danger you could have an abortion, I suspect. It's rare, but in some states if your health was threatened by something like cancer or kidney failure, you could maybe have one."

"What if the girl was going to go crazy or something like that?" I said. "Could she get an abortion then?" The white moon of Sue Ellen's face in the theater floated into my mind. Her lips was pinched, and her eyes was watery.

"I don't think so, Pert. I know of one case in which a young unmarried girl claimed to be going crazy because of the stress of her unwanted pregnancy. The doctors put her in a psychiatric unit. The baby was born there."

I sighed. I wondered if being born in a loony bin was any different than being born in the regular world.

Doc Jenkins' stethoscope was dangling from his neck like two question marks. "Didn't those doctors care about how life would be for a baby whose mama didn't want it?" I said. I pictured Maxine Boggs's little girls. They was hungry and dirty. Their teeth was as run-down as their shoes.

"Of course, Pert," Doc Jackson said. "Doctors *do* care about those babies and those women."

"So why can't they do it, then, Doc?" It seemed simple to me. "If you can go to a doctor to take out your appendix, why can't you go to take out a baby?"

Doc Jackson moved closer to me. I could smell the thick

215

creamy odor of the soap he had used. "It's not that simple, Pert. Removing a baby isn't the same thing as removing an appendix."

"But maybe you're *not* removing a baby, Doc. Maybe you're just taking out a glob of cells. Maybe it's just like clumps of frogs' eggs setting in a pond. They're just speckles in a glob of jelly. They ain't frogs yet."

Doc Jackson folded his arms again and looked at me from under his bushy eyebrows.

I don't know why I thought of Rae Jean right then. I pictured her in church, on her knees at the communion rail. Her lips was parted to receive the round white wafer of bread from Father Joe. Rae Jean was different from me. I thought that the bread and the wine just *stood for* the body and blood of Jesus Christ. Rae Jean thought the bread and wine *was* His body and blood. Which one of us was right? It seemed something like frogs' eggs. Did the clumps of cells *stand for* a frog or *was* they a frog? And what about the cells Sue Ellen carried in her belly? *Was* they a baby? Or did they just *stand for* a baby?

Then Doc Jackson said, "Have you talked to Rae Jean, Pert? Does Rae Jean know about this?"

"Sure, Doc," I said, rubbing my ear. "My ear's on fire. It's been throbbing like the devil. I reckon Rae Jean knows I couldn't sleep."

"No, Pert. I'm not talking about your ear. I'm talking about your questions about abortion. Does your mother know about them?"

I stared at the frizzy hair sticking from Doc's ears and wondered about Sylvia Jackson, Doc's wife. Did she ever kiss him on the ear? If she did, didn't all that hair bother her?

"I'm not sure," I said. It was true. Rae Jean probably *didn't* know about my questions, but I couldn't be positive. I didn't know *for sure.*

"You watch yourself, Pert."

I stared at the diplomas on the wall. One said HENRY HAROLD JACKSON, M.D. The other said HENRY HAROLD JACKSON, D.V.M. I was pretty sure Jimmy Wilson would never have a diploma on his wall. About the only thing my brother'd ever have for hanging was a girlie calendar for the wall of the gas station.

"Oh, don't worry about me, Doc. Old Pert Wilson can take care of herself if anyone can." I heard myself say those words, but I wasn't sure I really believed them.

"Pert, I mean it," Doc said. "Terrible things happen to girls. Their mothers, too. Lots of women die trying to take care of things for themselves. There are people out there who hurt lots of girls, girls just like you who want to get rid of babies. The girls are desperate. Some of them contract terrible infections. Some of them die, bleeding to death."

"Who are those people who do those things, Doc?" I said. "Are there any of them in Kinship?"

He took my hand. He held it hard. "Do you want me to tell your mother about this conversation?"

I shook my head.

"Then I want you to promise me two things."

I hung my head and said nothing.

Doc squeezed my hand tight. "Promise me," he said, "that you won't try to do anything stupid and that you'll come back and see me at the end of next week."

"If I do, Doc, will you promise not to tell Rae Jean?"

He tightened his lips and nodded his head.

217

Odette Coates,

TRAILER 6

Well, now, everybody in the park's mad at James Wilson. They're hotter'n hell on a Saturday night. They'd have killed him dead by now if they could afford a rifle.

What worries me most is little Pert. I seen her go from up to down quicker than a Georgia barometer, but I ain't seen nothin' like that gal now. That gal's bein' pulled like taffy.

First Pert runs over to check on her mama. Rae Jean's been paintin' outside in the yard now. Don't do them paint-by-numbers no more. I been catchin' snatches of her pictures, things like flyin' animals and golden swirls and strange faces that look like folks you know but just can't place. I been seein' Rae Jean outside on the lawn chair strokin' that cat every day, talkin' to it like it was a baby.

Then Pert runs off to check on her daddy. He's been tearin' up the roads between Kinship and Claxton for a while now, and when he come home, Pert run over with hot coffee. Sometimes when he's been gone for hours and she don't know where he was, I'll see her waitin' by the stoop and pacin'.

Like I say to Alvin, somebody's picked up that gal's heart and throwed it on the ground.

Well, now, I even seen Pert goin' over to Weevils, and you don't go to Weevils for nothin' good. Like I say to Alvin, you only see a Weevil when you is at the end of your rope and it's startin' to fray. Seein' Pert over there kept me talkin' with

Sophie and Farley and Alvin. We're gettin' ready to go to town to see that lawyer fellow and kick those old Weevils out of this park. Don't know what we plan to use for money. It's always a bad sign when you get to needin' a lawyer. Nothin' but know-it-alls makin' a livin' off of other people's troubles.

Worst of all was thinkin' about Pert and Rae Jean and Jimmy out of a home. I'd bet Pert was countin' on her daddy to bail 'em out, but like I say to Alvin, some folks is just all vines and no taters. Ain't no amount of tongue waggin's gonna change that fact.

Bein' out of a home ain't nothin' nobody'd ever wish for. Alvin and Odette knows what it is to be sittin' on their suitcase on the sidewalk. Bluest kind of blue there ever was.

24

I'd only been inside Weevils' trailer that time I was small, when I had asked for help with falling asleep. Even when I asked for the love potion a short while ago, I had stayed out under the awning. When I collected rent, which I did every month, I stood outside the door and let them pass their money to me through the screen. Nobody with a lick of sense would spend much time with Weevils.

I knocked on the door, then jumped. The sound of the hollow rap had scared my own self.

"Come in." I knew that scratchy voice. It was Ida's.

It was as dark inside as out, and damp. Candles flickered on a dresser under a cracked mirror. Wax pooled hot near the candlewicks.

Ora Weevil set on a high stool in the middle of the crowded room, an open shoebox under his beard. Ida was standing beside him, a pair of scissors in her hand. Ida was trimming Ora's beard, the fresh-cut strands falling into the shoebox he held. When I stepped across the threshold, the floorboards squeaked, and a few of the strands of beard missed the box and fell to the floor.

Ida Weevil swung around and glared at me, her eyes like

the slit marks on one of Gram's birthday pies. "Ain't it just like a Wilson to bring trouble to the door!"

Both of them bent to the floor, crawling around on their hands and knees, feeling for something in the dark.

"Have you got 'em, wife?" Ora said.

"Feels like it, husband," she said, picking up fallen wisps of beard and whisking them into the shoebox. "But we's got to get 'em all. You knows that when you trims a beard you's got to get every cut strand."

"I'm sorry I interrupted," I said.

"Sorry never did no good, Missy," Ora said. "By the time you get to sorry, it's always too late. Got 'em all, wife?"

"I think so, husband."

Then Ida Weevil came closer. "You gotta watch out for the devil, Missy. If he get ahold of one of them cut strands from Ora's beard, the devil'll put a curse on us sure as the dawn."

I knew all about the devil. It was Ida Weevil herself who had whispered in my ear when I was small, telling me all kinds of things about him. How the devil can't come into a place with light. How he enters a body through the mouth and you'd better watch what you say when you open it. How blue jays spend every Friday with the devil, telling him all the bad things we've done all week. I'd been scared of the devil for years. That's why I'd kept away from Weevils.

Ora slid off the stool and came up behind Ida. I felt a shiver when I looked at his gray beard. Half of it was cut to his neck. The other half was hanging all the way to his waist. "How's that love potion working, chile?" I didn't like the way Ora winked at Ida.

221

"It's working swell," I lied. "Fact is, it's working so swell, I came to ask you for another potion."

The Weevils looked at each other and smirked. Their missing teeth reminded me of jack-o'-lanterns.

My palms was starting to sweat. "Ida Weevil," I said, "can you tell me how to throw a baby?"

She cocked her head like she was listening for something. Then she raised a bony finger and came closer. She smelled musty.

Ida's finger poked at my belly. "A baby, Missy! Ain't that a wonder!"

I swallowed hard. It felt like trying to keep down dry heaves.

I saw Ida's green eyes under eyebrows bushy as black caterpillars. "So our young missy's old enough to be a mama, Ora!" The thin white skin of her finger glowed in the candlelight. I felt like Hansel, poked through his prison bars, growing fat for a witch's supper.

Ida turned her back on me and faced Ora. "Husband," she said, "get you out the back door and cut me one of them juniper branches."

Then Ida Weevil faced me again. "Best idea for fixin' the problem of a gal what don't wants a baby," she said, "is a potion from a juniper bush."

Then she paused and brought her green eyes next to mine. "Unless the gal's got a mountain of money." She threw open her mouth and laughed.

My blood heated up. Ida Weevil knew I didn't have a mountain of money. Not even a tiny hill.

Ora had dragged himself to the kitchen and out the back door. I could hear the wheezing sound of a handsaw. When he came back, he handed Ida something with dark green leaves. She shoved the juniper limb in my face.

"They's folks what will help you throw a baby, girl. Granny women and such. But they's costin' money. This here," she said, waving the branch in front of my eyes, "will bring down a baby good as anything, Missy. But you's got to follow the directions exact, hear?"

I heard. "I swear," I said. "I'll follow them exact. But why ain't you going to charge me?"

Ida laid the juniper branch on the table and folded her hands across her chest. "Ain't gonna charge you *money*, Missy. But it'll cost you, just the same." When she talked, her chin slid back and forth like a blade that sharpened her teeth.

I blinked. I didn't understand.

"Not everything what costs means money, Missy." She looked at Ora. He nodded at her. "It won't take no money for this potion. Only a promise." Her eyes was glowing.

I took a deep breath. "What do I have to promise?"

Ida Weevil looked at Ora. Some kind of secret signal passed between them. Ora nodded again, and then Ida said, "They's tryin' to zone us out of here, Missy. Folks in the court—Miss Mulch and Coateses and Mr. Ewing—is trying to keep Weevils out of Happy Trails. Says this here park is zoned residential and our business makes it commercial. Says we has to leave on account of that."

Ora combed his half beard with his yellow fingers. "Heard they hired a lawyer, ain't that right, wife?"

Ida grinned. "For once you're right, husband," she said. "But if they gets rid of us, Missy, they has to get rid of Coateses, too, that's the truth. Barbecue's a business, ain't it, Missy?"

223

I knew it was a business to Coateses. Barbecue was their whole life. I nodded.

"So's Mr. Ewing's puzzle project, if you ask me, wife."

Ida nodded. I saw the way Weevils fed off each other. They was like those parasites we studied about in science.

Ida Weevil shook her finger at me. "So if they's tryin' to get rid of Weevils on the ground we's commercial, not residential, more folks than Weevils has to go, too."

What they said made sense to me. Near everybody in the park had something to sell. Iris Breeding sold aprons in Gram's shop; Highwaters peddled vegetables from the tailgate of their station wagon; one time a man had even drove all the way from Waterloo, Iowa, to trade for one of Charlie Hale's hubcaps.

Ida put her face right next to mine. "Looka here. You has to promise to keep us here in Happy Trails, Missy."

I looked back at her and swallowed. Even if I promised, it would be a hard thing to do; everybody in the trailer court was dead set against Weevils.

"How am I going to be able to do that? No offense, ma'am, but Weevils ain't got many friends around here."

Ora snapped at me. "Don't have to be friends to live around someone, chile. No law that says you gotta be friends with your neighbors, ain't that right, wife?"

I knew you didn't have to be friends with neighbors. Gene Nugent didn't howdy a soul. But folks let him be.

Ida began to pace. I heard her long skirt swish across the floor. "Folks listens to you, Missy. They's glad to see you drop by, even if it's just for rent. They respect your mama, and you know how to talk. Little Missy can talk slicker than a car salesman at an auto auction."

As I listened to Ida, I didn't know whether she was paying me a compliment or insulting me. From my daddy I was beginning to see that fast talkers wasn't always fine company.

Ida stopped pacing. She brought her black brows down to me. "Pert Wilson could talk folks into living in a *horse* trailer and make 'em think it was a palace."

I looked at the Weevils and shuddered. If Weevils could talk me into a promise, I could talk them *out* of one, too.

"If I promise to try to keep you in the court," I said, "will you promise something for me in return?"

"Why should we?" Ida snapped. "If you help us stay, we'll give you the potion. That's an even split. Why should we promise anything else?"

I was clear about what I needed. I would just say it flat out. "Because I won't help you," I said, "without it."

Ida looked at Ora then turned her eyes on me again. I could see the red rims of her lower lids. "What's the promise, Missy?"

"Promise me," I said, gulping air like water, "you won't tell anyone in my family that I've asked about throwing a baby." All I could think of was Rae Jean. I pictured her in my mind, her blond hair like a halo. Rae Jean would die of heartache if she knew I was doing this.

The Weevils looked at each other and then nodded their heads in my direction. "That's an easy promise, Missy," Ida said. "Now I'll tell you about that there juniper branch."

I listened close while Ida picked up the branch and thrust it in my face.

"First off, Missy," she said, "you ain't gonna find nothin' better'n juniper branches for throwing a baby."

I didn't know whether to feel relieved or scared.

"You makes a tea, Missy," Ida said, her long skirt dragging the floor. "You takes about half an ounce of the leaves and flowering tops of this here limb, and then you boils about a quart of water separate. Once it's good and hot, you pours the water over the plant material." She made a pouring motion with her wrist and hand. "You steeps it for no more'n twenty minutes—else it'll fell an elephant—and you drinks it hot, and you takes about one or two cups a day, at bedtime and in the morning. It'll throw a baby every time." Then she slapped the branch into my hands.

I closed my eyes and concentrated on her directions, willing myself to remember correctly. Half an ounce of leaves. A quart of water. No more'n twenty minutes. Hot. One or two cups.

Then I looked at the branch in my hand. It had dark green leaves. I knew that green was the color of grass and piney woods and hope. My heart sank. It was a color far away from Pert Wilson's black deeds.

Ida Weevil moved to the dresser under the mirror. She opened the top drawer. It was filled with straw mats, cigar boxes, hankies, strands of elastic, and old candle stubs. She found what she was looking for and pulled it out. It was a lipstick tube.

"Here's something else for you, young Missy," Ida said. "To remind you about your promise to keep Weevils in the circle called Happy Trails."

Ida slipped the case off the tube. The lipstick was a blood red. I saw the pointed end moving toward me like a missile. I wanted to cover my face with my hands, but I couldn't let go of the juniper branch. Before I realized what was happening, Ida Weevil had smeared a red ring around my mouth, grazing my skin with her sharp fingernails as she drew her circle.

Ida stood back and squinted at me. "I suppose you can't recall what I tole you about circles when you was small, can you now, Missy?"

I had no trouble remembering her words. " 'You gots to make a strong circle, Missy,' is what you said. 'Devil can't come into a circle what's kept tight.' "

Ida Weevil was ruining everything. Years ago she had taught me to keep the circle tight against the devil by getting in and out of bed on the same side. Now the devil herself was asking me to help her get inside the circle called Homestead Park. That circle included Miss Mulch and Coateses and Charlie and Pee Wee Hale and all the rest. It didn't include folks like Weevils.

"That there red stain will help you remember your promise," Ida said. "To keep Weevils in the court."

I glanced at myself in the cracked mirror. The candles wavered in the smoky glass, and I felt hot as the wax that ran down their sides. I stared at the red ring around my mouth and bit my lip against the anger. Red was the color of my family, my kin. The blood that circled in our veins meant we was home to each other. The red O that ringed my mouth now meant Weevils would live there, too.

I looked back at Ida. In the flickering candlelight her turban seemed to twist and wind like a snake. "And your promise to me, Ida Weevil?" I said.

"I promises not to tell no one in your family about the potion." I heard a catch like a caw at the back of her throat.

I hid the limb up under my shirt, so anxious to run away that I left the door open behind me. As I rushed across the yard to my trailer, the juniper branch scratched my belly.

It was dark out now, and the air was damp with fog. I felt like a goblin with my red mouth and black heart and my green branch hidden under my shirt.

I jumped when I saw my daddy. He had the TV on a dolly, and he was rolling it in the direction of his truck.

"Whatcha doin' with the TV, Daddy?" I said, pressing the juniper branch tight to my chest. I tried to sound calm.

He grunted. "Got things to make up to Miss Mulch. I'm trading this here TV in at the pawnshop in the morning."

I couldn't believe it. I was glad my daddy was trying to help Miss Mulch. But if he traded in the TV, I couldn't watch *I Love Lucy* anymore. Worse than that, trading in the TV was like trading in the wheelbarrow; it was like trading in a family memory.

Daddy set the dolly upright and moved closer to me.

I didn't want him to notice my red lips or the branch hidden under my shirt, so I talked quick and tried to back away, but Daddy was quicker than me.

He stared at the stain around my mouth and gave me a worried look.

"It's nothin', Daddy," I said. "Just trying out some makeup for Halloween. I'm fixing on scarin' folks something good this year."

Charlie Hale,

TRAILER 10

We just made a deal on the concrete. I confess I was able to get a special price. About half what that fellow over in Claxton had charged James Wilson. A few days ago Farley Ewing came forward with some money to loan to folks. Slagles said that was a hopeful sign. Said if folks would put down concrete and plan to stay, Slagles would think about holding on to the park. I *b'lieve* Farley Ewing helped out on account of Miss Mulch.

For a few days folks were as sour as crabapples. They griped about having to put up more money. They complained about all the struggles just to keep a roof over their heads. I confess people would have thrown in the towel if it hadn't been for Pert. She saw that folks didn't have much heart for concrete work just yet, so she'd sing and play her comb harmonica, and in the evening she'd call everybody over to play cards, and then she'd tell jokes. I *b'lieve* Pert's the reason things perked up around here.

I confess the job itself didn't look too hard on account of I'd been working in concrete all my life. We were getting the foundations marked and the trailers moved. It was a help the way Pee Wee offered to mark the plots and Jimmy offered to haul the trailers out of the way. I *b'lieved* we'd be ready to pour by the weekend.

Just this morning Highwaters and Alice Potter finally came through with their money. Made Slagles glad. Slagles said they promised not to think about selling the park for at least another year now. That meant Gene Nugent was the only one who'd be leaving.

I was worried about Rae Jean. Pee Wee heard Rae Jean telling James Wilson something in no uncertain terms. Something about how they'd be staying. No ifs, ands, or buts. I confess it made me glad. But I didn't know how Rae Jean was going to manage it. Farley Ewing was letting folks borrow some money, but it wasn't enough for Rae Jean. The concrete cost near two hundred dollars, and Farley only had fifty dollars to loan her. But Pee Wee was sure about Rae Jean wanting to stay. He had heard Rae Jean shouting about it. I confess I wouldn't think such a little bit of a thing could be so strong.

I try to help when I can. Rae Jean had put up some of her paintings in her mama's craft shop. I *b'lieve* I was her first customer. The picture showed a young boy in a car with wings, flying above a town that looked like Kinship. The car had silver tail fins. The young boy had a face like Jimmy Wilson's. The town had a grocery store with an awning like Shriner's and a bank building with columns like the First National Bank of Kinship. I liked seeing the dimple in Rae Jean's cheek when I said I'd be honored to buy it. Gave her five dollars for it.

25

I'd never in my life had words with Sophie Mulch, and what happened made me feel like the weight of the world was back on my shoulders, pressing down on me like irons.

Miss Mulch and me had been tight as a screw and a washer for years, but now I was defending Weevils as Miss Mulch attacked them.

Miss Mulch and Farley Ewing and Alvin and Odette Coates had called a meeting. Odette had climbed up on an old tree stump and announced how they was trying to hire a lawyer to keep Weevils out of the park. Everybody seemed interested, but nobody had any money. It felt like my blood was draining out my toes. I knew how to talk, but I didn't know how I would talk down a lawyer.

I cleared my throat. "Excuse me, Odette," I said. "You better be careful about getting up on any high horse that means a lawyer. If Weevils can be run out of this park because they're doing a commercial business, so can everybody else."

"Well, now, Pert," Odette said, putting her big hands on her hips, "just what in tarnation does you mean by that?"

"Barbecue's a commercial business, too, ain't it, Odette?"

I saw my words sink in like a hammer. Odette's knees got weak. She was fixing to faint. Alvin grabbed her by the elbow and helped her off the stump.

Ashamed, I turned to the rest of the trailerites. I'd been trying to cheer them up ever since Earl Shivers didn't show. I'd been singing with Farley Ewing on his ukulele and even cracking jokes with stick-straight Carter Breeding.

"And ain't you fixing on boxing and selling those puzzles of yours, Mr. Ewing?" I said.

Farley looked at Miss Mulch. All he said was, "Hmph."

"And what about you, Emil; Myra? Ain't Highwaters selling their vegetables for more'n a little pocket change?"

Then I stuck out my thumb and pointed to my own self. "And what about Wilsons? What about Rae Jean and her pictures? She's started sellin' 'em. Doesn't that make *our* trailer commercial instead of residential?"

Nobody said much. I confess I don't think folks had thought of their own businesses as something commercial like Weevils'.

Then Miss Mulch piped up. "I swannee," she said, shaking her gray curls, "those Weevils are doing something *wrong* over there. The police have been snooping round for years." Everybody had their eyes on her. Just like she was the teacher and they was in her class. "Help me up on that stump here, Mr. Ewing," she said. "I want people to listen."

I could tell Farley Ewing was afraid she'd fall, but Miss Mulch got that stubborn look in her eyes, and he handed her up on that stump like it was a carriage. Then she settled her lace-up shoes, caught her breath, and started scolding. "We're *fools* if we don't do something about getting those lowlifes out of here before they turn their place into some-

232

thing as permanent as concrete." There was a quake in her voice that reminded me of Alice Potter's stutters.

I stepped up to the stump and looked into Miss Mulch's face. "I beg to differ with you, Miss Sophie," I said. "We're fools if we *don't* let them stay. Where would Coateses be without barbecue? What would a Highwater live on without a produce stand?"

Miss Mulch wasn't budging. "What Coateses and Highwaters are doing is legal, Miss Pert Wilson. Weevils are doing something *illegal.* Decent folks got a right to a decent neighborhood. *Laws, we know* Weevils are doing wrong."

Before I knew it, my fists had balled up and my eyes had bugged out and my words shot out like bullets. I went right over to Sophie Mulch and turned my face right up to hers.

We was nose to nose, and I said, "Prove it, Miss Sophie Mulch! I *dare* you to prove it!"

The color drained from Miss Mulch's face. She looked like she'd been slapped by her own daughter. It was dead silence.

Then Miss Mulch spoke, and her voice was steady. "Mr. Ewing, dear," she said, "will you kindly help me off of this stump?" Farley Ewing got a sudden sunburn, and then he took her old hand in his older one and helped her down. Her knees looked a little shaky, but her voice was clear.

"Miss Wilson," she said, letting go of Farley's hand and turning to me, "step into my trailer for a minute, please." It wasn't a question.

I never much liked what followed *step into.* All my life I'd been asked to "step into" the line or "step into" the principal's office or "step into" detention hall.

Folks drifted back to their trailers, and as I followed Miss

Mulch, I knew I was tired of carrying things. I was tired of carrying the weight of the world in my hands, on my shoulders, in my heart. Ida Weevil had asked too much of me.

It took Miss Mulch forever to sit down. No wonder old people never was eager to get up.

"Would you get me some iced tea and then come sit, Pert? And some sugar? You know I can't take it plain."

I knew. Miss Mulch had a powerful sweet tooth. Once a week she made fudge. When I was small, I helped stir the marshmallows and chocolate chips in a double boiler on top of her stove. She always had homemade butter cookies and pecan tarts that she set on a tiered plate; the layers went from large to small like a Christmas tree.

I brought the tea and sugar. Then I watched Miss Mulch measure out two heaping spoonfuls of sugar with an iced-tea spoon. Miss Mulch was the only person I'd ever known with iced-tea spoons. Iced-tea spoons was something I always wished Rae Jean could own. One year when I didn't have a thing for Rae Jean for her birthday, Miss Mulch had given me one from her set of six iced-tea spoons. "I swannee," she'd said while she'd helped me wrap it up, "what's an old lady to do with six iced-tea spoons? I've never had six people drinking iced tea with me at one time in my whole life." When I remembered the swishing sound of the tissue paper we had used to wrap the spoon, my lower lip started to quiver.

It was quiet in the room for a long time. The only sound was the clinking of Miss Mulch's spoon against the glass.

I cleared my throat. "I'm sorry I yelled, Miss Mulch," I said.

She took a careful sip of her tea and then set the glass on

a plastic coaster. You couldn't drink anything in Miss Mulch's trailer without having to set it on a coaster.

"I accept your apology, dear," she said. "You must have felt very strongly about keeping the Weevils here." The way Miss Mulch talked to me reminded me of Rae Jean. When I did something wrong, Rae Jean never got angry.

Miss Mulch picked up her glass again and made quiet sipping sounds. Then she took a cocktail napkin and rested the glass on the napkin in her lap. Miss Mulch was the only person I knew who used cocktail napkins.

I twisted the ring on my finger. The band had grown thin and the stone was coming loose from the setting.

Miss Mulch gave me her little string-bag smile, her upper lip pulling into gathered stitches. "That's real progress, Pert Wilson," she said. "Time was when *I'm sorry* just wasn't in your vocabulary."

She was right. I always had trouble owning up to things. I was good at blaming. I was skilled at giving things a fist. I was a regular expert at always thinking things was somebody else's fault. *I'm sorry* hadn't been in my dictionary.

I cleared my throat again. "I wanted to say I'm sorry . . . and something else, too." I noticed that apologizing for the second time made the words come easier. Maybe they was words that got easier the more you practiced them.

"What else did you want to say, Pert?"

I guess I got it from Daddy. I guess Pert Wilson was one to have the last word, too. It went like a seesaw, Miss Mulch banging down on one side and me crashing down on the other. I said I still thought Weevils should stay in Happy Trails. She said she still thought they should go. I said it wasn't right to turn people out of their home. She said it was, too, right, if those people was making it hard for others to make a decent home for themselves.

When I said that turning out Weevils because their trailer was a commercial business would hurt near everyone else in the park, Miss Mulch nodded her gray head in agreement for the first time.

"*Laws,* Pert Wilson, that's the only thing you've said that makes a lick of sense to me. I don't see how we can move Weevils out on the grounds that they're commercial without hurting our other neighbors, too."

I nodded. I was glad Miss Mulch was seeing the light.

"Unless," she said, "we can prove that the Weevils' business isn't legitimate, that they're engaged in work that's illegal."

"You ain't going to be able to prove it, Miss Mulch."

"You're probably right, Pert," she said, picking up her Bible and setting it on her lap. "But you've just reminded me that there's something else bothering me about the words we had outside today."

"Something else?"

She nodded her head. Her gray-and-white curls was the same colors as Mittens's fur.

"What bothered me was those two words you used, Pert. Those two words: *prove it.*"

I scratched by the side of my nose, wondering what she meant.

She slid on her reading glasses. I watched her open her Bible and flip through the pages. They made the same swishing sound as the tissue paper we had used to wrap Rae Jean's birthday spoon.

Miss Mulch found what she was looking for. "Here it is," she said. "Hebrews. Eleven, one. 'Faith is the substance of things hoped for, the evidence of things not seen.' " She looked up at me over the tops of her glasses.

I blinked at her. I wasn't sure what she was getting at.

"You know as well as I do, Pert Wilson," Miss Mulch said, "that Weevils are up to no good."

I felt guilty. I knew how to be up to no good myself.

"You also know that I can't prove it. You challenged me with your words: *prove it.* But you knew I couldn't. Some things you know and just can't prove. You take them on faith. There's such a thing as evidence you can't see, facts you can't prove." She shut her Bible.

I didn't know what to say to Miss Mulch. She had found me out, of course. I'd asked her to prove what Weevils was doing wrong when I knew she wouldn't be able to. I had turned the tables on Miss Mulch, but somehow she had now turned them back on me. Maybe that's what made her such a good schoolteacher.

Miss Mulch put the Bible on the table and the iced tea in the coaster and rose from her chair. The way she pushed herself up, her knees unsteady, reminded me again how old she was. I saw the way her shoulders was hunched and the way her ankles turned out in her heavy lace-up shoes. When had Miss Mulch gotten old? Why had I never noticed before?

She bent close to me. Her cheek against mine was soft and warm as a fresh loaf of bread. "Smart as you are, Pert Wilson," she whispered, "you don't yet convince me. I don't see the sense in letting Weevils stay."

That was just like her. Sophie Mulch was ruled by sense. She brushed with tooth powder after every meal. She never wore hose with runs. She started her taxes on January first. The only things Sophie Mulch ever did was things that made sense.

"Miss Sophie," I said. "What if I think of a plan to keep Weevils in the park without hurting anybody else?"

"Even a girl smart as you, Pert Wilson, doesn't have that much brainpower!"

I figured she was right. I felt dumb as a loaded-down ox.

"Thanks for the visit, Pert," she said. "I swannee, I never thought I'd hear the words *I'm sorry* from Pert Wilson's lips." I heard the *hee-hee-hee* in Miss Mulch's laugh.

She put her knobby fingers on my shoulder and drew me close. She smelled of lavender water. "Take some fudge before you go, Pert," she said.

I never could resist Miss Mulch's chocolate fudge. I went over to the kitchen table. The fudge was on the bottom tier of the three-tiered plate. While I loaded up, I saw a pile of bills next to the cookie server. The one on top said, "Fenwick Florists." I bent a little closer. The bill said, "One (1) wrist corsage. Pink sweetheart roses. $3.95."

My mouth fell open as I turned to Miss Mulch. My fingers squeezed into the pieces of fudge.

I only half heard Miss Mulch as she talked.

"We disagree about this business with Weevils, Pert," she said, her gray hair soft as dust on my cheek, "but I want you to remember one thing." I could feel a tiny tremble in her chest as she pressed me close to her again. *"Laws,"* she said. *"Laws,* but you mean the world to me, child!"

Pee Wee Hale,

TRAILER 10

Ever since that Shivers fellow stranded folks high and dry, Pert'd been looking me up more. She had been working to cheer folks up. It was downright tiring, she said. Watching her made me wonder how clowns kept up all that smiling.

One time Pert just up and asked me a question. "Pee Wee," she said, "what do you think makes a good father?"

I near about fell off the stoop. "I don't rightly know, Pert," I said. "Never thought much on it."

She kept those blue eyes on me. I felt like somebody was looking at me through a rifle sight. "Well, Pee Wee, what would you *guess*?" she said.

I said, "I reckon what makes a good father is the same thing as makes a good mother. Or brother or sister. Or a good kid. Or any kind of good folks, Pert."

Pert's dark-blue eyes had a look that was sweet but sad. It made me go on. "Well, if I had to guess, Pert," I said, "I reckon it'd be trust. Trust, Pert. I guess it would be that. Trust is likely what makes a good father."

I thought about Uncle Charlie. Even though he wasn't my father, trust was the best thing about him.

Then Pert just up and left.

She come over again last night. Knocked on my window late. I was tired as a mule after all that work getting ready to pour concrete, but I went out to the stoop anyway and switched on the flashlight. She came right to the point. That was just how Pert Wilson was.

"Pee Wee," she said, "would you let something bad happen to folks you know if it could keep something worse from happening to your own family?"

"You mean like if it was raining and you only had one umbrella, you'd let other folks get wet while you held it open over Jimmy and Rae Jean?"

"Yeah, sort of." She wrinkled her nose like you do before you sneeze. "Except rain never hurt nobody. I'm thinking about something real bad."

"You mean something downright life-and-death?"

She nodded. "Uh-huh."

"You mean something like there's a bunch of people getting ready to drown and you're on shore with only one life preserver, who do you throw it to?"

"Yeah, that's it, Pee Wee." She snapped her fingers like she was finally glad I had caught on. "And you don't even listen to the other folks shouting. You just make sure you throw it to your family." She was twisting her ring over and over.

"So what bad's gonna happen to your family that you're gonna keep away, Pert? And what are you gonna let happen to the other folks?" I didn't say it, but it seemed to me bad stuff happens to folks all the time, family or not, and you can't prevent half of it even when you try.

"Pee Wee," she said, serious as a preacher, "I don't really know what bad is going to happen. Just know it is."

I yawned. "Well, Pert, I guess family's more important than anything else. Your first loyalty's to your own kin. I reckon there's nobody that comes before Uncle Charlie. I'd do anything to keep him safe."

"But what if somebody not in your family *feels* like family—only they ain't? What if I had to hurt Odette and Alvin? Or Farley Ewing? They feel like kin. What if I had to hurt them to keep my own family circle tight?"

I thought about Pert and the difference between her and me. A choice like that would never come my way. I wasn't 'zactly social. Didn't have too many friends I cared about the way Pert did. "I reckon I can't say. I'm not close to anyone except Uncle Charlie. Don't reckon there's nobody I feel that way about."

I thought about Sue Ellen Jenkins. She was cute. Nice, too. I could have cared about her if I'd had a chance. I'd asked her to the movies, but she had smiled and said Jimmy Wilson was the only fellow she went to the movies with. Now Sue Ellen and Jimmy were engaged. It didn't look like I was going to find anybody to care about real soon.

"I reckon a choice like that would be hard for Jimmy, too," I said. "Jimmy might have a problem worse than you with a choice like that. My guess is that Sue Ellen feels like family to him. What do you think, Pert? Do you think he'd let her get hurt in order to save a Wilson?"

I don't know what I said wrong. It was pitch dark out, so I couldn't see it coming. But Pert reared back and punched me in the stomach. I tried to grab her arm, but she slipped it away and run off.

She disappeared into the darkness. I rubbed my stomach where she had punched me. Across the lawn I heard her yell, "Shut up, Pee Wee Hale. Why don't you just *shut up*?"

26

The thoughts in my head was like dirt kicked up in a dust storm. I wondered about Miss Mulch. About how she had bought me those sweetheart roses. What she said about faith. How I meant the world to her.

When I got back home, I set the smashed fudge on a saucer; my hands was shaking and my lower lip was quivering and my mind was in such a whirl I could hardly taste the chocolate I licked off my fingers.

Rae Jean scared me near half to death.

Before my words with Miss Mulch, I had started making the tea. I'd decided to fix two pots. One for the juniper leaves. One for regular tea. The tea with the juniper leaves was for Sue Ellen and was on the back burner. The regular tea was for the folks in the court who'd been working so hard. It was on the front burner. I reckon I was brewing that tea on the front burner for the same reason that Rae Jean said all those Hail Marys on her rosary.

I was fixing on taking the juniper tea over to Sue Ellen's this afternoon. I had measured out a quart of water into the back pot—just like Ida Weevil said. Then I'd got out a big mixing bowl and cut the leaves and flowering tops of the juniper limb into it. It looked like about half an ounce.

While I'd worked, Mittens had wound herself around my ankles, stroking me with her soft fur. Daddy was off seeing if he could get back the down payment on the new trailer he had ordered over in Lawrenceville. Jimmy was outside helping Pee Wee and Charlie Hale with the concrete work. Rae Jean had gone to town to help Gram out at Kinder Krafts.

As the water'd begun to boil, I'd thought about the promise I'd made the Weevils. It was the hardest promise I had ever made, and I'd wondered if their recipe was worth what I owed for it. I'd tried not to think about Miss Mulch and Coateses and Farley Ewing and the rest, all living permanent residential with Weevils on my account. I'd shut my eyes and concentrated instead on Sue Ellen Jenkins and her bawling baby. Sue Ellen had three choices, all bad. She could marry Jimmy, live in disgrace, or get rid of the baby. Getting rid of the baby seemed the best choice, didn't it? If she got rid of the baby, the other bad choices would go away, too, wouldn't they?

I'd looked into my two pots; the hot bubbles was rolling in both of them. I'd added regular tea leaves to the front pot, then poured the water from the back pot into the bowl of juniper leaves. I'd stirred the juniper brew, then dumped it back into the pot again to let it steep. I'd wanted it to get good and strong.

Now, my fight with Miss Mulch over, the tea on the stove had cooled. As I stared into the brew I had made, I knew I wasn't so sure about what I was doing. Like what Weevils had asked, Sue Ellen's request was beginning to seem too hard. Before my promise to Weevils and my fight with Miss

243

Mulch, things had seemed different. Things had seemed only about keeping my own family safe.

I shut my eyes and let pictures of Sue Ellen float across the inky night that fell. I saw her pig hands holding mine at the supper blessing and her pig ears at our Monopoly games and worst of all, Jimmy Wilson rassling and boxing with her pig self instead of me. Then I opened my eyes and knew Ida Weevil was right: You had to keep the circles tight.

I began to worry. Had the potion on the back burner steeped too long? Ida Weevil had said no more'n twenty minutes, hadn't she? With all the time I talked to Miss Mulch, the tea probably steeped near twice as long. I strained the leaves and tops of the juniper branch out of the tea and hid them in the bottom of the trash.

That's when Rae Jean scared me.

She came out from the bedroom with a paintbrush between her teeth and an empty glass in her hand.

I jumped. "Thought you was with Gram in town, Rae Jean!" I tried to sound calm.

"I was. Came home early. Business was slow."

Rae Jean dipped her empty glass into the pot on the front burner. Then she took the paintbrush from between her teeth and laid it over the edge of the counter like a lit cigarette, opening the tiny freezer compartment inside the Frigidaire.

"Good tea, there, Pert," she said, plopping some ice cubes into her glass. "Hits the spot." She grinned.

I gasped. "You shouldn't have had that yet, Rae Jean," I said. "I ain't strained it yet, and it ain't good and cold."

"That's okay, Pert," she said. "The ice cubes cool it off."

"How much tea you drank already, Rae Jean?" Something

244

like panic was climbing up the rungs of my spine. I remembered how Ida Weevil had said to steep the tea no more'n twenty minutes and how more'n that could fell an elephant.

"Makes my second glass. Why, Pert?"

I tried to stay cool as a cucumber. Had Rae Jean's first glass come from the front burner—or the back? And two glasses couldn't hurt, could they?

"No reason," I said. "Just wondering if I'd have to make more for the folks in the park. That pot's for them. They've been working hard and worrying long. Wanted to serve 'em tea. Needed to make plenty. Working on concrete makes folks powerful thirsty."

Rae Jean smiled at me. Her eyes made those crinkly lines at the corners that I always loved. They reminded me of streams feeding into a pale blue lake. "That's nice of you, Pert," she said. "Real nice."

Then Rae Jean put her paintbrush between her teeth, picked up her tea, and walked back to the bedroom.

I leaned up against the Frigidaire and blew out my breath. I wiped my damp forehead with the back of my hand.

Then Gram came through the door. Jimmy had picked her up from town in Charlie Hale's truck, and she said she planned on spending the afternoon outside watching Jimmy and Charlie and Pee Wee work. But I knew Gram was more like to roll her stockings down to her ankles, set her feet up on the chaise lounge, and crochet until she fell asleep.

Then Charlie Hale came in. He was explaining about the moving equipment that was being delivered this afternoon. It normally cost a pile of money, but Charlie had once done a big favor for Huck Grimes, so Huck was donating all the equipment.

245

When I turned back to check on the stove, my blood turned to ice water.

Mittens was bent over the back pot. Some of the tea had spilled over the rim; the stains made tiny orange puddles across the counter and the top of the stove. When Mittens lifted her head to me, her pink mouth was dripping tea, and her eyes was glazed. They reminded me of the girl who was forced to have a baby in the loony bin, and I thought of Sue Ellen's eyes, floating in their sockets.

I reached out to pick Mittens up. As I held her to my cheek, her gray fur felt as soft as Miss Mulch's hair. Then the convulsions began. They started with a tiny tremor like Miss Mulch's chest when she held me close. Then the tremors grew stronger, and I could feel them hard against my own face and neck and hands. They came from way down deep in the center of something like an earthquake. I tried to squeeze Mittens tight to my chest, holding her there, protecting her, using the pressure of my arms to calm her down the way you bundled a crying infant tight in a blanket.

But the force of her shaking was too strong. She seemed gripped by something outside herself. A demon. A storm. The something pushed her from my arms and onto the stove. As she fell, her white paws dragged across the rim of the pot, and the pot flew over, spraying the kitchen with orange rain and drenching the front of my shirt and shorts.

I screamed. "Help!" I cried. "Mittens!"

Gram and Charlie Hale and Jimmy ran in from the front room. Rae Jean ran in from the bedroom.

"Oh, my God," cried Rae Jean when she saw the cat. Mittens was flailing across the counter like a mad animal. "Get

246

her off the counter before she falls, Pert! She could fall off there and break her neck!"

I grabbed the twitching cat by the nape of the neck, holding her in my grip the way a mother cat holds her kittens. As I picked her up, I felt something inside her melt and soften like a stick of butter set out in the sun. Now she let me cradle her in my arms, and I held her against my waist, the waist that had carried a little kitty to Trailer 5 in a T-shirt, rocking her like a baby. I watched in horror as the pink tongue fell out of her mouth, the hazel eyes rolled back in her head, and the belly under her white fur was still.

Rae Jean had just put her fist to her mouth and Jimmy had just put his arm around her waist when Daddy came in.

"What's all the commotion in here?" he said.

Gram scowled at him. "It's the cat. The cat just died."

Daddy brushed by everyone to look at the still bundle I held in my arms.

"At least it was over quick," he said. "At least she didn't suffer."

Gram shot her words right over to Daddy. "How quick you think it *was*, James Wilson? *Was you here?*"

"No," he said. "Ever'body knows that, Wilma. I was out trying to get back the deposit on the trailer."

It was like Gram had put up her dukes and started swinging. "And how do you know she didn't suffer, Mr. Vet-er-in-ar-i-an? What animal school did *you* graduate from?"

Jimmy moved from Rae Jean and put his hand on Gram's shoulder. "That's enough, Gram," he said.

"No, that's not enough, Jimmy," Gram said. Fact was, Gram never quit until she had won. "I'm asking your daddy a question here. How does *he* know the cat didn't suffer?"

247

Daddy turned to look at Gram. I did, too. Everybody did.

Gram was on a tear. She started with Daddy's coming back. "Everything in this family's gone wrong from the first Sunday you set foot on our steps, bud." Gram didn't say about the fun at the Lucky Buck or the fruit crate heaped with money.

Daddy opened his mouth to talk, but Gram interrupted, slugging words at him.

"You just breeze in here like you're as welcome as the flowers in May after running off on your wife and these kids, leaving 'em without so much as a can of beans." She was huffing, and Daddy started to talk when she drew in a breath.

"Wilma," he said, "I was only—"

"Don't you 'I was only' me, buster. You just blew right in like you owned the park, selling metal skirts but letting everybody else do the work."

I looked at Charlie Hale and Jimmy on either side of Rae Jean. One of them shuffled his feet; the other one swallowed. Gram didn't mention all the hard work Daddy did riding up and down the hills of Georgia selling skirts, or the way those skirts had perked up everybody in the park.

I could see Gram's knees was beginning to give out. She grabbed the back of the metal chair and leaned on it for support. I was glad it wasn't the wobbly one.

"Wilma," Daddy tried to say, "It wasn't that way . . ."

"Don't 'wasn't' me, sonny. You bought them things they didn't need. You messed up their family routines." I knew Gram was partly right and partly wrong. Things was messed up for sure, but we needed the food, we needed the money, we needed to gobble down peaches from the front stoop and

248

tear up the back roads with the radio blasting. Fact was, we *needed* to mess up our family routines.

Gram pulled out the chair. She gave up and set down, and I heard the metal creak, but she never stopped talking. Her knees was spread out, and her housedress barely covered them, but Gram's great big arms was still swinging their fists in Daddy's direction.

"And then the icing on the cake's when you stole Miss Mulch's money to buy that concrete and made that stupid business deal with a fellow halfway across the state who's like to be all the way to Mexico by now." Gram swallowed air and started up again. "And now you've got to pawn all those things they didn't need but had come to think of as theirs."

Then Gram pointed to the cat. It was heavy in my arms, and I now knew what they meant about things that was dead weights. "And now you're telling us about how something didn't *suffer.*"

Everybody looked at Mittens while Daddy tried to answer Gram. His words sputtered like an engine fixing to die.

I was tired, and I couldn't stand to look at the bundle in my arms. The white paws was limp as ladies' gloves laying across a gray pocketbook.

"Cats don't feel nothin', Wilma. Ever'body knows that. Animals don't feel pain like people."

Rae Jean shuddered when he said that, and I now wished Daddy would shut up.

Gram lit into him again. "How do you know, Mr. James Wilson Know-So-Much? *Was you ever a cat?*"

It was one of those family fights we had so often now. They seemed to be about one thing but they was really about something else. It was like connect-the-dot puzzles.

Only after you'd hooked the dots up could you see what the picture was all about.

As I held the cat in my arms, I looked at Rae Jean. She was a soul mild and meek. I looked at my brother Jimmy. He was, too. Rae Jean and Jimmy was different from Daddy and me. I guess I'd been right when I told Daddy I was fixin' on scarin' folks somethin' good this year. I guess I finally did.

I stared at Mittens and wondered how it was that you could cause so much hurt to people you loved when all you ever wanted to do was love them. I wondered how you took back that hurt. I wondered how you could ever say *I'm sorry* hard enough. I wondered if Daddy ever wondered those things, too.

"You don't know the first thing about suffering," Gram said. "You just drive on in one day, and when it gets too hard, you'll just drive on out. You're the kind to set things in motion, bud, and then you take off and let everybody else deal with them." Gram wrote the book on carrying on, but I'd never before heard her carry on like this. I wished she'd stop.

I couldn't hold the dead cat anymore. It felt like the weight of the world had moved from my shoulders to my arms and hands. I was tired to death of all the things I had carried over the years. The rent checks. The TV dinners. The wagging tongues of folks like Nympha Claggett. I was tired of trying to make things come out right. Trying to defend my family. Trying to pretend that everything was just fine. Trying to say that we wasn't suffering when, fact was, we was suffering every single day of the year. I didn't want the weight of the world on my shoulders or on my arms or on my heart anymore. I just wanted someone else to help me carry things for a while.

I shoved the cat into Daddy's stomach. He looked startled at first, and his blue eyes blinked; then he held Mittens at a distance, away from his body. Like it was a cootie he didn't want to touch. There was something young in Daddy's face I had never seen before. I had never seen age before today in Miss Mulch's face, neither. How had I not seen how old she was? How had I not seen the youth in my daddy? Except for a few wrinkles and the beard, Daddy looked like the young boy in the photograph Rae Jean had framed for me.

Daddy stared down at the cat. He looked startled. He was a boy who'd never sat by a crib but was asked to nurse a sick baby, a young man on a bus who didn't know enough to give an old lady his seat, a teenager on the way to the prom who'd forgotten about the tickets, the flowers, and showing up on time. How had I not seen how young he was?

Quick as a jif, Daddy passed the dead cat to Rae Jean, and I caught the look in her eyes. The blue turned as gray as Mittens's fur, the corners and lids as blurred and feathery as brushstrokes in a watercolor. I saw her eyes look up like that picture of Mary on the wall at St. Jude's, searching for a light from someplace better than earth. As I ran from the trailer, I heard her mumble words like a kind of prayer, and I understood for the first time in my life why my mama always turned to Jesus.

Part Six

27

I was starting to understand Gram when she said be careful what you wish for. I was starting to wonder about things. I'd been thinking on the cat and the corsage and Mr. Shivers not showing up. Daddy had asked me to help him make sales this weekend, and fact was, I wasn't real sure I wanted to go. Hadn't I already helped Daddy make plenty of sales? Hadn't we rode off with piles of money already?

Still, I liked it that I'd be spending the whole weekend with him, joking and laughing, traveling around, not having to lie about skipping school. I liked it that I'd be doing something for Miss Mulch and Rae Jean, too. I knew Charlie and Pee Wee and Jimmy'd be pouring concrete this weekend; it might help them to have Daddy and me out of their hair.

I had brought Daddy some coffee after dinner. We was eating separate now. Rae Jean and me and sometimes Gram ate Dinty Moore beef stew or Franco-American spaghetti off our laps in the front room. Jimmy spent all his time either working or messing with Sue Ellen; don't know when he ever ate. Daddy ate at the Lucky Buck or off the Sterno stove

255

in his truck. But I brought him coffee every night so we could talk, and that Friday night I did the same.

He was setting on an upturned crate inside the bread truck, thumbing through a plumbing supply magazine, and when I came up he slapped it down. "Hey, thanks, Pert," he said as I handed the steaming coffee across the back fender. Then he took a sip and smiled at me. "Ahhhhh. It's just like I like a woman, Pert: strong and hot."

I stared at him and blinked. What did he mean by that? Did he mean Violet Lumpkin? Or Janice, the waitress at the Lucky Buck? Or Janice's friend from the five-and-dime in Troy? Or Rae Jean?

"That's a joke, Pert," Daddy said. "You're supposed to laugh."

I smiled without showing my teeth. That was something I learned from Gram. She said grouchy folks smiled without showing their teeth. I wondered, though, why I didn't laugh. Near everything was usually funny to me.

"Where we going, Daddy?"

"Anyplace you want."

Time was when the sound of "anyplace you want" was the best music in the world.

I said, "Don't you need to think about what the best trailer towns might be? Places where people is most like to buy?"

"Don't have to plan like that with you around, Perty. Any place *you* are is a place where folks will buy. You're my sure-fire salesman." He'd never called me Perty before. It was the name he had wrote on my birth certificate.

Daddy shook out the map. Red lines and blue lines criss-crossed the state of Georgia like arteries and veins.

"You pick the spot, Pert," Daddy said.

Time was when looking at a map could start a thumping in my heart, when I longed to drive from the mountains to the prairies to the oceans white with foam. Now the shape of the state looked like Mr. Shivers's belly, and the arteries and veins dipped and swooped, looping and knotting. I felt tied up in them.

"No, you pick, Daddy."

He insisted. "No, Pert, you just close your eyes and point your finger. We'll make this an adventure. Stir things up. Keep things interesting. We'll pick a town just like numbers in a lottery. Wherever it lands, that's where we'll go."

I closed my eyes and pointed. I heard a thump when my finger hit the map.

I opened my eyes. "Atlanta!" I'd only been to Atlanta that one time with my friend Maggie Pugh, and we'd just stayed one day for a wedding. We didn't have time to snoop around. If Daddy and me went to Atlanta, we could see the Coca-Cola offices and I could apply for a receptionist's job in person. We could eat at the Varsity Drive-in.

I looked at Daddy and laughed. "Are you sure you want to go to Atlanta, Daddy? It's a big city."

"I'm sure, Pert. We can sell concrete and skirting along the way."

My heart was starting to pump. "What time you want to leave in the morning, Daddy?"

"Let's leave early. And then how about a big breakfast at the Lucky Buck before we get going?"

I thought about that. "They'll be pouring concrete early, so folks will be up at the crack. It'll be noisy. Why don't we leave right before they get started? How about eight?"

"Okay," Daddy said. "Meet me here at seven forty-five." He threw the map across the back of the truck.

I picked up his empty coffee cup and got ready to leave.

"Let me ask you something, Pert. I'm needing a change. Going to Atlanta will help. But I think I'd like to shave off my beard before I go. What do you think?"

He gave me his profile. It looked just like the high-school boy in the picture. The eyes was the same dark blue. The nose was straight and even. The smile was half up. Only thing different was the beard.

"I don't know," I said. "It might look good, Daddy. Only way I've ever seen you is with a beard." He'd look handsome in a paper sack. If he shaved his beard, I could compare what he looked like now to what he looked like as a boy.

"I like it that you can break the routine, Pert," he said. "Do things different. Your mama's still a young woman, but she's already set in concrete. Know what I mean?"

I nodded. The nod meant both yes and no. There was a queasy rolling in my belly. I didn't like Daddy saying bad things about Rae Jean. Even if they was true.

He pulled the mirror off the wall. "Well, I'd better shave it off tonight if I'm getting up early in the morning. Won't have much time to shave then."

I watched him gather things together. He poured water from a big glass jar into a bucket. He got out his razor blade. I noticed the toilet tank was gone.

"Let's stand outside where there's more light, Pert."

It seemed like a lot of trouble to shave outside. "I'm sure you can step in the trailer and use our bathroom, Daddy. Wouldn't that be a lot easier?"

"Don't feel too welcome over there of late," he said. He pointed to the mirror. "Would you hold the mirror for me?"

He sat on the back fender of the truck, one knee over the other, the heel of his right boot digging squares in the dirt.

I watched him splash water on his face. Then he looked at his face in the mirror, and the way he admired himself told me something new about him. I reckoned I wasn't the only one who knew he was handsome.

When Daddy pressed the razor to his cheek and started scraping, I thought about all the ways me and him was the same. Blue eyes. Big talkers. Widow's peak. Elvis Presley smile that went half up and half down. Clever and wild.

"Can I ask you something, Daddy?"

"Sure, Pert." He pointed to the mirror with his razor. "Hold that still, Perty."

I tightened my grip on the mirror. The right side of his face was scraped smooth, and I saw how firm Daddy's cheek still was. Like a young boy.

"Where'd you pick up that wrist corsage for me, Daddy? It was the nicest thing anybody's ever given me."

"Oh, some store in town."

"In Kinship?"

"Uh-huh."

"A florist's shop?"

"Yeah, I think so."

"Which one?"

"Now, I don't remember the name of every store I set foot in, Pert." He was scraping his left cheek, and he rinsed the razor in the bucket of water. I thought of Ida and Ora Weevil, saving beard strands in a shoebox.

"Was it on Fenwick Street? Was it called Fenwick Florists?"

"Yes. I think that was the name. That sounds like it."

"You sure?"

"Yes," he said. "I'm sure now. I remember talking to the girl and saying I wanted sweethearts for my sweetheart."

I clenched the mirror tight. I had two views of Daddy now. I could see him across from me, working on his jaw, and I could see him below me, reflected in the mirror.

He was scraping the corners of his mouth. Then he pushed out his chin. As he scraped, I saw the crater in the middle of his chin like a landmark on a map. It was a cleft, a valley. The closer I looked and the more he scraped, the more I saw it was something smaller than a crater. More like a dip or a dimple.

I dropped one hand from the mirror and my fingers jumped to my own chin. I felt its shape over and over again, the hard bone under the point, the way it angled up to my jaw. My fingers searched for just one sign that I was different from Daddy.

"Watch it, Pert," Daddy said, waving the sharp end of the razor at me. "Don't let the mirror slip."

From where I stood, I had two views of Daddy. I wondered if either one—or both—or none—was truly him.

"Okay, Daddy," I said. I tightened my grip and held on.

Gene Nugent,

TRAILER 9

It was dark out, and early. Sun hadn't come up yet.

I'd just come in from walking Sarge when I saw him drive up. Looked like a pretty fancy mobile home, if you ask me. Bay windows and a body sided just like a house. A dark-haired fellow knocked on the bread truck. He must have woke Pert's daddy up. When James Wilson rubbed the sleep from his eyes, I saw he looked different, and then I realized he had shaved off his beard. The other fellow hiked up his pants and buttoned them at the waist. Pert's daddy swung a knapsack over his shoulder and climbed into the mobile home. He looked like a private off on a mission.

Gotta leave this trailer court, thank you very much. Guess they don't call it a court. Call it a park now. Reminds me of the army. Use words like *pacification* when they mean blowing people to bits. If you ask me, it's time to leave when folks start talking like that.

The hell of it is, I'm not sure where to go. Sarge likes walking in the woods at night. I like it that no one bothers me much. But if you ask me, once they start making you decide whether you want a metal skirt or a permanent block of concrete, that's a signal flare for me to go. Can't stand to do what everybody else does. Like my privacy. Like to keep to myself, thank you very much. Didn't even like public showers in the army.

28

I ran to the woods straight off. My heart was thudding as I plunged into the pines. I was fixing to drown, and the forest smells saved me, buoying me up like water in a swimming hole.

He was gone. I'd showed up at seven-thirty in the morning, and when I didn't hear him stirring inside the truck, I had pounded on the rear door. Then I'd ran around to the front of the cab. I'd climbed up on the running board and peered through the window. I'd pressed my nose to the glass and called for him. "Daddy?"

I'd looked at the windshield. Something white was flying under the wiper. It looked like the back cover of a plumbing catalog. I'd grabbed it.

I ran way back, deep down, to the darkest part of the pines. It felt like kerosene in my belly, something that only needed heat to make it ignite. I felt for the matches in my pocket.

I picked up the note. My daddy wrote me this before he left:

DEAR PERTY HON—

*LEFT THE TRUCK FOR YOU AND JIMMY—KNOW
HOW MUCH YOU NEED WHEELS—*

KNOW ABOUT THE POTION, PERT—SUE ELLEN
COME TO ME FOR THE SAME THING—
WEEVILS CAN EXPLAIN—

HAD TO GET GOING AND IT WAS TOO HARD TO SAY
GOOD-BYE—

YOU CAN BET I'LL BE BACK—

YR DADDY

I wadded up the note and stuffed it in my pocket.

I had trouble striking the match. My hands was shaking bad. Finally the match caught, and I dropped it to the forest floor. I watched the flame bury itself in the damp pine needles. I struck match after match, dropping each one to the forest floor, watching them catch hold and burn. The flames leaped in yellows and reds like autumn leaves.

I looked down at the ring on my finger. The brass band was worn thin from all the twisting I'd done since Daddy gave it to me. It didn't sparkle in the piney gloom. I had to wiggle it a tad to slip it over the knuckle, and I held it between my thumb and index finger. Then I reared back my arm and threw it hard as I could into the woods. It disappeared without a sound.

I heard a crashing, then turned and saw Sarge sniffing the ground, pulling Gene Nugent after him.

Gene looked at me and grinned. I glanced at the scar that ran up from his right eye over the top of his head. He'd got his brains blowed out in Korea and the scar was from where they stitched them back in. "Cooking your breakfast over a fire this morning, Pert?" he said.

Sarge was poking his head around the fire, and I could feel myself blushing purple. Gene Nugent stomped on the flames with his big army boots.

"How'd you know I was out here, Gene?" I said.

"Been in Korea. Can spot a signal flare from a mile away."

He looked up at me. I was a full head taller than Gene Nugent. He was small, but he was wound tight as wire.

It was quiet. Gene never talked much. He was friendly in his own way, handing me a Goo Goo cluster without saying a word when I brought him his newspaper. He was the only trailerite who wanted to move, and I was going to miss him.

"Ain't you going to ask what I was doing out here?"

Gene Nugent's tiny eyes was like BBs in his face. When he squinted, the BBs disappeared. "Already know."

"What do you mean?"

"You come out here every time you're troubled."

I hung my head. "Do you know what I'm troubled about?"

"Sure do," Gene said. "Anybody with troubles is troubled about the same thing."

I didn't understand Gene Nugent. Troubles came in more colors than Rae Jean's paints. There was troubles about money, about work, about love. Jimmy's troubles was different from Gram's, and Gram's was different from Coateses and Breedings. I couldn't figure how everybody was troubled about the same thing, and I said so.

"The dark places, Pert," Gene Nugent said. "Everybody's troubled about the dark places. Everybody wants to understand them, Pert. Wants to get rid of them, too."

I thought about the dark places that I knew. The piney

woods. The Bijou after the lights went down but before the movie started. The black curtain that fell across my eyes when I squeezed them tight. The place inside me where it smoked and burned.

Gene Nugent's voice was raspy as radio static. "Maybe you thought the dark places would turn light once your daddy came back."

I swallowed hard. Then I nodded. And listened.

"The hell of it is, Pert, the dark places are always with us."

I looked at the camouflage suit that Gene Nugent wore for clothes and the metal tag he always wore around his neck for jewelry, even when he went bowling. I wondered about the dark places that was Gene Nugent's troubles.

"Got a smoke, Pert?"

I laughed and fished in my pocket. "How'd you know I smoked, Gene?"

He didn't answer me. He just grinned.

"Only got one cigarette, Gene. Want to share it?"

He smiled. I passed him the cigarette and lit the match for him, then watched him suck in the smoke.

"How do you know about the dark places, Gene?"

He passed me the cigarette. "Same way everybody does."

I took a drag, feeling the smoke dive deep into my red-black heart.

I passed the cigarette back to Gene and didn't talk. Somehow, without words, he could hear my question.

"By living through them, Pert. You in Kinship. Me in Korea."

Alice Potter,

TRAILER 2

I 'spect it's time to paint Pert's bottle. I gots Rae Jean up there on my tree in *p-p-pink* and Jimmy Wilson in gold. Red's the right color for Pert, don'tcha know. Red's the color of fire. The granny woman says *Fire in the eye, Heart won't lie.* There's another one, too. *Fire in the heart, Feels love's dart.* It don't much matter in Pert's case. She's got fire both places, and don'tcha know fire's always *r-r-red.*

29

The next morning I was still mad as fire. I went over early, Daddy's note pressed in my pocket. I didn't need Daddy to send me here. I would have gone my own self.

As I crossed Weevils' yard, the chickens set up a racket, squawking and fluttering enough to wake the dead. I knocked on the door. I smelled sausage frying.

"Get the door, husband," I heard Ida call.

"Just a cotton-pickin' minute, wife. Hold your horses."

I heard Ora shuffling to the door. When he opened it, I saw the red pajamas and the slippers he wore for shoes and the gray beard. He looked like a lowlife Santa Claus.

As he let me in, he called, "It's little Missy, come for breakfast."

"Didn't come to eat, Ora. Came to talk," I said.

Ida's turban peeked out from the kitchen. "Well, Weevils is eatin' whether Missy's hungry or not. She can come in *here* and do her talkin'."

"This won't take long, Ida. Then you can get on with your meal."

"Make it snappy, Missy. Husband and me doesn't like our food cold." I saw a plate of sausage links setting on the counter. Ora rooted in the Frigidaire, while Ida scooped a wad of grease from a can and threw it into the skillet.

"My daddy left yesterday morning," I said. "I come—"

"We knows, Missy," Ora said, piling bowls of food onto the counter. "We was likely the last folks to see him afore he drove off." I saw that Weevils didn't cover up their food when they stuffed it in the Frigidaire.

"We lets him gamble one last time," Ida said. "Almost didn't. Your daddy's stinged us for a lot of money. We's been tryin' to get him to sign an IOU for a month."

"But he had some cash on hand night before last, didn't he, wife? Said he'd traded in a TV at the pawnshop." Ora picked blue mold from a bowl of yams.

"Husband here give in and lets him wager."

My mind swooped like bats in the dark navigating by radar. So my daddy had gambled the TV money instead of giving it to Miss Mulch? And he owed Weevils a pile of money?

"What's he owe the money for?" I said.

Ida's laugh was a cackle. "Gambling, Missy. What'd you think?" She spooned cold cooked okra into the skillet. My stomach churned.

Ora set some bowls back into the Frigidaire, and then he leaned against the counter. "First time he come he had a hundred dollars, ain't that right, wife? Said it was an inheritance from his pappy."

Ora watched Ida drop okra wads into the hot grease. "Next time was after folks started buying metal skirts," he went on. "He had some loose change, and Wife and me knows about loose change in a gambler's pocket. Can't wager it fast enough."

The grease on the stove popped and sputtered.

"Had a good long winning streak, too," Ida said.

Ora nodded. "Had enough to buy stuff for Wilsons and enough left over for mobile homes and the ladies, to boot."

I knew about the stuff for Wilsons. Record players. Hula Hoops. I could only guess about the other things.

Ida peeked under the okra patties with a spatula. "Problem were, Missy, your daddy had the wrong religion."

"Religion?"

"I'll bet you don't think gambling's a religion, does you, Missy?"

She was right. Religion was kneeling and genuflecting and sending babies to hell if they hadn't been baptized. And Daddy didn't have any religion at all.

Ida must have seen my wrinkled brow. "Religion ain't no more'n what folks believes in. Jesus. Lady Luck. It don't make no difference. Crucifixes and rosaries, lucky pennies and rabbits' foots is just different ways of gettin' saved."

"Ida's right there, chile," Ora said. "And gamblers is the most religious folks in the world, ain't that right, wife?"

"Okra's near done, husband," Ida said, peeking up under the okra patties.

Ora spread a dirty kitchen towel across the counter while he talked. "You should have seen your daddy that last night, chile. He was in a trance like someone praying. After he won, I got to thinking it might be the last time Weevils would see him, ain't that right, Ida?"

Ida grunted and lifted the okra patties out of the skillet. "Said he'd be putting the money he won down on a mobile home for you and Rae Jean."

I wondered about that. Daddy told us he was getting *back* the down payment on the mobile home.

"I couldn't figure how Rae Jean would ever want to settle down with the likes of him," Ida said. "You, maybe. But not Rae Jean." I hung my head. There's nothing worse than shame. "Besides," Ida said, "he looked different. Made me wonder if he'd be taking off. He'd shaved off his beard."

"Didn't save the clippings, neither," Ora said. "Devil'll get him now for sure."

"Think about it, husband. Fella's marked by the devil anyway. Ain't you seen that big pit in his chin? Don't you remember that chant? *Dimple on the chin, Devil within.*"

My insides froze up. I remembered what it had looked like, that deep pit that appeared in his chin when I had watched him shave. I had seen it right after he had told me that lie about the sweetheart roses. A crater. A valley. My fingers jumped again to my own chin, and I fingered for the pit where the devil hovered within me, too.

"That's right," Ora said. "But we got the IOU out of that devil anyway, didn't we, wife?"

"Patties needs drainin', husband," Ida said.

The Weevils traded places. Ida had laid the okra patties across the dirty kitchen towel. Now Ora pressed on the top of each patty with the spatula, pushing out the grease.

Ida put her hand to her turban. It was coiled around her head like a snake. She pulled the paper out of a fold in the turban and waved it under my nose.

I stared at the paper. I saw the familiar handwriting with the dashes flying off the page. It said, OCTOBER 30, 1961— I.O.U. $1000—FOR GAMBLING DEBTS—JAMES WILLIAM WILSON. I counted zeros. That was three zeros, not two or one.

270

It was also what Miss Mulch wanted: proof the Weevils was doing something illegal.

I looked at Ida. "But you said he *wouldn't* sign an IOU."

"That where *you* come in, chile," Ora answered for her.

Ida shoved the paper back into her turban. "When your daddy wouldn't sign the IOU, we tole him about you. Tole him about you askin' to throw the baby."

Firecrackers was going off inside me. I wanted to take that skillet of hot grease and dump it on their heads.

"Your daddy got a funny look on his face when we told him about giving you that potion." Ora looked up from the okra. "That news pulled him up short. Never saw such a sad face before." He put the okra on a chipped platter. The towel that had been under the patties was sopped with grease.

I turned on him and grabbed at the platter of okra. It slipped from his hand, and the okra patties slid to the floor.

"You *promised*! You swore not to tell my family! I've been working hard to keep you folks in the park and it ain't been easy." I thought of how much I had hurt Miss Mulch, the Wilsons' best friend for all these years.

"Didn't," said Ida, picking the patties off the dirty floor and setting them back on the platter. "Didn't break our promise!"

Ora picked up the fork he'd been using to mash the yams. He pointed it at me. "Promise was about *family*, chile."

I didn't understand.

"We's promised not to tell no one in your *family*," Ora Weevil said. "Your daddy's just *kin*. He ain't *family*."

I grabbed Ora Weevil by his red pajamas and shook. "What are you talking about? He's my *daddy*. I've got his

271

blood in my veins. I look like him, I talk like him, I act like him. What do you mean, he ain't *family*?"

Ida Weevil pulled me off of him. She stuck her face right next to mine. I could smell her stale breath. "You looka here, Missy. They's a powerful difference between family and kin, hear?"

I heard. I just didn't understand.

"You needs to know who your real family is, Missy. Family ain't the same thing as kin."

I looked into green eyes that snapped like turtles. What was she talking about? I saw I'd been tricked. I wanted to find out why. "What's the real reason you told Daddy, Ida?"

She turned away to the stove and said her words slow into the skillet with her back to me. "Your daddy knew you'd never want Rae Jean or Jimmy or your Gram to know about that juniper tea and that baby you planned on throwing. That's how we got him to sign the IOU, Missy. Tole him if he didn't, we'd tell your family."

My mind was whirling. Did Daddy really sign that paper so Weevils wouldn't tell Rae Jean? Could Daddy have known how much keeping that secret meant to me? I thought on what Weevils had said. About family and kin and the difference between the two. What *was* the difference, anyway? We had the same blood in our veins, didn't we? What made the difference between family and kin? Was it like the bread and wine? *Was* they Jesus, or did they just *stand for* Jesus? Was it like the sperm and the egg? *Was* they a baby, or did they just *stand for* a baby? Was family and kin like that? *Was* kin family, or did they just *stand for* family?

Ora and Ida moved out of the kitchen to the dinette. They pushed a pile of old newspapers and shoeboxes to the end of the table to make room. They set down. Neither one asked me to join them.

Ora reached for a pitcher in the middle of the table. He poured molasses over his yams and okra.

Ida shoved some okra in her mouth. It must have been hot because she dropped her jaw a spell before she chewed.

She turned to me, chewing her okra and words. "But you still have a promise to keep Weevils in this park, Missy. I don't care how many lawyers they hire. We's stayin'." She wagged her fork at me like a finger. *"And don't you forget it!"*

"What? What are you thinking about, Ida Weevil, reminding *me* about a promise? You're the one who broke a promise. Why would you expect me to keep mine now?"

Ida poked at her yams with her fork. "Because we's givin' you something you want in return."

"And what is that, *may I ask?*" I looked down at her turban, twisting and coiling like a snake.

She reared back and laughed, and her mouth flew open. It wasn't a laugh so much as a chuckle; it wasn't a chuckle so much as a caw; it wasn't a caw so much as a cackle. "Because you *still* don't want us to tell no one in your *family!*"

I looked down at Ora Weevil, wiping up puddles of molasses with the okra on his fork. My stomach rolled over and over. I knew what Ida said was true. I knew I was ashamed of what I had done. I knew I'd never try to do something like that again. But I still didn't want Weevils telling my family.

Farley Ewing,

TRAILER 8

Hmmph. It's not too often that I get stumped by a puzzle. Come to think of it, the harder, the better. But I've been stumped as a dunce the last couple of days. Can't make heads or tails of all those folks showing up at the park in the middle of all the trick-or-treaters. Goblins, devils, Red Riding Hoods running all around knocking on the trailer doors every five minutes. Miss Sophie just leaves a big bowl of Tootsie Rolls outside her door.

But in between the hobos and the clowns are all these other folks we've never seen before. One of them drives up demanding money back, as if we could just pass it out like candy corn. Says he's from a trailer park in Milledgeville. Says the residents there paid for metal skirts that never got delivered. Fellow's pale as a vampire, but it's not a costume, see. That's his real skin color. When he showed up, it was the first time I ever saw Pert Wilson without something to say.

Another one had a face red as a devil. Brought a petition. Signed by everybody in his park. Seems folks over in Statesboro want their metal skirts, too.

The nastiest one was that fellow who said he was president of the Lawrenceville Mobile Home Company. Said Mr. Wilson and Mr. Shivers must have taken the keys to the mobile home they'd been test driving while the salesman had his back turned. Wondered if maybe they'd driven this way.

Gene Nugent piped up, and he hardly ever talks. "Is Mr. Shivers the one that hikes up his pants?"

Some other fellow had come over from Claxton asking questions. Either Mr. Shivers or Mr. Wilson or both owed a big bill in the tavern there.

They've been showing up at our doors right and left, hollering and begging day and night. A young lady even came by. Violet something. Seems James Wilson took her for lunch at the Lucky Buck every Tuesday. Where was he? I told her it was a puzzle about a hundred folks wanted to solve.

Hmmph. Weevils even came over to watch all the fuss. Shook their heads like they expected this. Come to think of it, I'd expected it, too. I'd seen Pert's daddy slipping over to Weevils now and again. Shared that information with Miss Sophie. We just didn't know what to do.

Miss Sophie's broke up about Pert. Some of the folks that stomped over recognized Pert and let out a stream of cuss words. Pert says she's seen some of them, never laid eyes on the rest. I can't blame those folks, though. They want either their metal skirts or their money. Folks in Happy Trails know how they feel. See, we've had the same experiences with concrete.

Miss Sophie and I watched out her window when Sheriff Keiter's cruiser showed up. Pert sat in it with him for an hour or more while the sheriff wrote down what she said.

Hmmph. Charlie Hale and Odette Coates have been talking to Miss Sophie and me about how to help out Pert. Know we'll try. But *how* is still a puzzle.

I do admire Miss Sophie Mulch. She understands that *everything's* a kind of puzzle. Must have learned that from all those years of teaching school. Hmmph. I *do* admire her, see. Just don't know how to tell her. That's *my* puzzle.

30

Each time the shovel bit into the red dirt, my hair fell down over my right eye. Now and again I'd lean on the shovel and push it back with my forearm. I was digging out by the edge of the woods where we had buried Lickety. I thought it might help for Mittens to have company. The Popsicle-stick cross that had marked Lick's grave was long gone, but you could still see the hilly mound we'd buried the shepherd under.

I'd told Rae Jean I would bury the cat for her. I knew the job would be hard on her, and I didn't think it was something she should have to do. Besides, this was all my fault.

As a casket, I used the box my boots had come in—the boots Daddy had bought for me, the boots with tooling on the side and the tab you used like a shoehorn. I had lined the box with strings of yarn Gram left laying around, so the bottom was a swirl of yellows and blues and greens and pinks. Mittens's gray fur looked pretty against the colored wool.

As I dug the hole deeper, I thought of all the routines we would miss without Mittens. She wouldn't jump up on the couch anymore. She wouldn't play with Rae Jean's ear, and

Rae Jean wouldn't bat her paws. She wouldn't lie on Rae Jean's tummy on the chaise lounge and listen to Rae Jean talk baby talk to her.

Rae Jean watched me shovel. She had brought the rosary and the Jesus statue from the shrine. She held the rosary in one hand and stuck the Jesus statue under her arm. Then she stood at the edge of the hole I was digging and fingered her cross.

"I know how hard it's been for you, Pert," Rae Jean said.

I stared into the hole that got deeper and the pile of dirt that got higher. "I'm just like him, Rae Jean," I said. "I'm not anything like you."

Rae Jean stayed quiet. She just listened.

"I've got his eyes," I said.

She nodded. "Yes, they're the same dark blue. Mine are paler."

"I've got his mouth."

"Yes," she said. But she didn't bring up to me about the same crooked grin.

"I run off at the mouth like he does, Rae Jean. I'm like those false teeth you get at the drugstore. Wind them up and they go yapping in every direction."

Rae Jean smiled. When that dimple sprung up on her right cheek, I felt the power of my own shame. What Alice Potter said was plain-out true: "Dimple on the cheek. Soul mild and meek." I tried not to think about the rhyme that went with Daddy.

I looked into Rae Jean's face and wondered why her routines had once liked to drive me wild. Rae Jean and I didn't have iced tea in the afternoons now. We didn't joke about being dog tired. We didn't hold hands over grace; we just bowed our heads over bowls in the front room. Now I ached with missing our routines.

Rae Jean pressed her silver cross to her mouth and bounced it off her bottom lip, thinking. "There's one thing different, Pert."

I leaned on the shovel and looked over at her.

"Your daddy's got that cleft in his chin. You don't."

I felt my breath catch on something like thankfulness.

Rae Jean came close to me and put her doll-hands to my chin. She touched the spot there that was different from my daddy's: It was flat as a pancake. Then she stroked my cheek with the back of her hand.

I bit my lip. The words came slow. "I'm . . . so . . . sorry . . . Rae Jean," I said, glad for the practice session with Miss Mulch. I took her hand from my cheek and turned it over in my own. I couldn't look her in the eyes. I had seen the gleaming water there. The colors that floated on the surface had fancy names in her paint-by-numbers sets. Aquamarine. Viridian. Cerise. I bit my lip harder. I could taste my own blood. "I'm sorry, Mama. I truly am."

"I know, Pert," she said.

Rae Jean knew something else, too. Doc Jackson had stopped by the trailer to talk to her. I had forgotten that I was supposed to go back and visit him. They asked me to step outside, then they talked for a long time. I didn't have to guess what was said.

I stuck the shovel into the dirt and pushed on the edge of it with my heel, feeling the blade dive down in the red clay. What was hardest was that Rae Jean hardly ever got mad at me. She never said I was an ugly, hateful daughter who killed her cat on the way to getting rid of a clump of cells that either *stood for* or *was* her own grandbaby. All she said was that the only trouble I ever caused was the trouble I caused for myself. She was right.

I worked steady for a long time. The only sound was the crunch of shovel in dirt.

Then Rae Jean said, "I want you to have something, Pert." Rae Jean looked straight at me. "It's something that says how I feel about you."

I blinked. "What is it, Mama?"

She put the Jesus statue on the ground and began to twist the ring on her left hand. She had to wiggle it hard to get it over the knuckle, but she held it to the light the way Father Joe held up the host for a blessing, and when she reached for my hand, I let the shovel fall with a thump. My fist was clenched tight from gripping the shovel, but my mama's touch was soft. I felt my fist melt into fingers of sunlight, and I thought of the handprint ashtray and the only other time in my life when I'd been sure my fists was unclenched. When Rae Jean slipped the wedding band on my finger, I was glad I hadn't given the ashtray away.

I could feel the salt sweat stinging my eyes. Through the blur I could see how the ring made a gold circle around my finger and how Rae Jean's arms around me and mine around her made a braided circle like the fingers of ladies leaving the communion rail. The circle of the ring and the circle of her arms said that Rae Jean was someone I could trust, someone Pee Wee Hale said was the only thing a good person had to be.

Rae Jean's eyes glistened with pale prism colors. She swiped at the damp corners with the back of her hand so they wouldn't spill over.

"Here, Pert," she said. "Give me that shovel. You need a rest. You look *dog tired*." Her laughter made the clinking music of ice cubes in a glass.

I grinned and bent down to pass her the shovel; it was straight and strong as my mama. When I put it into her hands, I felt the weight of the world lift off of my shoulders.

Rae Jean stuck the shovel into the dirt. "Let's finish this job, Pert. It's as hot as an iron out here."

I placed the boot box in the hole, and Rae Jean held her Jesus statue over it and whispered a prayer. As she shoveled the dirt back over the box, I saw that Rae Jean and me was finally putting something to rest, and I thought of Lucinda Adkins, up on the hill. Had she been lucky enough to have a mama like Rae Jean Wilson?

When we was done, Rae Jean smiled at me.

Then she said, "Don't you think a cold glass of iced tea would just about hit the spot right now, daughter?"

Sophie Mulch,

TRAILER 4

Laws, but I'm worried about Rae Jean Wilson. Came over here late yesterday afternoon. She'd been dabbing at her eyes with the tail of her shirt, and that tail, bless her heart, was wet through.

I swannee, I thought I'd known about heartache before, my own and that of the school kids I used to teach. Seeing Rae Jean weep like that made me think of little LeRoy Patterson, killed by his own father in a drunken rage. It made me think of Dawn Wilson, James William's sister, sleeping out in the peanut fields at night rather than under the same roof as her daddy. It made me think of Charlie Mac Leonard, Martha's retarded boy, and the kids that locked him in Grangers' barn that winter after stripping him naked and stealing all his clothes.

Rae Jean was crying so hard she almost couldn't talk. The words came out all stuttery, and she choked now and then on bubbles of spit. The words, when they came, said something about Doc Jackson and a visit. It seems Pert was due to pay the doc a visit, and seven days had passed and Pert hadn't showed up.

I'd never seen such swollen eyelids. Rae Jean said the worst part of it wasn't about what Pert had done, but what *she* had done, and she said she couldn't rightly stand to keep it all tied up in her heart anymore. Said keeping it all tied up made the burden even heavier than it was.

That was when I went over to sit next to her on the couch, bless her heart. I said things like "there, there" and "it'll be all right," things I'd heard her say to Pert and Jimmy when they were kids. I told Rae Jean I knew there were times that if you didn't talk about things, you could die from keeping them all stuffed up. I told her that's what friends were for: keeping you alive.

Bless her heart, Rae Jean put her head on my shoulder then, on the same place Jimmy and Pert had laid theirs on hers when they were babies. She took a deep breath and said the worst part was that, near sixteen years ago now, James Wilson had sent her to Doc Jackson for the very same thing. Jimmy was just starting to walk and the money just wasn't coming. He sent her to ask about throwing their baby.

I swannee, Rae Jean was sobbing when she said how everything fell apart after that. She couldn't throw the baby and James William couldn't see why, so she had gone off to have the baby, and he had gone off in his own way, too. Rae Jean said by then she had learned he was one for lighting out, not one for staying. She had told him to get going. For good.

She sputtered and blubbered while she talked. I put my hand on her soft yellow hair and stroked her like a kitten. *Laws,* I thought this old heart of mine would just sit down and die!

31

Jimmy asked me to meet him at the filling station. Mr. Hanks had been working him harder than ever. The station was doing business hand over fist, but it had been Jimmy's hands that had helped put the money in Mr. Hanks's fists.

I walked uptown to the station. Jimmy'd said he needed to see me and he'd buy me lunch. When he first spotted me, he had one hand on the gas nozzle filling Selma Adkins's car, and he waved the other hand at me. Mr. Hanks's station was jumping like the tavern on a Saturday night. There was only one pump—Mr. Hanks was fixing on buying another—and Lem Patterson's hay truck and Arnold Hardin's clunker was lined up behind Selma Adkins, waiting on service. Inside the garage, a Rambler was up on the lift.

Mr. Hanks came out and waved Jimmy off. "Go eat, son," he said. "Take a break." I liked the way Mr. Hanks said *son*. It told you he liked my brother.

Jimmy punched me in the arm. "Hey, sis," he said. "Okay if lunch is on me?"

I laughed. Jimmy knew my pockets was filled with nothing but lint.

We stepped inside the garage and Jimmy slipped change in the vending machine. He bought orange squares of peanut butter crackers and packages of Tom's peanuts. He bought a Coca-Cola for me and a Nehi for himself. Then we went around the side of the station and set on the curb beside the rest rooms, where it stunk like pee.

Jimmy pulled a bandanna from his pocket and spread it out on the curb. Then he opened the cellophane wrappers and placed the food in neat piles. "All we need is a little candlelight, Pert," he said, "and a toast." We clinked soda bottles, and I felt the way I had when he'd showed up at the dance and treated me like a queen.

"Got something for you, Pert," Jimmy said. He pulled an envelope out of his shirt pocket. He opened the envelope and passed a picture to me.

It was the picture they took at the dance. We both had on captain's hats, and we was standing in front of fake portholes and rails made out of cardboard boxes and tempera paints. Our faces was peeking through two white life preservers. You could see my pink wrist corsage on my right hand, holding on to the side of the white circle. On the bottom of the picture was the words HAYES COUNTY HIGH SCHOOL FATHER-DAUGHTER DANCE, 1961.

I was thrilled to pieces to have that picture, and I said so.

"I'm thrilled to pieces for you to *have* it, sis," Jimmy said back. "Maybe I'll get you a frame for Christmas."

I was so happy I'd maybe even forgive Jimmy for ruining the dance at the end by saying he was going to marry Sue Ellen.

Then Jimmy said there was another reason he wanted to talk. Fact was, the reason was Sue Ellen Jenkins.

"Sue Ellen's not going to marry me, Pert," he said. In the sunshine, the orange crackers looked dry as Georgia dirt, and Jimmy Wilson looked sad as an undertaker. I felt like jumping for joy and crying my eyes out at the same time.

I was learning to figure out the places where I didn't have to talk, and I could see that Jimmy just wanted someone to listen. I was glad that the someone could be me.

"She gave me back my ring last night, Pert. We had a long talk. Sue Ellen said getting married wasn't a good idea. Especially getting married for the wrong reason. Said she wanted to go to school more than she wanted to be a wife or mother right now. I was glad she could be so honest. Gotta admit it hurt, though."

I stopped chewing my peanuts and took a quick drink. "What about the baby, Jimmy?" I said.

Jimmy barely ate. I knew he'd had peanut butter for breakfast and now peanut butter crackers and peanuts for lunch, and I wondered how he could work so hard all day with nothing but peanut clumps in his stomach. It was like Arnold Hardin's clunker. It was always out of gas, but Arnold managed to drive all over Hayes County on fumes.

"Sue Ellen's parents have been talking to the Breedings. They've offered to adopt the baby after it's born."

I knew Iris Breeding wanted a baby in the worst way. But it gave me heartburn to think of Jimmy's baby wrapped in that yellow afghan or dressed in fancy baby clothes Iris stitched herself. I'd bet money Iris Breeding could smother a baby half to death.

Jimmy looked serious. His lips was straight as a ruler. "I'm

285

not going to let them do it, Pert. I'm not going to let the Breedings adopt our baby."

I waited for him to say what he needed to tell me.

"I'm going to keep the baby my own self."

I wanted to start flapping my jaw. What was Jimmy thinking? How was he fixing on taking care of a baby and working, too? What was the baby going to do without a mother? Would Sue Ellen change her mind about the baby after it came and hang around it anyway? What was Jimmy going to do for money? For food? For a crib? It was powerful hard, but instead of talking, I bit my tongue.

I looked over at my brother, at the big body that took up half the curb, at the long arms resting on bent knees, at the pants legs too short to cover his ankles. He left a mess in the kitchen every morning; he had no high school diploma to hang on the wall; he owned no car to take him where he needed to go. And yet what I finally said was true. "You'll make a good daddy, Jimmy Wilson."

He smiled, and punched me in the belly with his fist. Then he bear-slapped my arm, and I bust out laughing, spraying cola from my mouth like a hose.

I moved right up next to him and grabbed on to his arm. There was just one thing I had to ask him about, one thing I had to know. "Whatcha going to do with the ring, Jimmy?"

He frowned. I could see the oil streaks across his forehead. "Why, Pert?"

"Just askin'." I didn't want to tell him that I knew he stole Rae Jean's money to buy it. But if he could sell it back to wherever he got it, we maybe could come up with two hundred dollars for Rae Jean, and our family might have at least enough money for concrete.

"Hadn't thought about what I'd do with it, Pert." He pulled it from his pocket, the one on the front of his shirt, the one under the red star. "Figured I'd just give it back to Miss Mulch."

"Miss *Mulch*?"

I looked at the tiny ring in his big hand. It was an old-fashioned ring with scrolls and curlicues like silver lace around the small clear diamond.

"Yes, Pert," Jimmy said. "Miss Mulch gave it to me when she heard I was engaged. Said an old lady didn't have much need for a ring she got forty years ago from a fellow who ran off with her sister. Said I was welcome to it."

"You mean you didn't steal Rae Jean's rainy-day money to buy that ring?"

"What are you talking about, sis?" Jimmy said. Somebody behind me was fiddling with the rest room key. "You know I wouldn't steal from Rae Jean."

"Well, if *you* didn't steal that money, who did?" I heard the toilet flush and water running in the sink behind me.

Jimmy took my hand in his. His fingers was greasy with motor oil, and my fingers was greasy with peanut oil and salt. "Pert," he said, "think about it."

Jimmy didn't have to say it outright. I knew.

And I didn't like it. I wanted to close my eyes and call out into the darkness. I thought about the chant I'd used so many times over so many years. *If my daddy can hear or my daddy can see, help him receive this message from me.* I wanted to send Daddy an ESP message and I wanted him to send

287

one back to me. I wanted him to tell me that all the things I'd been thinking about him wasn't true. But I kept my eyes open. I didn't send the message.

"Jimmy," I said, "can I take the ring back to Miss Mulch for you?" I thought of all the things Sophie Mulch had given our family over the years: school shoes, math lessons, pecan tarts, an iced-tea spoon. I was hoping I could get her to give us one thing more.

"Sure, Pert," Jimmy said, passing the shiny ring to me. "Just be sure to thank her for me. And try to explain."

Jimmy moved his leftover crackers and peanuts into the middle of the bandanna and then tied the bundle into a knot. "Think I'll save this for supper, Pert," he said. I wondered what Nympha Claggett would say about Jimmy's choice of food groups.

Horace Bertram, the banker, was laying on his horn. He drove a Cadillac and didn't think he had to wait in line.

"One more question, Jimmy. Do you think you could teach me to drive?"

"What for? We ain't got a car."

"But we got a red bread truck," I said.

Jimmie dropped his jaw. "You're not sixteen yet, Pert."

I winked at my big strong brother. "I won't tell if you won't," I said.

Jimmy went back to work, and I watched him for a long while. First he made change for a customer and showed the man's little girl the cracker machine. The girl's eyes lit up as she pulled the lever and her crackers came out. Jimmy smiled and rippled her hair with his fingers. Then Joey Stoddard, the white barber's son, rode up on his bike, ringing the silver bell on his handle for service. Jimmy pointed him in the direction of the air pump. Clarence Adkins, who owned the sawmill, must have been taking his family on a trip. His wife turned from the front seat to tell her kids to stop that fighting while Clarence climbed out of the car to talk to Jimmy. He climbed back in with a road map. Then Jimmy took over the gas pump, and Mr. Hanks went back into the garage. Jimmy waved at me, and I waved back, looking at the red star over his pocket and remembering the Texaco commercial I'd seen before we had to give back the TV. The chorus of filling-station attendants sang, "You can trust your car to the man who wears the star."

I looked again at the picture from the father-daughter dance. The ship and the rail reminded me of all the times I felt fixing to drown, and I knew I loved the big blond grinning face next to mine in the picture. I figured there was lots of other folks in the water with me, too, but the handsome guy on shore had picked *me* out of the crowd and thrown the one life preserver to me. I was grateful.

As I walked off, cars was moving in and out of the station, driving up and driving off, hubcaps sparkling like the silver sides of Airstream trailers. I watched them come and go, their engines revving up and stalling out, their wheels stopping and starting up again. People was flying through the world on wheels, and I knew that, even with only a bread truck, Wilsons was starting to move through it, too.

289

Pee Wee Hale,

TRAILER 10

It wasn't 'zactly what Jimmy Wilson had in mind when he wished for wheels. But the bread truck moved, and it took us places. Don't think nobody'd call it traveling in style, but it was still traveling.

I'd see the red truck spinning up the road past the pines, and then Pert would throw open the cab door and tell me to get in. Sometimes Jimmy let Pert drive, and when she popped the clutch and squealed the tires, we laughed our fool heads off.

The first ride we ever took together was downtown with Miss Mulch to pawn her diamond ring for cash money. Mr. Ewing handed her up into the truck cab like she was the queen of England, and Pert rode in the back next to all the crates. Sophie Mulch nearly fainted when Roy Gander offered her five hundred dollars for that ring. I'd never seen anything like it. That old lady flipped through the pile of bills, handed two hundred dollars to Jimmy straight off and three hundred dollars to Pert. "That's for your mama for concrete," she said to him. "That's for you to start making good on all that skirting," she said to her. "Now let's go home and make fudge."

Pert and Jimmy and me had gone to Madison and Covington and Conyers, towns where Pert said she'd sold sheets with her daddy. Uncle Charlie helped them out. He got a good deal on metal sheeting through the contractors he knew, and Pert outfitted a park in Milledgeville right off. Folks there were downright steamed when we first drove up, and I couldn't 'zactly blame them. Once we got to work, Jimmy and me hammering the skirts down tight and Pert telling jokes, folks were laughing so hard they were holding their sides.

Pert said she was glad to get out of Kinship, even though it wasn't 'zactly the way she had planned. Said maybe someday we'd all get to Atlanta.

When the money got low, Uncle Charlie helped Pert and Jimmy out. His credit was good, and the contractors would ship them sheeting on his say-so; Jimmy and Pert could pay for it later.

I never did tell Pert about that day worker that showed up. Uncle Charlie knew him. Name was Andy Harris. Andy was looking for Wilsons and showed up at our door by mistake. Andy had a toilet tank that James Wilson had sold him, and the tank didn't work. Andy said James Wilson ought to be able to give him his money back because when Andy first met Pert's daddy up at the job site in Latonia, James Wilson said he was about to come into money. His business partner in Claxton had learned about a notice in the *Troy Tribune*. It said his pap had some unclaimed bank funds just sitting in the bank. James Wilson'd come back to Kinship to find out what that was all about. Figured there might be a little business in plumbing fixtures while he waited for his cash.

Don't think nobody would see much point in telling Pert. Wasn't nobody in Happy Trails that didn't like seeing her smile again.

It was good for me to get out. We'd head up and down the

hills and valleys of Georgia, the radio going full blast, Jimmy elbowing Pert in the ribs, all of us hooting and hollering. I breathed in the fresh green smell of pines mixed with exhaust and gasoline and thought it was the downright sweetest smell in the world. I added two more people to the short list of folks I care about.

Maybe Jimmy and Pert was disappointed in the bread truck. Don't nobody 'zactly go to a showroom to buy a red suitcase on wheels. But I thought of that truck like I thought of the Wilsons: not much style, but style in its own way.

32

Gram had planned the whole thing. We'd worked hard, she said, and it was time we all sat down to a meal together. Thanksgiving was as good an occasion as any. Gram was right. We'd poured all the concrete a few weeks ago, and Huck Grimes had even dragged the old yellow school bus to the dump. Gram put flyers up all over town and in her shop. The signs said KINSHIP COMMUNITY THANKSGIVING PICNIC AND CRAFT SHOW, FREE ADMISSION, HOMESTEAD PARK. She told folks they'd never see such a pile of bargains again in this century.

Everybody cooked. Highwaters brought red tomatoes big as wagon wheels and yellow squash big as sunflowers. Iris Breeding brought her tuna-and-potato-chip casserole, her red flannel hash, a pecan pie, and artichokes special for her Carter; nobody else knew what they was. Miss Mulch brought the desserts and five iced-tea spoons; I ran in our trailer and got the sixth. 'Course Coateses brought barbecue and Farley Ewing brought bowls of Birds Eye vegetables. Jimmy and me asked Rae Jean if we could bring mashed potatoes, noodles, and white rolls with gravy since the best

Thanksgiving we could remember was the one where we had that all-white meal.

Weevils brought okra. Fact was, Miss Mulch and Mr. Ewing and Coateses was still sour about having them there, but part of it was that the lawyer was too expensive and the other part was that they liked my plan. I had promised Miss Mulch I would try to come up with a plan for keeping Weevils in the park without hurting anybody else, and I reckon I did.

The plan had to do with circles. Before they poured the concrete, Charlie Hale and Pee Wee and Jimmy and me got folks to change the positions of the trailers. We'd moved a few bushes and arranged the trailers in a circle. It was the same way the pioneers had arranged their covered wagons, and the circle helped us feel safe.

Now the front entrance was like the opening of a horseshoe, and Pee Wee and me put the sign up there. Then we placed Miss Mulch to one side of the opening and Weevils to the other. I'd got the Weevils to move the chickens and the peacocks to the rear of their trailer to keep the front lawn nice and to keep Mayor Cherry off our backs. I'd seen how the chickens set up a racket every time somebody came near; I figured any shady characters coming in the back would let us know by setting the birds to squawking fit to wake the dead. And Miss Mulch could keep her eye out for any lowlife that came in the front. Fact was, I now knew something important. The devil can come into a circle anytime he wants: The trick is to get him out in the open so you can keep your eye on him. Pee Wee and me had changed the sign. Now it said HOMESTEAD *CIRCLE* PARK: WHERE THE NEIGHBORS IS JUST LIKE KIN.

Besides the food, everybody had their stuff set up to sell. We agreed that whatever anybody made would go into a fund for the park. The zoning commissioners was holding off on us right now, but you could never tell what politicians was going to do. At the craft tables, Farley Ewing had his puzzles and Miss Mulch her fudge. Iris Breeding had a stand for her aprons. Alice Potter sold bottles in every color of the rainbow. The Hales stacked their hubcaps in piles like big silver bottle caps, and folks came from as far away as Macon because they knew Charlie would charge a fair price.

Gene Nugent had decided to stay after I swore Jimmy and me would come watch him in the state bowling tournament a week from Saturday. We tried to get him to sell bowling lessons to anyone who was interested, but Gene just stood at the outside edge of the park with Sarge and smoked.

Everybody in Kinship came. Ida Perls and Fenwicks and Zeke Freeman and Cinda Samples on Stumble Martin's arm and Iris Breeding's aunt Olive and uncle Sam Shriner and Lumpkins with all their kids. The commissioners came and Lucy Tibbs, the switchboard operator. I knew Mayor Howard Cherry was impressed by our work when he blew out his breath in a sound that was just shy of a whistle. Folks was saying how the craft fair should be an annual November event, and everybody was having a good time.

By looking at Farley Ewing setting in a lawn chair next to Sophie Mulch, you'd swear there's a way to make love stay. Mr. Ewing had one of the Highwaters' tomatoes, and he was sticking pins in it and spelling S-O-P-H-I-E-M-U-L-C-H. Miss Mulch was slapping her knees and laughing like a hyena. Ain't nothing sweeter than old folks in love.

I was proud of Rae Jean. She set out her paintings for

folks to buy. They was strange and wonderful at the same time, and she had thought of the ideas out of her own head. One was a gold circle like a ring, but when you looked at the painting up close, you saw a dog with gold fur circling two sleeping children and reminding you of Lickety. There was another of a silver moon shining off a trailer roof, and one of an old man that looked like Ora Weevil with a lilac beard that looked like a mess of hydrangeas. My favorite was one of a fruit crate with wings flying over a house with white columns and green boxwoods; inside the crate was a baby with a face like my daddy's except for no cleft in its chin; the baby's face was red, and it was bawling its lungs out. I remembered the look that had passed between Rae Jean and Daddy when Daddy had dumped all that money into my fruit crate; I knew that look had something to do with me. When I told Charlie Hale how much I liked that one of the bawling baby, he up and bought it for me.

As I looked around, I saw that Homestead Circle Park was like something in one of Rae Jean's paintings. You couldn't really understand it, but it talked to you just the same, and it didn't expect you to talk back; fact was, it begged you to keep quiet. The sky was a gray blue like Rae Jean's eyes, and the crape myrtle was giving a second bloom of purple like the color on one of Alice Potter's bottles. The rust on the tops of the pines meant winter was coming, and it was the same color as the bottoms of the cars Jimmy worked on. I breathed air wet as the nose of Gene Nugent's Sarge and cool as Lucinda Adkins's stone in the cemetery. Inside, I felt something snuggling down, warming me through the damp air like a woolen scarf crocheted by Gram.

I reckon nobody told me about Miss Mulch buying those sweetheart roses because they knew I thought my Daddy hung the moon and they didn't want to take his shine off things. 'Course they was right. I *had* thought my Daddy hung the moon, only now I knew that the moon had two sides, dark and light. You couldn't have one without having the other; they was both part of things. Fact was, I still disagreed with Sophie Mulch. She still believed in getting rid of Weevils, but I knew you never can get rid of their kind of darkness. Gene Nugent said it: The darkness is always with you. Now that I know my daddy, I don't close my eyes against the dark things anymore. I look at 'em with eyes wide open.

I wasn't so restless at night anymore, but I never did see Daddy in my dreams; maybe now I didn't need to. I knew what he looked like and how he smelled behind the ear, and I knew I could fix him hash browns just the way he liked them and make him smile. In my dreams it was always just Rae Jean and Jimmy and me and sometimes Gram. We had our hubcaps out, trying to catch falling money. And sometimes it rained things like we was eating today: barbecue and chocolate fudge and tuna-fish casserole. When my dreams went the food way, the hubcaps looked more like dinner plates, and they was loaded with stuff that could really fill you up, not just stuff you could take to the bank.

It was getting dark when we set down to eat. The table was groaning with all that food. I saw that a little pile from someone over here and a little pile from someone over there added up to a whole lot of food for everybody in Kinship, and I knew how happy Jesus must have felt feeding all those folks with a few loaves and fishes. While we filled up our plates, helping ourselves to mashed potatoes and deviled eggs and baked beans and ham, inside I had to admit that I missed my daddy. Even though he was gone, I felt his presence just the same. Daddy had helped me see that the place we call home is broader than one roof and that everything's temporary anyway. I grinned when I pictured Rae Jean and Jimmy and Odette and Miss Mulch and Daddy and Pee Wee and even Weevils up there on that hill with Lucinda Adkins, feet up, laying down after our last big meal, napping together in the only place in the cotton-pickin' world that could pass for a guaranteed permanent residential home.

Before we ate, we made a circle and held hands. I'd told Charlie Hale how the devil can't come into a place with lights, so he had hooked everybody's old strings of Christmas-tree lights together, rigging them up on poles that circled the whole park. Darkness was falling, and the lights winked in blues and reds and yellows like the stained-glass reflections on the walls of St. Jude's. Rae Jean said the blessing. It was about thankfulness and family, and the words went out from the circle of the Wilsons to the circle of Homestead Circle Park to the circle of Kinship to all the tight circles of things that kept the darkness out. Rae Jean believed in Jesus, and Daddy believed in luck, but I had a religion, too. Pert Wilson believed in circles. Maybe the circles was like ESP. They wasn't things that you could prove exactly. But fact was, you had faith in them just the same.

Alice Potter,

TRAILER 2

By the time *s-s-summer* come, I's gots a new bottle for my bottle tree. It's just a bitty one, no bigger'n that new baby what's born over at Wilsons'. Cute little thing. Borned with a head of black curly *h-h-hair* just like her mama. Her daddy's spoiling her good, same as her gram.

Near everybody's painted they trailer this spring, don'tcha know. Coateses' yellow one was already done, but now everybody else's is colored in pink and blue and *g-g-green* like the dabs of color on my bottles. Trailers in Homestead Circle Park's set like pretty horses on a carousel, *m-m-moving* in circles to nowheres, but givin' folks a good ride anyway.

You hears that baby gal cryin' of an evening, cryin' for her mama, don'tcha know. Pert Wilson's bundlin' her in one of her great-gram's afghans and holdin' her, rockin' and singin', till the wee hours. Can't carry much of a tune.

Bottle trees is different from kinship trees just like families is different from *k-k-kin*. Bottle trees tells stories, stories about livin' folks and dead folks and folks whose stories I just *m-m-makes* up inside my own head, don'tcha know. Kinship trees just gives names. Kin drops by now and again. They sends letters or sometimes money. They comes around holidays. They ain't up on my tree. Only folks up there is *family.* Family's folks what builds a *f-f-foundation* under you—folks what *s-s-stays.*

About the Author

Trudy Krisher was born in Macon, Georgia, and grew up in South Florida. A freelance writer and teacher, she is a former book reviewer for the *Dayton Journal-Herald* and the author of a picture book, a textbook, and the critically acclaimed young adult novel *Spite Fences.* She now teaches at the University of Dayton and lives in Dayton, Ohio, with her three children, Laura, Kathy, and Mark.

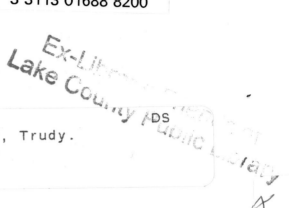